Readers who adore Amish fiction will quickly fall in love with *Grace Given*, book two in Beth Shriver's popular new series, Touch of Grace. At the heart of this novel is the powerful triple-threaded theme of forgiveness, mercy, and grace, and Beth weaves them together with a deft touch. *Grace Given* gives readers the best of all worlds—romance with a bit of mystery and a storyline that will make you burn the midnight oil. Highly recommended!

—DIANE NOBLE
AWARD-WINNING AUTHOR

In *Grace Given* a young couple and their family learn to overcome the hurt of betrayal and prejudice with love and forgiveness, leaving us wanting to make our own fresh starts. With a full cast of characters and compelling storytelling, Shriver reminds us of how complex even the "simple life" can be when it comes to matters of the heart—and what matters most.

—CATHY LIGGETT
AWARD-WINNING AUTHOR OF *BEADED HOPE*

Beth Shriver's smooth writing style and lovely characterization make *Grace Given* a joy to read. Beth Shriver is truly an author to watch in the Amish genre.

—SHELLEY SHEPARD GRAY
NEW YORK TIMES AND *USA TODAY* BEST-SELLING
AUTHOR

GRACE
Given

Touch of Grace
BOOK TWO

GRACE
Given

Touch of Grace
BOOK TWO

BETH SHRIVER

REALMS

Most CHARISMA HOUSE BOOK GROUP products are available at special quantity discounts for bulk purchase for sales promotions, premiums, fund-raising, and educational needs. For details, write Charisma House Book Group, 600 Rinehart Road, Lake Mary, Florida 32746, or telephone (407) 333-0600.

GRACE GIVEN by Beth Shriver
Published by Realms
Charisma Media/Charisma House Book Group
600 Rinehart Road
Lake Mary, Florida 32746
www.charismahouse.com

Scripture quotations are from the King James Version of the Bible and from the Holy Bible, New International Version, copyright © 1973, 1978, 1984, International Bible Society. Used by permission.

Although this story is depicted from the real town of Beeville and the surrounding area, the characters created are fictitious. The traditions are similar to the Amish ways, but because all groups are different with dialogue, rules, and culture, they may vary from what your conception may be.

Martyrs Mirror was written and published in 1659 by a Dutch Mennonite, Thieleman J. van Braght. One of the reasons why van Braght compiled this massive work was to strengthen the faith of his fellow believers, now that persecution of the Mennonites in the Netherlands had largely ended. *Martyrs Mirror* contains classic accounts of more than four thousand Christians who endured suffering, torture, and a martyr's death because of their simple faith in the gospel of Christ. It also includes more than fifty finely detailed etchings by noted Dutch artist Jan Luyken.

Visit the author's website at www.BethShriverWriter.com.

Library of Congress Cataloging-in-Publication Data

Shriver, Beth.
  Grace given / Beth Shriver. -- 1st ed.
     p. cm. -- (Touch of grace ; bk. 2)
  ISBN 978-1-62136-017-9 (trade paper) -- ISBN 978-1-62136-018-6
(e-book)
 1. Amish--Fiction. 2. Christian fiction. I. Title.
 PS3619.H7746G73 2013
 813'.6--dc23

                    2012034652

First edition

13 14 15 16 17 — 9 8 7 6 5 4 3 2 1
Printed in the United States of America

To Carmen Webb,
my friend, my encourager, and Christ follower

If we don't forgive, we won't be forgiven.

—*Amish Carpenter*

- Claping [claping]: verb, clap, clap-ing, noun, adjective.

- Pronounced *clay-ping: hate crime against Amish victims*

    1. assaults, physically or verbally, harming or harassing

    2. vandalism and property damage

R IPPLES OF PINK clouds covered the blue Texas sky. The sun slowly dipped behind a large oak tree, almost invisible against the fading darkness. Elsie and Katie Yoder strolled down a dirt road leading to their family farm after a day at a neighbor's quilting bee.

"I like the orange with the yellow patches." Katie flicked her thick, amber curls away from her cutting, blue eyes.

Elsie shook her head as she tugged the shawl around her for warmth. "Not me. I like green with the yellow."

Katie frowned and kicked a rock down the lane.

Elsie thought of a compromise, a frequent gesture she made on her part involving her sister. "What if we do all three?"

As they chatted about the patches needed to complete their quilt, an unfamiliar rumbling noise made them pause. Elsie stopped and glanced behind her as a blue car drove up, causing a cloud of dust to fall around them. Her kapp blew off, and the driver let out a low whistle.

The three other young men in the car heckled them and laughed. "Hey, sweetie, show us more."

"How about some leg, Amish girl?" the driver called out to her.

"Hey, ladies, stop and talk to us," another yelled. "No harm in being friendly."

Elsie had never felt dirty like this. With each word she felt as if they'd thrown a handful of mud at her. She sucked in a breath when the car came to a halt and the driver got out. His dirty, blond hair stuck straight up, and his blue eyes hardened as he took her in.

The passenger side door opened, and a tall, skinny young man sauntered around the front of the car. He looked Elsie up and down and moved toward her. She took two steps backward then took off. Her heart beat out of her chest, but she kept running until she got to the gravel road leading to their house, then she bent over, puffing and holding her side. Katie was close behind, trying to catch her breath against the cold air.

Katie turned around. "They didn't follow us, thank *Gott*."

Elsie followed her sister's gaze. No one was in sight.

"Elsie, Katie. Are you all right?" Their daed's booming voice came from behind them. "I saw you running all the way up the drive." Though he was a gentle man, his height and hefty build made him appear intimidating.

"*Nee*, we're fine," Katie answered before Elsie could think of what to say.

He eyed them suspiciously and then nodded. "Okay then." He lumbered away but looked back once.

"Do you think he believed me?" Katie watched him until he was out of sight.

"Why didn't you tell him?" Elsie twiddled her thumbs. What they kept secret had now become a lie. She didn't want the burden of either.

"I don't want to upset him or Mamm. Nothing really happened anyway." Katie shrugged.

"It might have if we hadn't gotten away from them. They had something bad on their minds." Elsie frowned. "What those boys said to us was embarrassing. What if someone thinks we invited the attention?"

"They would know better than that with *you* involved," Katie scoffed. "They didn't have a chance to do anything with the way you ran off so quickly."

But Elsie wasn't so sure. Katie liked attention, especially when a young man smiled her way. "Well, I guess it's done." Elsie tried to put it out of her mind as they walked to the house, hoping they made the right decision not to tell anyone. And she prayed it wouldn't happen again.

Three weeks later Katie disappeared, and Elsie's heart was broken for more than just one reason when Jake left with her.

~ Chapter One ~

ELSIE BLINKED, OPENED her eyes, and then peered out the window. Darkness hung in the morning sky. The storm clouds moved slowly, turning like smoke in the wind. Her heartbeat quickened as Elsie remembered where she was.

She knew, but drawing in a breath, she tried to forget. The four walls around her seemed to close in, suffocating her thoughts. It was her sister's birthday, but not a day to celebrate. Katie wasn't here.

At times she felt Katie was right there with her, even imagined what they might say or do. She wondered what Katie was doing now. Where was she? Elsie also thought of Jake. Her stomach roiled with anger and hurt. She didn't know which of them she resented more. The absence of one was hard enough, but both? When was the last time she hadn't been weighed down with such sorrow? Five months now, or was it six?

Soft rain hit the windowpane as she sat up in bed and gazed out at the endless rows of golden wheat fields. There would be no outside chores today. Even so, knowing she would have her five-year-old twin brothers in tow indoors made her tired. She immediately chastised herself for the thought.

They had moved from Virginia a year ago when young men in their large community needed land of their own. Finding a parcel size sufficient to make a living was becoming harder to come by in the areas up north. Here in Texas her family had more land than they could manage, but as Elsie soon learned, they were not welcomed by some of the locals.

Forcing herself to get ready for the day was becoming less painful. Even the simplest tasks used to irritate her and seemed pointless. Opening the closet door, she studied her black dress and white apron. They were wrinkled, in need of a good pressing. There were only a few of Katie's clothes left in the closet. Elsie thought of packing them up and putting them away in the attic with her other belongings, but she didn't. She left them there to see each morning and night, as if she needed something to hold onto to feel her sister's presence.

She had just walked over to the window when she heard her mamm come into the room. "Elsie, you're awake."

Without looking, Elsie knew her mamm's hands rested on her hips, her blue eyes sharp and blonde hair in a tight bun. She didn't want to discuss the significance of the day but turned to face her anyway.

"Sizing up the weather. There is plenty of work to be done indoors as well." Even as she spoke, Elsie knew her chipper voice didn't fool her mamm. When she turned, she could see it on her mamm's face.

"I'm sure your daed can find you something to do." Her mamm fell silent, seeming to analyze Elsie's every movement and word.

Elsie laid her clothes on the bed, smoothed her black dress, and then smiled at her mamm. "I don't want to leave you with the boys."

"I'll manage." Her scrutinizing stare made Elsie turn away. "Today will be hard."

Elsie stiffened her lower lip. She wanted to talk about it, yet didn't. Birthdays received little attention in the community. Elsie wondered if Katie and Jake were celebrating her day together right now.

"It'll get better. She'll come home." Mamm shifted forward and rubbed her hand along Elsie's arm. "Soon it will be your birthday. Twenty, that's a special one."

Her mamm's certainty hadn't waned over the last couple of months since Katie left. Elsie wasn't as confident of her sister's return, but then she knew more as to why Katie left than her mamm did. Telling anyone now about the harassment would only add more shame and suspicion to Katie's troubles.

The incident still gave her nightmares, and she shivered as the memory returned. Even in broad daylight she remained careful and watchful, especially when she was alone, listening for the sound of a car, picturing the boys with their leering expressions and hearing their dirty words.

If it weren't for Elsie's friend Rachel, Katie's absence would have been even harder. But Rachel had four brothers and her daed to tend to, with little time for conversation or consolation.

The five-year-old twins, Aaron and Adam, flew into the room freshly scrubbed, bringing the clean smell of soap with them. Her fair-haired brothers came to a halt when her mamm stepped in front of them. "Slow down, you two. Save your energy for your chores." She caught them both and gave them a tender hug until they wiggled free from her embrace.

"I'm starving." Aaron scrunched up his freckled nose and held his stomach for effect.

"I'm hungrier." Adam frowned, his chubby cheeks taut by the scowl he held.

"You two set the table, please." Mamm patted each of them on the bottom as they headed for the stairs. Adam glanced at Elsie. "Are you coming down?"

"I'm right behind you." Elsie smiled at him then turned to her mamm. "Are you sure about that?"

"About what, Elsie?" Mamm's brow furrowed, as if not wanting to go.

"About it getting better." Elsie let her gaze drift from her mamm's eyes. She didn't want to put pressure on her to talk about it only to make her feel hopeful. She wanted to see them both again. To scold and then hug Katie, and then to ask Jake how he could turn on her so abruptly, so cold. "And that she will come home?"

"I have great hope in my heart that it will get better, that she will come home, and we'll be a family again." Mamm's touch to Elsie's shoulder warmed her. She would try to hold the same good hope that her mamm did, and even more so the forgiveness she already gave Katie. "You're a strong young woman. You have so much ahead of you and Gideon—"

Elsie held up a hand, tired of her parent's references to Gideon. He was perfect. That's why she couldn't be around him. She was tainted with bitterness, yet Gideon never seemed to make a mistake or say a wrong word. And he was five years her senior, so he was more mature and grounded.

"If not him, then at least let someone in." Mamm waited for a reply, but Elsie couldn't share her thoughts about that horrid day that made her feel so dirty, and worse, that she'd kept the secret from those who loved her. From the whole community.

Mamm turned and went down the squeaky, wood stairs and sighed. "I wish I knew what went on in that head of yours."

Elsie merely smiled then slipped on her shoes and made her way to the kitchen to help with the morning meal of pancakes, eggs, and toast.

Her daed was up before dawn, tending to the morning milking, and was ready to eat. He lumbered in, ducking under the doorway, and rubbed his calloused hands together. "There's a chill in the air." He tapped each of the boy's heads and put his arm around Mamm's waist as he inspected the scrambled eggs. "Smells *gut* to me." His customary comment still made her smile. When he turned to Elsie, he tapped her on the nose and then sat down. "How's my girl this morning?"

Since Katie's departure Elsie was the only girl in the house, and she had to admit she liked the extra attention. She knew he meant more than his regular greeting due to the importance of the day, and she felt a small sense of peace. "It's going to be a *gut* day." She sounded more like her mamm than herself, but it was a heartfelt answer.

Elsie walked across the spotless white kitchen and took four plates off the shelf, placed them on the table, and then took the matchbox that hung on the wall. She lit an oil lantern and placed it on the large counter in the middle of the room.

As they ate, Mamm went to a shelf by the back door to gather dirty clothes and place them in a laundry basket. Today she and Mamm would do a week's worth of laundry, come rain or shine. Monday was wash day even if they had to set up a clothesline in the house. Daed had purchased a wooden washing wringer from their neighbor Jonas, who lived in their community, which helped the process along.

The boys sat at the spindle table their daed made and finished eating. They couldn't wait to get outside and see the baby birds. The chicks were new entertainment for them—until the next animal to come into the world, which made them very busy come spring time. Aaron stopped at the door. "Can you help me with my carving today, Daed?"

"*Jah*, son. I have a whittling knife just your size." He grinned at his son, obviously pleased Aaron wanted to learn the proper way to work with wood.

Elsie put away the last of the dishes and turned toward her daed as he walked to the door. "What do you need me to do today, Daed?"

He stopped with his hand on the door handle and told her his needs. "Axle on the wagon. I need one of the Fisher boys to come fix it for me." As Daed ran a hand over his dark, short hair, he studied Elsie's face for a moment, and then added a smile.

Elsie's heart nearly pounded out of her chest. Mamm stared at Daed as if he didn't know what he was saying. Elsie asked the question both she and Mamm were wondering about. "You mean go to the Fishers' house?"

Daed opened the door. "Only if you're up to it, Elsie."

Elsie thought of every reason she could say no. The memories of her time there with Jake would be painful. Their families hardly spoke since Jake and Katie left. The awkwardness of being with the Fishers would make it hard to go through the emotions that would arise. She avoided them, not knowing what to say and unsure where to find forgiveness in her heart for her sister or Jake. But she couldn't stay away forever.

Neither could she overcome her fear of being alone along the countryside. Since the vile harassment by the young English men, Elsie made a point to stay put on the farm or have someone with her. She often wished she'd confided in her parents right after it happened. As more time passed, the secret she held ate at her. She and Katie should have told what happened, because now the secret seemed no different from a lie, making the telling harder.

Elsie didn't know if she was physically up for the walk. She hadn't felt well all morning, and the temperature changed abruptly, making the day warm and muggy. The Fishers' place wasn't far but enough to complain about. Maybe it was an excuse. Her family worried about her adjusting to Katie and Jake's leaving. Maybe this was one way to show them she was better. Even more so, she needed to prove it to herself.

"Okay, I'll go." She stood tall but didn't look into their eyes. She was too close to saying no.

Mamm stared at Daed as if she didn't approve. Her lips parted, but she remained silent. Daed avoided her gaze, an act of will power to avoid both of their stares. "*Gut* girl." He nodded and walked out the door. Elsie followed, but her mamm stopped her.

"Elsie, you don't have to go." Mamm took her hand.

"It's okay. They're our neighbors, and I've been to their *haus* since...since they left, remember? I'll be all right." Elsie had to believe it herself before she could convince Mamm.

Mamm nodded. "*Jah*, you did well at the *haus* raising for their mammi and dawdi." Mamm stared at her with hopeful eyes.

She didn't need to know the pain Elsie felt that day. She was fine on the front lawn and preparing the food, but she couldn't go up to the porch where she and Jake had spent so much time together. And seeing the Fishers with their three boys left a big hole where Jake had been. Being the oldest, he assisted his daed not only with their blacksmith trade but also with caring for his brother Chris, who was a little slow.

"It'll be *gut* for me and make Daed feel better."

Mamm nodded. "Okay then." She patted Elsie's cheek and kissed her on the forehead, then caught up to Daed, who was on his way to the barn. "Solomon."

"*Jah*, Meredith." He stopped but didn't turn around.

Elsie heard his reluctant reply, but she turned away when they began to talk in hushed tones. Not wanting to be a burden, she walked on and didn't look back.

Chapter Two

THE WALK TO the Fishers' house was less than a mile, but Elsie felt it was twice as long in the heat of the sun slowly rising overhead, burning off the threat of rain. Her simple task was to ask them if they could help her daed with a broken axle; she could do that and would think of nothing else. But she couldn't let her mind rest with the thought of those young men finding her again. Elsie turned and glanced over her shoulder once, twice, and then again. After the third time she made herself keep her head facing forward, but even so she found she still listened for the sound of a motorized car. *I will not live in fear,* she repeated in her head.

She wiped the beads of sweat from her brow and turned down the dirt lane, lined with oak trees that led to the Fisher home. Her vision blurred as she tried to make out the distance. Her parched mouth and weak knees told her she needed water. It was foolish not to have drunk her fill before leaving, but she'd known if she didn't leave right then, she wouldn't go at all.

Wagons and buggies were lined up by the workshop. The large wooden building held tools and had stalls for horses needing shoes replaced or repaired. Although there were other blacksmiths in the community, the Fishers were usually chosen. They did the work more quickly due to the number of sons who knew the trade, and their skilled daed, Eli, oversaw the quality.

Elsie squinted as she looked ahead and saw a figure standing on the white porch. She couldn't make out the face until she was closer to the house and saw him turn to go inside. It could be Fishers' youngest son, Chris, who was shy around her and a bit slow. She squinted as she got to the house to see someone standing still right inside the door, not moving or speaking as she approached.

"*Hallo.*" The need for water overtook her usual instinct to withdraw. She anxiously stepped up to the porch. One step and then another, and she was standing at the last place she'd seen Jake…

The rocker squeaked each time Elsie pushed back with her toes. They had a perfect view of the barn raising the community was building for her cousins, John and Annie Yoder, whose barn burned to the ground.

"You need some oil," Jake informed her with a hint of a Texas accent.

"I don't need o-il." She enunciated the word. "The chair does. And if you keep talking like a Texan, Minister Zeke will scold you for not speaking our native tongue." She grinned, thinking that was a clever way to make him stop.

"Zeke doesn't concern me like he does you and the rest. He leaves his work to the deacons." The wind played with his blond hair that was too long.

Elsie sucked in air, having never heard anyone bold enough to say such a thing. "You shouldn't speak that way." She glanced around them to see if anyone was within hearing distance. It was true to a point, and now that he got her thinking about it, she thought maybe he was right.

"What way, the truth?" Jake continued to whittle a piece of wood with his knife as the men gathered together to begin their work. The women set out egg sandwiches, macaroni and cheese, fried chicken, and the sweet tea they'd become accustomed to.

Elsie eyed the shoofly pie and was satisfied. "You're gonna get yourself in trouble talking like that."

"I didn't think you could be persuaded so easily." He stopped for a moment to get her attention.

Elsie was about to defend herself when a herd of animals came running at them like a stampede; sheep and a couple pigs with the dogs nipping at their tails ran through and around the porch. Adam and Aaron's job was to herd the animals away, which wasn't an easy task with the new sprung grass in the front lawn. Jake started after a sheep that zigzagged to dodge him, but he fell, landing on his side with a sore arm that was on the mend.

Elsie waded her way through the mass of people and animals until she reached him. She took one step closer, lost her balance, and came tumbling down, landing on top of him. She put out her arms to push away, but he stopped her. His blue eyes shimmered against the sun, and for one second it was just the two of them, the noise and commotion mute for an instant. The warmth of his body made her uncomfortable, and she slid away.

Jake stood and offered her his hand, looking down at her with a grin. The combination of senses never left her mind, or the way he looked at her that day.

Small flecks of light drifted across her eyes, making her dizzy. She put a hand on the side of the house. Her brain told her to move away from the place where Jake told her he was leaving. Forcing her feet to go forward, she was distracted by the sound of footsteps inside the house walking away.

Figuring whoever it was hadn't seen her, she called out, "It's Elsie Yoder." Her voice was too parched to carry all the way into the house, so she stopped and sat down on the top stair. A slight breeze blew through the wisps of brown hair that escaped her kapp. She gave herself a moment to watch streaks of sunlight as they lit up the rolling hills.

Elsie again gathered the energy to go up to the front door. Maybe another family would hear her, give her water, and tend to the axle. Her daed would want her to at least give one of them the information.

"*Hallo*, it's Elsie." Silence. "Is anyone here?" She knocked again.

Elsie put her hands up around her eyes and her face against the screen. The smell of fresh bread drifted through the air, but still she heard no sounds. Even if she couldn't tell them about the axle, she needed water before she left. Her throat burned with the thought of going back home without getting a drink. She decided to go around to the back to see if she could find someone.

Elsie pushed her body forward across the porch, back to the stairs, and then heard the front door creak. She turned on her heel with newfound energy. Perhaps someone was finally here to help her.

Mose took a step out, held the door open, and started when he saw her. He was the second eldest son, a year older than Elsie. His blond hair and blue eyes were so similar to Jake's it made her pause.

"Elsie, come in. It's *gut* to see you." He spoke slowly so Elsie could understand him. She smiled as he held the door open so she could enter.

"Can I trouble you for some water?" She put a hand to her throat on impulse.

"Of course. Sit down." He helped her to the closest chair. She sat on the edge of it, impatient to quench her thirst.

Their home was plainer than hers—no colorful quilts or rugs or even a calendar on the wall to add a splash of color. There were only two chairs in the family room, but the kitchen was crammed with eight chairs surrounding a large wooden table.

As Mose walked away, Elsie remembered Katie talking about how handsome he was. The slight curl to his thick hair, along with his sturdy build, made it hard not to stare.

Mose returned quickly and handed Elsie the glass. She drank big gulps until he put a hand up to stop her. "Take slow drinks." He squatted down to see her straight on. "Better?" He reached for the glass, but she shook her head.

"Thank you, but I'm not finished." She took a couple more sips and felt the cool liquid soothe her throat and chest.

Mose didn't take his eyes off her and squinted in concern. "Are you okay?"

She nodded, but when Mose put a hand on her arm, Elsie felt awkward at his touch. It would have been proper to move her arm away, but she didn't. The resemblance to his brother was too strong.

Mose leaned back but kept his eyes on her. His slight smile made Elsie feel at ease. The dizziness began to fade, along with the burn in her throat. It was nothing more than the humidity and heat that caused the reaction. "I'm sorry. I'm not feeling well. I shouldn't have come."

"I'm glad you did, Elsie. I've missed your smiling face." He grinned as he said the words.

She was glad that's how he thought of her. This person she had become was not who she was. "I'm afraid I've let things go too long. I should have come sooner." She glanced across the room remembering happier times there. When he turned her way with questions in his eyes, she realized she should tell him why she came. "My daed needs help with a broken axle."

He tilted back slightly. "Oh, so this isn't a social visit."

She heard the disappointment in his voice as his expression became serious. It was then she realized she was a reminder for him. He was missing his brother in the same way she missed her sister.

Mose took her empty glass.

"I don't think it's urgent. If one of you could come to our place and take a look, my daed would appreciate it." Elsie stood and lifted her head to study his eyes. The bright blue eyes, Jake's eyes, made her stare as she waited for him to answer.

"I can go now and take the buggy so you don't have to walk back home. You look a lot better than when you first got here. Was it just the heat?" The compassionate glance appeared again, making her feel silly for bothering him with her discomfort.

"*Jah*, I'm fine. Thanks for coming over so soon." News of the buggy changed his focus. The longer they were together, the more comfortable she felt.

"Okay then, let's get you home."

With all the awkward emotions reeling in her mind, she couldn't agree more. She sat on the porch with Chris and watched Mose harness the horse to the buggy then got a metal toolbox and put it behind the seats.

Elsie scanned the fields and was sure it would be more than they could handle to run the blacksmith shop, plus grow as much crop as they did, without a household full of boys. Even Chris's disabilities didn't hold him back; he was good with the land and took more pride in it than most, sort of an obsession of sorts.

"All ready." Mose rested his arm on the porch beam and held out a hand to lead the way.

Elsie could hear the heel of his boot hit the ground with each step close behind her. "Bye, Chris." She turned to him as she walked across the porch.

He waved at her with a smile. "So long."

When she got to the buggy, Mose held up a hand to help her in then walked around and sat beside her. This was not ideal, the two of them being together alone, but was a necessity. She knew her parents would understand, but she hoped they wouldn't run into his mamm and daed. This isn't the way she wanted to see them; it would be uncomfortable enough without anything else to fret over. But sitting next to Mose with their shoulders touching did make Elsie a little uncomfortable; she needed to separate him from Jake. It was hard to do, with the similar appearance, voice, and lithe build. They could almost be twins.

"It is awful hot out here." Mose turned to her. "Are you sure you're all right?" His intense blue eyes were too familiar, and she looked away, watching the puffs of dirt kicked up by the horse.

"I'm fine. I feel silly to have bothered you." She wanted to forget about her weak moment and talk about something else. But the question lingering in her mind might not be well received. "Have you heard anything?" She didn't want to blurt it out but didn't want to miss the opportunity to get information about Katie.

Mose was quiet then finally spoke. "*Nee*. Have you?" He didn't take his eyes off the road, but his monotone response made her think he was trying to push it away. Elsie wondered why talking with Mose was so different from talking to Gideon. Was it because

Mose seemed more like her equal, even though Gideon was probably the kindest person she knew?

"Have you?" Mose asked again.

"*Nee.*" She knew better than to ask but was still glad she did. She felt his stare but didn't want to talk about it. She kept her gaze straight ahead on her family's white two-story clapboard house and the cluster of oak trees that surrounded it.

Mose jumped out, tethered the horse, and then went over to Elsie as she stepped out of the buggy. He stood quietly in front of her for a long moment. "If you ever need anything, let me know." He nodded earnestly and headed to the lame wagon tilting to the side.

Elsie wondered if something was hidden in his words, took one last glance, and then hurried into the house.

Chapter Three

THE SUN EASING down behind the horizon gave Gideon just enough light to make his way to the Yoders' barn. Their farm was plentiful with rich soil, producing one of the best crops, and the Yoders were as strong as the harvest they sowed. Thank God, as they were given a great cross to bear.

Gideon entered the stables. Solomon stood with his back to him, rubbing his neck. A bay mare paced back and forth whinnying. She stopped, put her head down, then slowly knelt. As soon as she made the forward motion, Solomon rushed to help her.

Gideon came to his side. Solomon stared at him as a broad smile crossed his face. "I do not see you for days, and then when I need you, you are here, praise *Gott!*"

"There is still a lot of transitioning for those of you who have moved down here from up north. It takes awhile to settle in, and I'm glad to help them." Gideon knew Solomon appreciated his visits since Will owned a farm now and the twins were too young to be much assistance with certain chores. The needs of the community kept Gideon away, but his own family was blessed with five boys, of which he was the eldest, so he was able to tend to others easier than some. Bishop Omar gave his blessing for Gideon to do so as well. He was glad to be back with the Yoder family, and even more so with Solomon's daughter Elsie.

The two men helped bring the animal down as gently as they could. Not that they were much help to the nine-hundred-pound mare, but it was Solomon's nature to try and help. Solomon didn't call for the local veterinarian, having grown confident with the birthing process. Solomon was there for his wife, Meredith, when she delivered each of their children and was a great comfort to her as well. He learned much from the community midwife, Alma, who arrived too late for the twins' delivery.

The mare whinnied and threw her head back. Her labor had started, and if all went well, it would be over within the hour. Solomon put his hand up to the mare's head and stroked her. When the colt's legs pushed through, Solomon gently tugged on them to help the mare along. He spoke quiet comforts while she worked at bringing new life into the world—God's miracle right before their eyes. Within a short time the colt tried to rise on long jittery legs. The proud momma licked her new babe, nudging him to stand.

"You pick the oddest times to show up, Gideon Lapp." Solomon sounded exhausted but delighted to have a healthy new colt and Gideon there with him.

Gideon felt slightly fatigued from spending most of his days with families in need, but he knew Solomon's fatigue was worse. The last year had been difficult adjusting to the move to Texas. Katie's leaving the community made it even worse. It seemed to have been hardest on Elsie. The sisters were close, which explained Elsie's heartache. But she showed little progress working through her sister's departure. He felt there was something more behind her sorrow.

"Thank God you are back," Solomon said as much to himself as to Gideon. The man wept when Katie left. It was one thing to deal with a child leaving the community, but an abrupt abandonment was too much to bear. The wrinkles under his eyes were more prominent, and his weak smile never touched his eyes.

"I came for a visit, not to tend to your mare." Gideon tried to lighten the mood, but it seemed neither had the energy. Their job done here, he wanted to have a moment with Elsie. He only hoped she would receive him. The longer her resentment over Katie's leaving went on, the further she pushed him away.

He got up and followed Solomon to the house. Day was turning to night as the sun slowly disappeared, leaving them in darkness except for the lit candles in the front windows.

Gideon glanced to either side of the steps as he walked up. The usual garden of flowers hadn't been planted, a chore he remembered Meredith and the girls looked forward to each spring. The spring planting would start soon, and Gideon would need to tend to his own family. Courting would begin come autumn, and it was then he hoped to gain Elsie's attention. He had always planned to, and now with Jake's departure from the community he felt the time was right to spend more time with her.

"What have you been up to that's kept you so busy?" Solomon asked with a bit of desperation in his voice, obviously missing his presence.

Gideon forced himself to stay away. He was torn between giving Elsie time to sort out her feelings alone and offering his help. He found neither a good choice. "I thought Elsie needed more time."

"She's better when you're here." The pleading penetrated his words once again.

Gideon hoped that was true. He knew her spirit was drowning, but she seemed to improve with each visit. She was making an effort to stop the downward spiral, yet Solomon told Gideon he didn't think Elsie could pull herself from the place she had fallen into. Gideon was sure she could.

Solomon grunted. "I feel as if I've lost two daughters, not just Katie."

Gideon slowed when they reached the top of the stairs and stared at Solomon. "We won't let that happen."

Solomon nodded slowly then ambled across the porch. He wasn't one to let his emotions show, especially of late. Both men were silent except for the sound of their boots hitting the wooden planks.

The smell of baking bread and beef wafted toward them as they entered the house and went through the entry room and then into the kitchen. Gideon's mouth watered. It had been a long time since he'd last eaten. Knowing he would be seeing Elsie tied his stomach in a knot, a juvenile reaction he thought he'd overcome, until he let Elsie steal his heart.

Gideon watched Elsie work with her mother in the large kitchen. Elsie walked across the spotless, hardwood floor to the long table with a stack of plates in her hands. She lifted her eyes to Gideon and stopped abruptly, her expression unreadable. She was still too thin but improving, and the glow of her skin was returning. Yet her eyes told the story of her soul. The light brown color still appeared to darken more each time he saw her.

"Gideon, I didn't know you were coming." She glanced down at the plates and at the sixth place at the table, Katie's chair. Then she looked at him again.

He smiled. The familiar feeling filled his chest, twisting the knot tighter in his gut. Her mouth twitched as if to hold back a hesitant smile. He was about to speak, but she spoke first. "I'll get another place setting."

"I hadn't planned on dinner." The awkwardness was too much to stand. As hungry as he was, he didn't know if he could sit through a meal with her.

"It's no bother." She set the plates on the table and went back to the cabinet with swift steps, as if she was grateful to turn away.

Meredith continued to scoop mashed potatoes into a huge bowl then placed it on the table. "We're all glad you're here, Gideon. It's been too long. Have you been helping the downtrodden?" She smiled with admiration, but Elsie gave her a disapproving stare before returning to the table with another plate. When she walked back into the kitchen, Solomon spoke with Gideon in a low voice.

"Have a seat." Solomon settled into a chair at the head of the table and motioned for Gideon to sit next to him. "I don't understand her behavior." He shook his head and rubbed his hand over the many scratches on the once smooth table. "She should be making plans for her own life, *jah*? Finding a new beau." He winked.

"*Jah*, unless there is something we don't know." Gideon took the gesture lightly. It was Elsie's decision as to whom she chose. But he understood this daed's frustration with his daughter's slow process getting back into community activity...it was a life without her sister. A feeling tugged at him, telling him there was more to her pain than betrayal of the young man she was attached to and the loss of her sister's companionship, although he couldn't begin to guess what it could be. He wondered how much Solomon and Meredith knew about Elsie's feelings for Jake. Courting was kept a secret and usually done in groups. "I wasn't sure of the relationships they had for one another until this all happened."

"I didn't pay close enough attention, I suppose." Solomon moved forward and spoke softly, his gray eyebrows drawing together. "What else could be bothering her?" Solomon's patience was weary, and understandably so. Elsie had been reclusive over the last couple of months.

The patter of four little feet rumbled down the stairs. "Gideon!" Adam yelled and came running with Aaron right behind him.

Elsie walked from the kitchen and smiled as they ran toward him. She put one hand out to stop them. "Slow down; it's time to eat."

Gideon motioned for them to come to him. His youngest brother demanded the same attention as these two, and he was happy to oblige. He messed Adam's hair and snapped Aaron's suspenders. "Your daed will need help with spring planting since Will has his own to tend to."

"*Jah*, I'm big enough now," Adam said, and Aaron nodded with enthusiasm.

"You're *gut* boys." Gideon didn't know how much they understood about all that happened involving their sisters. He knew the best way to help was to keep them busy. The whole family was still dealing with the situation, but Elsie's demeanor seemed to keep them from coming out of the shame Katie's leaving created.

"*Jah*, we'll need two strong boys to do the work," Solomon added, causing their faces to brighten.

They sat together at the thick, wooden table Solomon made from oak trees growing on his land. Adam sat shoulder to shoulder with Gideon. Aaron copied him on the other side. After Solomon prayed over the food silently, the tinkling of silverware grew in volume over the silence. It grated in Gideon's head until he couldn't stand it any longer.

"How are Will and his new bride, Ruby, getting along?" He had heard of the vandalism that went on at their place—a mailbox hit from the post and knocked a couple of feet away. Others had much worse destruction since the Amish came to claim the land. Gideon didn't know if he should bring up the subject, knowing how independent Will was. He may not have told them. It was a blessing and a curse to have others confide in him; with the information came difficult decisions.

Solomon looked up from his food with fork in hand. "They are still settling into their new home. I'll miss having him come planting. We're still getting used to this Texas heat; planting comes too soon down here in Bee County."

"You know I'm always able to help, Solomon." Gideon almost felt guilty. As much as he meant what he said, his motivation was always Elsie first when it came to helping the Yoders.

"I miss Will." Elsie's voice was such a surprise Gideon couldn't help but turn his head her way. She hadn't taken her eyes away from her plate, but it was good to hear her speak her thoughts about something…anything.

"I'd like to see their new home. Maybe you could take me over sometime." Gideon thought he might have jumped at the chance for an outing with her a little too eagerly, but if his interest showed, so be it.

Elsie glanced his way and nodded, then turned to her daed, who was smiling his agreement.

After dinner Solomon read his Bible to the children by the fire. Gideon sang a silly song that got the boys laughing. Then they all sang a traditional hymn. Aaron began to rub his eyes and yawned.

"It's time for bed." Meredith wrapped her arms around her sons' shoulders and walked them up the stairs. Once they were in their room, they started calling for Gideon to tell them good night.

With the children asleep, Meredith and Elsie finished the cleanup of supper dishes while he sat with Solomon by the fire. A round rug of many colors lay at their feet, one Meredith made with Katie and Elsie to teach them the craft. Pillows the girls made set on two side chairs. The yellow and green coloring of one stood out to Gideon. He remembered Elsie's beaming face when she showed him her accomplishment.

Gideon studied Solomon as the older man slumped in his rocking chair. The lines around his eyes seemed more deeply etched, which made Gideon wonder if a parent ever got over a child's desertion. He supposed God wanted them to trust Him and not on themselves for understanding. "You have a fine family, Solomon, and a *gut* life. You should count yourself a blessed man."

"You go on and remind him of that, Gideon," Meredith chimed in as she wiped off the table.

"It would do you *gut* to stay out of this man's conversation," Solomon teased. He rocked at a livelier rhythm and then turned to Gideon.

Meredith came over to Gideon and put her hand on his shoulder. "We're glad you're here."

He grinned. "It's always *gut* to spend time with all of you, but I should be going."

Solomon and Meredith spoke at once, but it was Elsie's voice Gideon heard. "You're leaving?"

His eyes lifted to hers. For a brief moment he thought he saw a flicker of disappointment, which gave him hope. "Would you like to walk me out to the porch?" His heart thumped in his chest. Even a few moments alone with her could be enough if only she'd let him in.

Elsie stared at the floor and put her hands behind her back.

"*Nee*, I don't want to keep you." She turned toward the kitchen, her eyes still downward.

Gideon didn't know whether to let her go or offer again. He didn't seem to be able to make a single right decision when it came to her. "I'm not in a hurry, Elsie. I can stay." He sounded more like he was pleading than offering his time.

Elsie stopped as if she'd come to a dead-end and stared into the kitchen. He knew she felt the need to finish in the kitchen and thought of a solution. "I can help you with the dishes if you like."

When she turned to him, her drawn face relaxed slightly. "*Jah*, that would be nice."

"Do you mind?" Gideon asked Solomon.

"Of course not, son." Solomon moved his hand forward as if to physically shove him into the other room.

Gideon stepped lively into the kitchen and closed the door halfway. He hoped with more privacy she would confide in him. "I'll dry." He picked up a towel and reached for one of the plates she'd rinsed.

"*Danke*." She kept her eyes forward as she handed another plate to Gideon. It was all he could do not to talk, but he wanted her to feel some pressure to say what was on her mind. Small talk would only slow things down.

The repeated clatter of dishes and soft spray of water lulled him into the feeling he was only here for moral support, nothing more. "Elsie?"

She started as if in another world. Elsie glanced at him but avoided his eyes. "You need to go, I know. I'm sorry. I want to talk to you, but I can't seem to get the words out." She handed him silverware and wiped drops of water from her cheek.

"It might be *gut* for you to, Elsie. Maybe you can try. If it doesn't feel right, stop, and we'll wait for another time." His words were just above a whisper, slow and methodical.

When he put a hand on Elsie's shoulder, her resolve seemed to melt, and she stared straight at him. "How do I get past this, Gideon? What is this stronghold on me?"

Gideon put down the towel and turned to face her. He wanted her to hear his words clearly. "Take one step forward to show yourself you can do it."

Her eyes began to water. "What step?"

He held her stare, no matter how hard it was to see pieces of her fall apart. "Forgive Katie."

Her eyes widened, and she took a deep breath. "I've tried, but the anger and resentment come back."

"Don't give up. Think of the seventy times seven Christ asks of us." He lifted his hand and wiped off the remaining water on her cheek. "It means infinity."

She nodded her understanding, locking her eyes on his. For the first time Gideon felt she might care for him in the same way he cared for her.

~ Chapter Four ~

ELSIE WOKE FROM her dream, one that played over again in her mind, a wheat field in flames. To an Amish family a burning field was the same as burning money, especially if they were unable to do anything but watch their livelihood go up in smoke.

She sat up in bed and surveyed the dark sky. Closing her eyes, she pushed the vision away and thought of life in Virginia. Elsie enjoyed the memories of their home being built, the friends she'd grown up with, and Bishop Omar, whom she would have missed had he not come with their group here. He was the one person she wished she could confess everything to that was burdening her heart.

She understood why they needed to leave. With three sons to think of, her daed knew they needed to go some place where they could have the land they needed to continue living the Amish way. Some men avoided the move, finding jobs in nearby towns, but they missed working the land. Solomon wanted his boys to continue their farming traditions even if it meant leaving.

"Morning!" Her mamm sang as she came into her room and grinned when she saw Elsie fully dressed. Her mamm's bright mood was catching. It was enough to make her smile.

"I was up early." Elsie was working on a better outlook and determined she would succeed.

"What would I do without your help to prepare breakfast?" Mamm rarely ate a warm meal, always fetching something for one of the children, let alone have one made for her.

"*Nee*, no one cooks like you do." Elsie thought it would be nice to make Mamm breakfast one morning. She stored it in her mind. Mamm appreciated actions more than words or gifts.

"Put your apron on and remember its meaning." With that she stepped out of the room.

Putting on one's apron meant you were ready to work—a quality instilled in her since she was a child. "I'll be down quickly," Elsie called out behind her.

Gideon had told Elsie he had something to show her and had asked if she could come by when morning chores were done. Elsie frequented Omar's home more after Jake left, having more time once he was gone. She didn't realize how much she saw him until suddenly he wasn't there anymore. Elsie stayed awake all night after he told her his plans. He left before she got to his house the next morning. Then she came home to find Katie gone as well. Elsie rubbed her chest, still feeling the stabbing pain of her discovery. Her sister never told her she cared for Jake so deeply. But the ways of courting in their community were proper and subtle, especially in the Fisher and Yoder homes.

Once she cleaned the breakfast dishes, she waited for the boys and her daed to leave. "Mamm, can I meet with Gideon for a while later today?"

"Of course; he could have joined us for breakfast." She scrubbed a cast iron pan with vigor until its surface was smooth and clean.

"I'm meeting him at Omar's." Elsie removed her kapp and repositioned it firmly on her head.

"I suppose you won't need a chaperone there." She smiled and placed the pan on the white counter. "You and Gideon seem to be getting along well."

"He's been a part of our family since we came here." Elsie tried to make light of their relationship, not sure of how she felt.

"That's been over a year now. That's long enough to know how you feel about someone." Mamm couldn't hide her want for Elsie to marry a young man like Gideon. Elsie had seen Mamm watching and listening to them while she tended to her household duties.

"The person I felt for is with someone else." Elsie stuck the pins through her kapp then looked at her mamm. Her lips parted slightly as she forced a smile.

"Well, he wasn't the right one for you then." She drew Elsie to her and gave her a tight hug. "Gideon is more handsome than any young man I've yet to see."

Elsie scoffed at her mamm, not used to her saying such words. She shook her head. "I will be back to help with the noon meal. *Danke*, Mamm." Elsie appreciated her mamm letting her spend time away from the farm. It made her feel responsible and more mature. She would pick some bluebonnets for Mamm on the way home and put them in a vase for her.

When she got to the main dirt road, she noticed a rider and horse heading her way. It was Rachel and her bay. "Where are you off to?" she asked as she brought Charles to a halt in front of Elsie.

"To Omar's. Want to give me a ride?" Elsie reached up before Rachel could answer and pulled herself up on the horse's back behind Rachel.

"We haven't ridden together for ages." Rachel clucked to get Charles into a slow stride.

"You're too busy."

"I can't argue with that. But it will get better when my brother is married off."

Elsie sucked in air. "How do you know?" Couples kept their marriage intentions private until they made an announcement to the church, but it wasn't much of a surprise if they were courting.

"He's has been asking me a lot of questions. With no mamm to ask, I suppose it all falls on me." She kicked again for Charles to pick up his hooves. "Charles is lazy today. I hope you're not in a hurry."

"*Nee*, don't worry." Although she was anxious to see Gideon, she appreciated this time with her closest friend. "Do you mind knowing about their plans?"

"*Nee*, I just wish I had a mamm to talk to when my time comes."

They were both quiet for a short while. Elsie wished she hadn't asked the questions, so she switched to a more teasing tone. "And when will that be?"

"Much later than you," she teased, and Elsie tugged at a long strand of her dark hair.

"Are you and Gideon spending more time together?" Rachel asked.

"*Jah*, I suppose it's become common knowledge. He's helped with...well, everything."

"You seem better." Rachel turned her head to let Elsie see her smile. "He's a *gut* man."

Elsie sighed at hearing the familiar compliment. "*Jah*, I know. I only wish I could live up to him. I felt more comfortable with Jake for that reason."

"Then you were selling yourself short." Rachel turned down the dusty road leading to Omar's house. "You need to stop that way of thinking."

"And you need to stop making us a couple, or people will think we are." When they got to the house, Elsie jumped down off Charles and frowned at Rachel. She loved her friend, but she was full of advice at times. Elsie expected it came from raising all those boys, but she didn't always appreciate it when it fell on her.

Rachel grinned. "Okay, whatever makes you feel better." She turned Charles and started back toward the road.

"We need to work on our quilt." Elsie was glad she thought of an excuse for her friend to spend time with her. It was good medicine to sit together and quilt; finishing their quilt was long overdue. It was one Katie started with Elsie before she left, but Elsie couldn't bear to leave it undone.

Rachel raised a hand to her forehead. "I'd almost forgotten."

Elsie waved and eagerly walked the rest of the way to the white house with black trim. She was anxious to find out what Gideon wanted to share with her. Omar's home was large for his many children, but some of them moved away to start their own families, leaving a couple of rooms for he and Gideon to study.

Services were held in the parishioners' homes, but Omar opened his home for meetings with the deacons and ministers.

Elsie knocked on the door, and Minister Zeke answered. He was a squatty, egg-shaped man, with a ring of dark hair around his head, and always in a sweat. His squinty eyes peered into hers.

"Elsie, Gideon mentioned you'd be coming. Come in." He opened the door wider, and Elsie stepped inside. A long staircase led upstairs, and a large dining room was to the right next to the kitchen. To her left were the meeting rooms. "So you're here to see Gideon."

"*Jah*, he's studying something he wants me to see." Elsie wanted as little assumptions made as possible. She had too much on her mind to have anything else to worry about.

"I see." A smile stretched across Zeke's face. "It's not usual for a young woman to study here at Bishop Omar's home. Is there something I should know about?"

Elsie leaned back, wanting to create a distance between them. "*Nee*, he wants to show me something is all."

He rubbed his hands together and hummed. "How is your family coping with everything that's gone on?"

"We're fine, Zeke. *Danke*." Elsie was tired of his nosy questions and tried to pass by him. "Which room?"

He smiled and pointed to the open door to her left. "Keep the door open."

"*Danke*." Elsie was already walking to the door, not wanting to have to answer any questions.

Elsie peeked in and searched for him. It was silent, so she walked to the back room where the ceremonial pieces were kept. Gideon sat at a small desk, reading a thick book with paper and pen at his side. His eyes moved across the page, and he scribbled something in a notebook. This was why she felt she wasn't worthy of him. His desire for knowledge and serving the people seemed to come so naturally for him. She felt compassion for others, but it didn't seem to be enough.

Elsie stepped closer. "What are you reading?"

He started and slowly turned to her. He smiled his greeting and pointed to the black book. "This is what I wanted to show you." The hardback appeared to be ancient. Chips were missing from the cover, and the title's gold stenciling showed wear from age and heavy use. The *Martyrs Mirror* was something she'd heard about in Sunday services, but she didn't know any of the stories specifically.

Elsie sat on the chair next to him that he obviously prepared before she came. "I've never seen a book this large." She felt Gideon's eyes on her, enjoying her fascination. "We have the book at home, but I've never read it myself."

"There are over twelve hundred pages from the years 1562 to 1660 describing the accounts of martyrdoms in the Christian faith." He stopped only long enough to see if she was with him, which she definitely was. "The book was created in an era when the Anabaptists were being imprisoned for their beliefs."

Elsie cringed. "This may sound disrespectful, but I really don't want to read about Christians dying."

"It's their final messages from jail that will not only explain the roots of your faith but tell you about our history. You've read of the disciples and how they met their fate due to their faith." He tapped the cover. "This is their story, and many more."

Elsie still wasn't sure she wanted the details, but she was intrigued simply because of Gideon's enthusiasm. "How were they able to record all of this?"

"Various sources. Some are memoirs, others written records never before made public. There is information from examinations, death sentences, and letters. Also documents obtained from magistrates, criminal authorities, and clerks. The list is long and substantial."

She smiled. "You know a lot about this."

He glimpsed at her, to the book, and back again. "These examples have strengthened my belief in more ways than I thought possible. Backed up with Scripture and the history found in the

Old Testament, I've found it to be second only to the Bible for learning our place in this world."

Gideon knew her diligence for the Bible. Comparing any book to it caught her attention. "If it's that relevant to all Christians, why is it partial to the Amish and Mennonites?"

"The persecution told in this book is what drove the Amish from England to North America."

She pursed her lips. "That's a well-known fact."

"But this explains our heritage from four hundred fifty years ago."

Elsie's brow lifted. "Can I see it?" She didn't look away and began reading before he could answer.

> The *Martyrs Mirror* is about Christians who discovered God wanted more for His people than they ever imagined. Because their transformed lives set them apart, they were criticized and persecuted, meeting in secret, anticipating arrest, but often winning the respect of their neighbors, winning converts who saw them sacrifice their lives.

"This *is* interesting." She sat back, and Gideon read more to her.

> "Those memorialized in this book wanted to restore the glory of God's original plan for His Church. They laid the plumb line of the Gospel to their lives, and as best they could, sought to adjust their lives to match Christ's example, instead of reinterpreting Christ's example to fit their lives."

They talked, exchanging questions that neither could answer. Their curiosities led to more questions that led to the foundation of their faith. Though Elsie had reservations about a book full of strife, she was intrigued by what they'd discussed. When the clock chimed, it didn't seem possible that an hour could have passed by.

"You know so much about the history of our faith. I can see why you are thought to be a minister." Elsie was almost jealous. Her fervor for the Word was so great she wished she could have a place among the men who studied and knew the Bible well. But that couldn't happen in the Amish community. "I wish I had the opportunity you do."

His dark eyes flashed. "You're always welcome to study with me. I know you spend time in the Bible and have a passion to learn more." He tilted his head. "I definitely know that much about you."

She laughed. "Do you think you know everything about me?"

"*Jah*," he responded soberly. "Pretty much anyway."

This made her pause. "Perhaps you're right."

They sat in silence until Elsie broke through the quiet by glancing away. "I should be getting back to help my mamm." She stood, and Gideon followed her out.

"If there is anything you want to share with me, you know I'll hold it in confidence."

Elsie stared down at her black leather boots and brushed off a chunk of mud with her toe. "Sometimes I think you can read my mind."

"There are times I wish you could read mine." He smiled gently and watched her go. Elsie turned once to see him still standing in the doorway, but she knew he continued to watch her until she was out of sight.

As she made her way along the road, she heard the creaking of a wagon behind her. She turned around to see Mose's blond hair blowing in his eyes and a smile growing across his face. "What are you doing out here in the middle of the day?" He pulled on the reins, and the horses slowed to a halt.

"I don't want to be late for the noon meal." She looked around hesitantly then lifted a hand to cover her eyes. "Would you mind giving me a ride home?" She didn't know if she should make the request. It might be frowned upon that they were together alone, but she didn't want to be late in helping her mamm with the meal.

"Sure, hop in." He helped her with a hand up and waited for her to get settled. "Are you feeling better these days?" His blue eyes rested on hers as he waited for her answer.

"*Jah*, I'm fine. I don't know what came over me that day." She looked away, knowing exactly why. Being there again without Jake, the heat of the day, and sitting there with Mose created a combination of both emotional and physical anxiety.

"I was glad to see you again, Elsie." Mose glanced at the horses but then gave his attention back to her. "I'm not sure why, but I feel better when I'm with you." He studied her, but she didn't know what he surmised.

"We have a common bond. It gives a body comfort to know someone else is going through the same hardship as they are." She didn't believe her words and hoped he didn't see her as downplaying the way he felt. "I do know what you mean though. It's *gut* to be able to talk about them." She didn't want to say Jake's and Katie's names. That would open up a conversation she didn't want to have. Right now she felt comfortable and relaxed.

They were quiet for a while, and Elsie enjoyed the common silence between them. Then Mose pursed his lips and talked but kept his head forward. "I hope this doesn't make you feel awkward, but I'd like it if we spent time together every now and again. Just to talk about them." He turned to her then with question in his eyes. "Does that sound okay, or would it make you uncomfortable?" His crystal blue eyes were intense as he waited for her answer.

She wasn't exactly sure of what he meant. It seemed innocent enough, but she didn't think it was such a good idea. "You mean to support each other?"

He paused, soaking in what she said. "*Jah*, it would be *gut* to have someone to talk to."

Elsie questioned how much it would help. And in the end she decided that some companionship between them might do them some good, but she'd rather not be reminded of Jake in any way, even if it meant keeping her distance from Mose.

⌣ Chapter Five ⌣

THE MILKING WENT slowly. If Gideon wore a watch, he'd be checking it every few minutes as he observed the tourists doing in town. He couldn't get to the fields fast enough, knowing Elsie would be there. Not used to this rushed feeling, he felt an unfamiliar anxiety. He paced down the row of Holsteins and watched as the machines pumped.

It seemed that something was different about Elsie this last time he saw her. Less pain in her eyes? A willingness to press forward? He couldn't put his finger on it, but something was there that wasn't before.

When the machines quieted, he went from one to the next, removing the suction cups and wiping them down. Once the milk was pasteurized, it was distributed into containers. Gideon took the bottles to the cooler and placed them on the shelves.

Studying *Martyrs Mirror* gave him and Elsie a common interest and, Gideon had to admit, also an excuse to spend time with her. Her parents' complete trust in him made him appreciative, but he also felt a great deal of pressure. His attraction for her was not only emotional but physical as well. He kept his thoughts pure in order to stay focused on creating a friendship in hopes it would eventually grow into more.

When he finished feeding the livestock, Gideon made his way to the first home where a number of men were gathering to help with spring planting. They proceeded from one farm to another until every one from the group had their crop seeded for fall harvest.

When he arrived at the Stolzfus home, a group of a dozen men stood on and around the porch talking and taking in the weather.

A few dark clouds threatened rain, but they would work through it unless it became unbearable.

"Gideon, my friend. We need your solid arms to steady the plow." Benjamin Stolzfus made the experience as much of a social gathering as a day of labor.

"You put me to work before I got a chance to say hello." Gideon stepped lively into the circle of men and exchanged their banter. With greetings aside, they each began their part in the process. Gideon found the horses and harnessed them. After hitching the plow, he was ready. Each horse team required two people, so Gideon readily grabbed his friend Yonnie to assist him. He didn't bother to slow down, teasing his friend by making him run.

Yonnie ran up and pulled himself onto the bench. "Thanks for stopping to let me get on." He grinned and brushed the blond hair from his eyes. "So how are things at the Yoders?" He rested his arms on his muscled thighs and waited for Gideon to answer.

"Why would you ask about another family other than my own?" Gideon played along, not knowing if he wanted to bare his soul to his inquisitive friend.

"I've heard you've been spending time there." Yonnie fed on others' relationships because he couldn't seem to have one of his own. His forward and brash ways weren't appreciated by most girls, and even more so their parents. He meant well but had a big personality.

"I spend time at many different homes, just not yours lately." Gideon laughed. "Do you miss me, old friend?"

"Not so much. I've been busy with a girl of my own." Yonnie turned to see his reaction. Gideon all but dropped the reins hearing the news.

"Who?" was all Gideon could manage to say.

"Beverly Zook." He waited for only a second then had to ask, "You don't approve, or are you jealous?"

Gideon didn't fall for the bait. He knew too well Yonnie's struggle with women, and he hoped he found someone who suited him. He just couldn't picture him with a bishop's daughter. "Neither; she's a nice girl."

Yonnie's face became somber. "How are the Yoders? Letting go, I hope."

Gideon paused at the words. "That's a *gut* way to put it. All but Elsie, but even she is coming along." If his prayers were answered, that would come to fruition. In the meantime, all he could do was hope.

"Did you hear about the Kings' fence line getting cut?" Yonnie winced as if it pained him to say it.

"*Jah*; did they lose any livestock?" Gideon usually knew first-hand when these incidents happened, but he had been preoccupied with the Yoders and studying *Martyrs Mirror*. It was worth it. He was sure the study was helping Elsie through her own time of trial. She seemed to be getting a grasp what their forefathers went through to create a peaceful and forgiving people.

"Found 'em wandering about. Thought this nonsense would stop." Yonnie sat up and tightened the reins.

"You don't think it was an accident?"

"*Nee*." He quickly answered then turned to look at Gideon. "Why, don't you?"

Gideon chose his words carefully. Spreading rumors without the facts would lead to more problems. "I'd like to think so."

Yonnie scoffed. "Always the optimist."

They dropped the plow and started refining the rows of soil. They were followed by those dropping the seed. Cotton and wheat grew best down south, unlike the tobacco they planted up north. Gideon's community taught the men who moved here how the crops differed. The newcomers from Virginia settled farther south on land that butted up against the land of the Texans, who also grew crops and raised livestock. That's where most of the trouble occurred, according to the authorities, but they could do little about it unless the Amish pressed charges. But they wouldn't, so it was futile.

They took a break at noon when the women brought sandwiches

and drinks. Gideon kept an eye out for Elsie but stopped when Yonnie noticed his distraction. Gideon watched as Mose walked up beside her and they began to talk. He supposed it was only appropriate considering they both felt the loss of a sibling. Elsie caught a glimpse of Gideon and made her way over.

"I thought I might find you here when I saw Yonnie." Elsie's voice broke into his thoughts as he turned to greet her.

"Elsie, I was looking for you." Gideon knew his face was beaming, but he couldn't curb his emotions.

"The boys wanted to help me milk this morning." That's all she needed to say. The boys added time to the chore that took awhile to begin with.

Yonnie shook his head. "My sisters won't set foot in the barn if there's milking to tend to. You're fortunate to have a girl who doesn't mind helping with the Holsteins."

Elsie and Gideon stared at one another. No one referred to Elsie as being his. He snapped back into the conversation and groaned thinking about when he had to be patient with his younger brothers as they learned the routine. "The cows are never in a hurry, and I'm sure Adam and Aaron aren't either."

Elsie nodded her agreement. "Once Will left, it became my chore. I don't mind it though. Gets me out of the house for a while, doing something different. When the boys are old enough, they'll take over."

Elsie dealt with a lot of the people in her life leaving, moving on while her own life hadn't changed. Will left first and then Jake and Katie soon after. Gideon hadn't thought about how close together their departures were.

She walked closer and glanced over the field he was working. "Looks like you're almost finished."

"This soil is better than most, much like your daed's." Gideon knew Solomon missed the fertile soil that didn't need the extra season of soybean or clover to replenish. The red clay of Texas had to be treated, or it wouldn't hold the water needed to grow healthy crops. The men worked together until they found a mix of acceptable fertilizer. Solomon continued searching for new ideas, hoping for results like he had in the fields up north.

Yonnie peeked into Elsie's basket even though his plate was full of food. "What 'cha got in there?"

"Don't tell me you want more." Elsie smiled and sat down on the picnic blanket then passed around the egg sandwiches she made. Yonnie stuffed one in his mouth just as Beverly sat down next to him. Gideon was glad to have a moment to talk with Elsie alone.

"Are you still interested in visiting Will and Ruby?"

"*Jah*, I've already told them. They said they would like you to come for dinner."

"I bet you miss him."

She sighed as if she didn't want to be reminded. "It's as if there's a hole in my heart for each person who's left."

"A lot has changed in a short period of time. It's understandable you feel that way."

"That among other things."

"You still don't feel settled after a year's time?"

She shook her head, perhaps out of frustration. He tried to read her expression. Maybe there was something she couldn't tell him. "It doesn't feel like home yet."

"Give it more time. It's hard not to compare a place where you were born and raised—your home—to a new place that's unfamiliar." He smiled. "But it must be familiar, in some ways."

"I spoke out of turn." She gestured broadly. "This is that place for you. This is home." She let her gaze drift away from him. "It doesn't feel like we should be here."

"Well, I'm glad you are, Elsie Yoder." He waited until she turned toward him, caught her eyes, and smiled again, playfully.

"There is one *gut* thing about being here," she said warmly. "If we hadn't moved, I wouldn't have met you." She turned around to see if anyone heard her. Then, as if embarrassed, she began to clean up the food, packing it away in a large basket.

Gideon didn't want to further embarrass her, so he didn't

respond, but he wished he could tell her how much she meant to him. But he sensed she wasn't ready to hear it. "You're here for a reason. You just don't know what it is yet." He glanced over at the older men who were sitting together, laughing and eating their fill. "Your daed is quite a fellow." Solomon belted out one of his thunderous laughs, confirming Gideon's words.

She grinned. "My mamm thinks the smaller community is better for us down here."

He watched as Elsie scanned the area filled with children playing and women talking and hoped she would someday agree with her mamm, enjoying the laughter and conversation filling the air.

The men started to get back to their planting but were diverted by a game of Eck ball, which was simply avoiding getting hit by a handmade ball wrapped with twine.

Some of the more conservative groups felt that sports destroy one's sense of modesty and emphasize pleasure. Gideon hadn't seen or heard of anyone from Elsie's group speak against it, so thought he'd join in. "I've got to get on the team against Yonnie."

"If you want me to encourage you, I can't. Where I'm from this is considered prideful." Elsie turned away, making it clear she was finished talking about the matter. She answered his question, but he was unsure how to handle the situation.

Gideon stood when Yonnie called his name. He stared him straight in the eyes and almost laughed at Yonnie's serious expression. That alone proved Elsie's point, but he still didn't think a simple game together caused any harm.

The game wasn't being played in a barnyard covered with hay like when they were boys. The spring grass had come in, but the ground would be hard when you went down after a spin to dodge a throw.

Spectators made up of older men, women, and children gathered around to watch. The men reminisced about the days they were young and agile enough to play the game. The women grimaced when a ball hit a player too hard, and the young children imitated their own game with a hardened piece of manure that was quickly taken away by a nearby mamm. He caught a glimpse of Elsie, her face unreadable, but he had a good idea of what she was thinking.

The sting of a few hits and the hard ground began to work the pain around until Gideon felt like his whole body hurt. He watched until Yonnie was struck out and ran to the side like he didn't have a single ache. If that wasn't pride, Gideon didn't know what was. "Good game, friend."

They shook, and Yonnie gave him one of his slaps on the back that hurt more than usual. "*Jah*, we haven't played that game for a while. That's the last time I play without a layer of hay under my feet."

"No doubt about that, or maybe not play at all." Gideon was beginning to lean toward Elsie's rationale, if for no other reason than to avoid the pain. "I'm ready to be a bystander." Gideon glanced over at him. "You don't seem to be hurting like I am."

"I'm tougher than you." Yonnie grinned. "But if we ever do play again, it'll be with tomatoes." He squeezed Gideon's shoulder and limped away just as he caught sight of Elsie walking away in the other direction.

Chapter Six

G IDEON JUMPED UP into the wagon bed and made a rough count of the chairs. The men were lined up from where he stood to the front doors of the Yoders' home, passing folded chairs to one another for church service. Although families usually took turns holding the services, Omar offered to have it at the Yoders' place again this Sunday. Their house was the largest of the twenty or more families who attended church, so the women and children were able to gather in a separate room from the men. This led Gideon to believe there was something out of the ordinary to be addressed.

John directed the men to where the chairs needed to be set up, and Annie guided the women and children into the side of the house they would be meeting.

"Gideon." John nodded and guided him to a corner of the room. "What's this I hear about Elsie Yoder?"

The gossip kept things turning even though there wasn't usually much to tell. Gideon was sure he and Elsie were big news, but no one was supposed to ask, John being the exception. "You would be the one to ask." Gideon smiled.

"You know me well enough. I'll ask to your face, not behind your back." He leaned against the wall, but his eyes shifted toward Annie, who was making room for more benches. "I gotta go help, so make it quick."

"You're going to be disappointed to know there's nothing to say." Gideon shrugged and John frowned. "Believe me, I wish there was more to tell."

"Well, hurry things up. Elsie's better off with you." One of his little ones ran between them, causing John to grin. "Our kids need to grow up together."

Gideon nodded in agreement, but it only made him wonder if Elsie felt the same way. She'd spent a lot of time with Jake, and at times he wondered if there was anything more than friendship between them.

Minister Miller, Zeke, and Omar seemed deep in conversation at the far end of the entry room. Gideon tried not to stare, but his curiosity got the best of him. The minister's serious expression and crossed arms gave away his anxiety. Omar, however, seemed calm, nodding slowly as the other man spoke. Gideon hoped there was not a problem involving Omar, a man he trusted and held in high regard.

Mose strode in carrying three chairs, whereas most of the other men could handle only one or two. He was a strong, cocky one in Gideon's mind. He instantly chastised himself for his negative thoughts toward Mose, knowing his disapproval stemmed from the knowledge that Mose took Elsie home the other day unattended by a chaperone. Not that this was unheard of, but usually permission was expected from the parents.

Mose arranged the chairs and then turned to Gideon. Their eyes locked until Mose nodded and went out to get more chairs. The tension was there, and Gideon wouldn't let it go. He was never one to avoid conflict. As it was written, however, a believer must approach the person they have wronged, and they must work it out together. That is what he set out to do.

When the chairs were unloaded, Gideon walked over to Mose, who stood talking and laughing with some of the other men. Gideon tapped his shoulder, and Mose turned to face Gideon without surprise. The others continued their banter as the two men stepped away.

"I wondered how long it would take you to feel the need to talk to me." Mose stared straight ahead, his eyes narrow and chin lifted.

As soon as he said the words, Gideon scorned himself for

taking the liberty to question Mose about the situation. He was too involved in Elsie to be impartial. So he diverted. "How is everyone getting along with Jake gone?"

Mose frowned at him before he responded. "I thought you were going to ask me about Elsie." He gave Gideon a sideways glance. When Gideon didn't answer, Mose continued. "We're making do, just like the Yoders." Mose stopped and turned to look at Gideon full-on. "That's what we talked about the day I took her home."

Gideon knew he deserved this. Mose should know better than to think Jake was on his mind instead of Elsie. He let out a long breath, caught in his misguided intentions. "I guess I've become protective of Elsie."

"You guess?" Mose chuckled and shook his head.

Gideon smiled as well. "It's more obvious than I realized."

Mose glanced at the sun rising above the acres of land, silos, barns, and white clapboard houses. "You have to understand we have a certain bond between us with our siblings going off the way they did. Married by now, I suppose."

Mose didn't bat an eye when he said it, but Gideon flinched at the word. "You sound sure of this. Do you really think they would marry outside the community?"

Mose shrugged. "I sure hope so. Living together would ban them from the community in a heartbeat. Coming back legally joined might get 'em back in."

His refreshing honesty surprised Gideon. No one was brave enough to talk about them, let alone speculate what their situation might be. "I hadn't thought about it that way." Gideon squinted into the sun with Mose.

"That's because you've been too occupied with Elsie," Mose said coolly.

"You might be right about that too." He turned to Mose. "But she also accepts my company." Gideon hated the way that sounded, justifying Elsie's feelings for him. He felt intimidated by

Mose, unsure of the man's intentions when it came to Elsie. "But then she may accept yours as well."

Mose scoffed. "If that's true, we'll never find out, will we?" He didn't do Gideon the honor of looking him in the face as he made the remark, but Gideon took the bait.

"Why do you say that?"

"Because you suffocate her. If you stepped away and let her breathe, she might finally come out of her shell." Mose's voice rose with frustration.

Gideon took a minute to lower his temper down to a simmer. "Are you saying this because you really believe it would help or because you don't like to see us together?"

Mose grinned. "Both." With that he strode away. Gideon didn't have a chance to answer, but when he thought about it, he didn't have an answer. His only recourse was to ask Elsie herself.

He watched Elsie talk with his mamm and daed and tried to push back the thoughts Mose just put in his head. The service started, and verses were read and hymns sung. Elsie sat with the other women and Gideon with the men, so he didn't get a chance to talk with her.

The minister stood and quietly looked over the congregation, his face crimson and full of emotion. He turned his head, and when he scanned the room again, his face relaxed. "I have news, both *gut* and bad, but more for the *gut*." He smiled, and his confidence seemed to grow. "There are more communities who have moved down this way, which I'm sure you know about. They are in the beginning stages of settling in and need some direction. I have been asked to tend to this flock so they can grow and be plentiful."

Mumbling buzzed around the room. Omar stood and gently moved his outreached arms with palms down so they would quiet. He began to sit down, but Minister Miller held up a hand to stop him.

"Omar, along with Zeke and the deacons, will be here for you during my time away. Please stand with us." He nodded at the men who, along with Omar, served the community when there were times of need or prayer. "Minister Zeke will be taking my place while I'm gone."

The volume level grew as the congregation buzzed at the news Zeke would be head minister, and not favorably. Annie and John were just two of the many who had run into difficulties with him in the past.

"I know you will be in *gut* hands, God's hands and these men who are here to serve you." Minister Miller dismissed them with prayer.

Gideon knew something was in the works, but he didn't expect this. The continuing migration of Amish to build new lives in the south continued to grow. The land was cheaper here, and when a man had three or more sons to parcel his land off, it wasn't enough in their former community. His thoughts changed to those of appreciation that he had settled here almost two years ago and finally felt it was home. He needed to help these new families feel that same sense of stability.

A touch to his arm brought him back, and as he turned, he knew it was Elsie. "Did you know about this, Gideon?" Her brown eyes lifted to his, flustering him momentarily.

"*Nee*, he didn't mention anything to me." She didn't seem to believe him, which both surprised and amused him.

"I can see the need for it. You all helped us out when we moved down here."

"*Jah*, I wonder how Minister Zeke will do in his place. Our elders are *gut* men. I suppose they will lead us for the short time Minister Miller is gone as well."

"I wonder how long he will be gone."

"As long as it takes the newcomers to get settled. As you mentioned, you remembered when you came here not long ago. There are a lot of differences to get accustomed to, and the settlers can adapt faster if some of us help them."

She nodded reluctantly. "Who all are leaving?"

"I've heard that one more may go with the minister."

She seemed to tense up, and Gideon started to console her, but then he remembered Mose's words and thought maybe he did coddle Elsie too much.

"*Jah*, he wouldn't travel alone."

Gideon shook his head. "There may be others who want to go." The thought of being away from her brought back the familiar knot in his belly he so often felt when he was around her. But this was for a different reason.

"Gideon, may I speak with you?" Omar motioned for him to come outside with him. He nodded to Elsie and pulled at his whiskers.

"I'll be right back." When Gideon turned to Elsie, he could see anxiety in her strained face. "Don't worry." He touched her cheek lightly and followed Omar. The older man stood with his hands behind his back, staring at the ground.

"Gideon, how are you, son?" His smile was barely visible under his gray beard, as were his twinkling blue eyes.

"I'm well." Gideon always enjoyed his talks with Omar, and he felt the same appreciation coming from him.

"It's a *gut* plan with the newcomers moving down this way, more every year." After a few seasons of not enough crops to make ends meet, more and more made the trek to Texas. He tried to think about his own family's struggle so he could have the compassion to help them if needed.

"Would you be interested in going with the minister?" He rested his folded hands on his stomach as he picked his words. "Minister Miller should have someone with him as he travels to the new community and see that the new minister gets adjusted there. I thought it would be better to send someone without family to tend to."

Gideon's heart beat double time. "But won't you need help here with the minister gone?" He knew better than to ask. He had been told what was needed and thoughtlessly responded for his own benefit. "But then if that's what you needed, that's what you would have asked for."

Omar smiled. "It might be wise for you to meet the new folks and help them settle."

"You may be right." Gideon nodded. "But I'm concerned about what rules to follow. Those of us who originally planted here who are of the New Order have learned to compromise with the group from Virginia being of the Old Order, but not without disagreements. I can't imagine how much more confusion there will be with this group of newcomers who are among the more progressive groups."

"That has been on my mind as well. I'll talk with Minister Miller on the matter and see what he thinks needs to be done." He tapped the flat brim of his felt hat. "But there are needs to be filled here as well. I'll see what those are if that's your preference."

Gideon said a quick prayer for wisdom and strength. "I will go where you need me."

The men took off their hats, and Omar stepped to his place up front. Gideon went to find a seat on the right part of the home, and the women sat on the left with the children. The minister selected songs from the Osbund, and when he preached the sermon, he moved his gaze from one side to the other so all were addressed.

After the sermon the men took the chairs and placed them in rows to sit and eat the noon meal together outside. Tables were brought out, along with plates and silverware. Elsie brought a platter of Salisbury steak. The tender beef slices smothered in garden fresh stewed tomatoes, green peppers, and onions with gravy caught Gideon's eye. "Your favorite."

"Did you make it?" Gideon was touched she remembered. And there was plenty. Living in a house with all brothers, getting your share was a big issue when it came to food.

"With a little help from Mamm." She set it on the table with the rest of the food that was enough to feed the lot of them and many more.

Rachel pulled a hand towel off of the whoopie pie she'd made and wiggled her eyebrows. The chocolate cake with crème filling was always a special treat. "Save room."

Elsie grinned. "You know I will!" She placed it on the table next to the steak. "This is all I need. Mamm's steak and Rachel's pie."

Elsie waved at her brother and his wife, Ruby. Will clasped his young wife's hand and walked over to them.

Gideon appreciated her playful mood and found it was catching. Thoughts of Mose and the possibility of him leaving were tossing around in his mind, knowing he'd have to tell Elsie.

Rachel's gray eyes lifted at the edges when she glanced at Gideon, and her full, round cheeks glowed as she unveiled her treat. She looked down at Elsie, who was a good three inches shorter than she was, and moved the pie away from Elsie's plate.

"What are you thinking about?" Elsie asked him while they waited for everyone to gather round the tables and find a seat.

Gideon thought about the words he needed to say concerning his conversation with Omar, and then glanced around him. The sky was blue with a few floating clouds. A slight wind kept the heat from becoming a bother, and the green grass went on forever, farm after farm. Children played tag while the men set up chairs and tables and the women readied the meal. This was not the time to talk of anything but the weather, crops, and good health. And he thanked God for it.

"Gideon?"

He watched Elsie's face change from concern to a slight smile as she admired their friends, family, and bountiful food.

"Nothing, nothing at all."

Chapter Seven

THE WIND WHISTLED through Elsie's window, causing her to rouse and finish gathering the clothes that needed mending. The billowy clouds spun in the sky and changed shapes due to the strong gusts flowing through the air. She knew Texas was known for its tornadoes, but she hoped she'd never experience one. The rumbling of her brothers bustling down the stairs drew her attention away from the weather and to her door.

She caught a glimpse of them as they rounded the corner. "Why are you two in such a hurry?" Resting her hands on the wood banister, Elsie waited. A moment later Adam poked his head out and looked up at her.

"Going to see Josaphat." He grinned, showing a space in his teeth. A wobbly, stubborn tooth refused to let go of its root, causing a hole between them.

"Who is Josaphat?" She couldn't keep up with all the animals Adam considered pets, let alone their names. Daed discouraged Adam's attachment to them, but it was a hopeless request. Elsie secretly knew her daed had the same affection for the livestock.

"The new foal." His freckled face disappeared, so Elsie went back to her room and dressed for breakfast.

She took the basket of clothes to the family room and set it down by the rocking chair. It would be relaxing to sway back and forth while sewing, but she first needed to help Mamm prepare the morning meal.

When she got to the kitchen, Mamm was stirring pancake batter while eggs sizzled behind her on the stove. "I'll start the bacon."

"I can't keep those boys away from that foal." Mamm smiled

and poured the batter on the hot griddle. "Will you flip the eggs for me, Elsie?"

"You mean Josaphat?" She grinned, and her mamm chuckled.

Elsie grabbed the spatula. "Have you heard when Minister Miller will be leaving for the new community?" Then Elsie wondered if she should have asked her mamm, but she felt she would burst if she didn't talk to someone about it. She worried Gideon might be asked to go with him, and it made her stomach roll. She couldn't stand to have another person leave her. But she would put her own feelings aside to serve the new Amish if need be.

Mamm glanced at her before pouring the pancake batter. "*Nee*, I've heard Omar is having some of the men get together to decide. You might want to ask Gideon if you haven't already."

Elsie was surprised that her mamm would suggest this, but then it might concern Gideon. And the older she got, the less her mamm intervened in Elsie's choices or decisions, but Gideon was the exception.

"I heard the Fishers' field was rummaged through." Mamm flipped three pancakes quickly and stirred the batter.

"The field they just planted?" A single jolt snuck up from inside her and dissipated. She would not live in the fear that every bad circumstance involved the English. It would take only one tire tread to know it was them.

"*Jah*, they'll have to replant."

Elsie thought hard. This conversation may help her figure out what to do. "Is it that bad?"

"I'm not sure." Mamm shrugged. "Without tillage it's difficult to harvest."

Elsie thought about how big the loss was to have to replant a field the size of the Fishers'. "And the cost of the seed?"

"Everyone will chip in on the cost." Mamm searched for the syrup in her large pantry and put it in a small pot with warm water.

"What caused it?"

Mamm shrugged. "I've heard the weather down here can get

pretty violent. I've seen those twisters hop around and do some damage." Her mamm hesitated, seeing the question in Elsie's eyes, and searched for another answer. "Unless it was done on purpose, and I can't imagine why anyone would do that."

Elsie started with surprise that her mamm would think of the possibility. "Was there a storm last night?" She turned away, hoping someone in the community would confirm it was due to the weather.

"Some rain." Mamm paused and put a hand on Elsie's shoulder. "Don't fret. These things happen. The Lord will provide." Mamm dug into breakfast preparations, her focus back to making the meal.

Her mamm was strong when she needed to be, an admirable character trait Elsie hoped she'd grow into. She knew it made life easier to depend on the Lord instead of herself. But it didn't seem to be as easy for her.

"Will you ring the dinner bell, Elsie?" She scooped up another stack of pancakes and placed them on the plate with the rest. Elsie worked methodically as she finished cleaning the breakfast dishes, deep in thought.

"*Jah*. Would it be all right for Gideon to stop by?"

Her mamm's eyes brightened. "He can stay for lunch if he helps you pluck some chickens."

Cleaning the chickens was a task she didn't think she'd ever become accustomed to. It would be nice to have him help her. "*Danke*, Mamm. I'm going to go and meet him." She wanted to hear Gideon's opinion of the incident. She was probably overly concerned, but she needed to hear that from him.

Elsie quickly helped with the dishes. Mamm let her go as soon as the last dish was dry. She walked down the road that led to three farms, including Gideon's. It was selfish of her to want him to stay, and she would tell Gideon that. She depended on Gideon more than she'd realized. She shamed herself for taking him for granted; looking back, she could see that clearly now.

The part of Jake she kept a tight hold on was slipping through her fingers the longer he was away. She had been in denial when he left with Katie, thinking he must have gone with her out of some sort of guilt. Katie may have persuaded him; she was good at that. She had been curious about the outside world, but maybe Katie didn't want to go alone. She shook her head as she pushed away the excuses. How vain of her not to think he simply chose Katie because he cared more for Katie than he did for her.

— ◈ —

The balmy spring afternoon held a blanket of moisture encompassing the corral Jake and his brothers were working in. The sheep bawled, protesting the upcoming shearing they'd soon be getting. It would take most of the hot, sweaty day to finish shearing thirty of them. Chris brought the sheep into the barn and kept them coming to his daed and bruders until the job was done.

Elsie's grip on the basket she carried tightened when Jake looked up at her. He stood and pulled off his gloves as he eyed the wicker basket. "Is it lunchtime already?"

"Nee, but I figured you'd be hungry." Elsie locked her gaze, unmoving, with a slight smile.

"I know I am." Mose addressed Elsie but stared at his bruder. "Hungry that is." He walked toward Elsie, demanding her attention and food. He reached for the basket. "If anyone cares to join me, I'll be under the cottonwood tree." That left them alone, but not for long. Katie appeared out of nowhere and made her presence known.

"Elsie, I thought I was supposed to bring the Fishers their meal." Katie grinned at Jake, and his smile widened. It was at that moment Elsie saw a spark between them, the same flicker Elsie thought she saw from Jake.

"Nee, you have the Sutters, remember?" Elsie heard the irritation in her own voice, annoyed with the game Katie was playing. Elsie waited for Katie to leave, but the only movement was closer to Jake. "I'd hate for the Sutters not to get their lunch."

"Jah, so I guess I'll take it to them." Elsie's tone would surely encourage her sister to offer to take the food to the Sutters. But what Katie did next

confused her; Katie blushed, which was something Elsie had never seen her strong-headed sister do before.

Katie's spell was broken when she'd seen Elsie, but began again when Jake's eyes shifted back to hers.

When Elsie got to the end of the dirt road leaving their farm, the sound of a motor vehicle broke through her thoughts. It was coming down the road behind her, a foreign sound that shot a jolt of panic through her. Her heart jumped as adrenaline pumped through her body. She picked up her pace, almost into a run, when the car's engine revved and came up behind her.

The *ping* of an object hitting something hard made her turn to see what made the noise. A young man about her age leaned out his window and threw a hand-sized stone at a windmill that was too far for him to hit. He tried again with a smaller rock that shattered a piece of wood and flew into a vegetable garden recently planted. He hollered along with the other men in the car, then ducked back inside through the window. That's when she got a good look at his face and went cold.

Elsie glanced around for a place of refuge. There was nothing but wide-open spaces, not even a ditch alongside of the road to hide in. Her instinct told her to run—fast. The minute she did, she was discovered. The men's voices grew louder. The car sped up, closer until they were right next to her. She tried to move her legs forward, but they felt leaden—as if in a nightmare. She urged them to move faster, and faster still. But the voices grew even louder...the rumble of the engine came closer...she felt the heat of the car and pushed herself forward. She lost momentum and rolled down into the tall prairie grass, wishing she could disappear. Elsie opened her eyes. Two of the men got out of the car and stood above her, looking down with hands on hips. The driver stayed in the car, sneering as he watched.

"What are you running for?" The driver was one of the English boys with a Texas drawl. At one time she thought the sound appealing, but soon it was an accent she'd come to despise.

She pushed herself up, trying her best to ignore all of them, and started walking again. The car crept alongside of her, and the two men walked by her on the opposite side. Elsie refused to look at them and kept walking with her head high. They matched her stride, snickering. Her insides jelled, but she wouldn't show her fear. Yet they had the upper hand, and they knew it. "Leave me be," she said.

"If you can't be friendly, why don't you leave?" The driver's voice rose, along with the beating of her pulse. He moved farther out the window, his chest leaning against the doorframe.

Elsie attempted to move away from him, but the other two men blocked her from doing so. She tried to hurry forward.

With a hoot the driver settled back inside and then pulled the car in front of her and stopped. "We don't want your kind around here." The other men stepped closer, laughing.

"Why?" She shook with both anger and fear. If they had something to say, they should say it to the bishop, not her.

"Be sure to tell everyone we warned you," the driver said.

She wanted to tell them her people don't work that way, that they would talk with them and make things right. But she knew it would be wasted breath. So she made an idle offer. "Then will you leave me alone?"

"Of course we will." His sarcastic chuckle made her shiver.

One of the young men next to her stepped closer. Elsie felt like a child, fearful and afraid of these strangers. "This land is no place for you northerners." He captured her gaze.

Elsie turned her head, a cowardly gesture, but his cold, blue eyes were unnerving.

Her body began to shake. She took a deep breath and willed her nerves to calm down.

He laughed and turned with the other young man toward the car. "She's shaking like a leaf," one said as they both crawled back in.

The taunting chuckles, the threats, sent her reeling with frustration and alarm. When the driver reached out to flick his cigarette, she moved away and managed to get a couple of feet ahead of the car. It was a feeble attempt, but she needed to do something. In an instant the car was beside her again. The men howled with laughter as they hit a rut in the road and splashed her with mud, then slowed and went into reverse as if to do it again. She stood on the road, scared and humiliated.

She lifted her head, her eyes filled with tears blurring her vision. She noticed movement down the road and blinked away the tears. A buggy came toward them, making her heart pound. The closer it got, the more it looked like Gideon, or did she just want it to be him? When he got close enough, he pulled back on the reins and jumped out of the buggy.

Gideon's eyes darted from her to the car that was now slowly rolling toward them. His brows drew together as his hands twisted into fists and released. "What's going on, Elsie?"

She shook her head. "I'm sorry, Gideon."

"Please stop your vehicle." Gideon's loud, even voice caught the driver's attention.

He took a double take, starring at Gideon. "Who are you?"

"Gideon, Gideon Lapp. And you are?" He didn't move but kept his arms firmly across his chest and feet planted. Elsie had never been happier to see him. Her helpless stare drew his attention. He motioned for her to come to him. "Elsie."

She took a step forward and walked as fast as she could to Gideon. For whatever reason she felt if she ran, it would entice the men to chase her, an animal instinct of some sort. These young men were nothing like she was used to; they were insulting and disrespectful, especially the driver—so opposite of the men in her community.

When she reached Gideon, she stood with her back to the Englishers, took his hand, and squeezed tight. Elsie leaned into his strong shoulder and found strength there, enough to turn around and look into the eyes of these awful young men.

"What's going on here?" Gideon's words were polite, but his tone was not.

The man stared for a long while, looking from Elsie then back to Gideon. "Just having a conversation."

Gideon stared at the mud dripping down the bottom of her dress and onto her boots. He gritted his teeth and closed his eyes, then she heard him ask for quiet strength. "Why don't we all sit together, share a meal, and talk. We mean you no harm."

"We don't want to be seen with goons like you. Pack up your buggies and go home." The Englisher's upper lip curled into a smile, and he tipped his hat mockingly Elsie's way. He made an extra effort to drive slowly and didn't take his eyes off her until they drove away.

Elsie let out a long breath, not realizing she held it. Gideon didn't move until the car was out of sight then stared down at his boots. Letting go of her hand, he stood with his muscled arms tight around his chest. Now with the immediate danger over, she lifted her gaze to Gideon and knew there was more coming.

Chapter Eight

HE COULDN'T BRING himself to look at her. Gideon kept his eyes to the ground and waited for Elsie to speak. All he heard was the breath she forced from her lungs. He slowly moved his eyes from her boots, up to her black dress covered with mud, and then to her face. She laid one hand on her chest and reached toward him with the other.

He lifted their clasped hands and pulled her in front of him. "Are you all right?"

She closed her eyes briefly and looked into his face. "*Jah*, I'm fine." Her eyes filled with tears that she blinked away to regain her composure. "Thank you for helping me, Gideon."

He nodded and turned to see the dust settling down the road. He wanted to fight those men for Elsie's honor. His humble prayer was the only thing that stopped him. "What was that about?" His usual gentle demeanor was replaced with urgency, feeling it was necessary to get the facts.

"Walk with me." She turned toward the lane leading to her home and glanced over the rows of freshly planted corn as tears slowly slid down her cheeks. "They want us to leave."

Her short response only brought more questions to mind. "Why?"

She shrugged. "I'm not sure."

He tried not to stare at Elsie but needed to see how this affected her. "For what reason? We cause them no trouble."

"I've kicked it around in my mind over and over again. They say it's the land." She shook her head. "I think they know they can pick on us because we won't fight back."

"That could be the reason, but it's a pitiful one." Gideon could understand if they'd done something that caused those men to want the Amish to leave, but they kept to themselves. They only recently started going into town to sell goods that the ranchers had no interest in, and the crops were in demand for all who grew them. As he studied her expression, he felt she was holding back. He waited for her to tell him more.

She slowed her walk. "I've been trying to think of *Martyrs Mirror* when it comes to these people—forgiving them because they know not what they do."

He couldn't help but smile. "*Jah*, you're exactly right." That made him stop and think not only in the way he should deal with this situation, but also how Elsie was applying the forgiveness part of *Martyrs Mirror* in her own life. That could also explain how she'd begun to come out of her shell. But if bullying was the case, it would be hard to reason with them. Still he would have to try. "Have you seen them before?"

She nodded but didn't meet his eyes. "Once. Before Katie left." Elsie said it quickly as if to get the words off her chest.

"Does Katie know about these men?"

She nodded again.

Gideon grunted without thought, frustrated with Katie once again but this time because of something that affected the entire community. "So you two kept this to yourselves?"

"They scared us, Gideon. We've never known men like this, full of anger and hate." She held back a sob, and he felt ashamed for asking the question. It was the protective side of him that didn't help now with what had already been done.

"I'm sorry, Elsie. I don't blame you. I'm just upset that this has happened. I wish you would have come to me when it first started."

"We didn't know what to do. I prayed it would all go away, that they would see we are peaceful people and let us be."

"Tell me how it started." He guided her to a wooden bench close to Mamm's garden and sat next to her.

"I've tried to shut this out for so long that it's hard to talk about." Elsie put a hand to her forehead and slumped down.

Gideon kept hold of her hand, not wanting to lose the physical connection, and spoke softly but clearly. "Did they tell you not to?"

"They told us to persuade the Amish to leave, that we weren't wanted here."

"What did they expect you to do? Convince the entire community to pack up and leave?" He couldn't hide his irritation at their irrational request. "If they had any integrity, they would have come to one of us men." He scoffed, knowing harassing the women would be more powerful; these young men obviously knew that too.

Elsie looked down at her muddy boots. "They thought we would leave after our first crop because it was so bad."

"Well, that changed after our men learned how to irrigate using the drip tape and found a fertilizer that worked. I don't think it's the land so much as they like to push their weight around."

"That's what they say, Gideon, but maybe they just want the power to decide who their neighbors are."

"I wish you would have told me or someone about this."

"We didn't know what to do." She twirled her thumbs. "Then John and Annie's wheat field went up in flames."

Gideon jerked his head back with the thought that it could have been these men who did this. How could anyone be so bold and heartless as to destroy a man's livelihood? He watched as Elsie wiped a tear from her cheek.

"Whether they did it or not, I feel as if I'm the one who lit the match. I should have said something earlier."

"You did what you thought was right. Don't punish yourself, Elsie. None of us have experienced something like this for no apparent reason." When he looked at her, he saw the guilt she must feel. "Losing that crop is what gave Annie and John the determination to start their bed-and-breakfast. It all worked out for *gut.*" He turned away, thinking about the position she'd been put in. "I probably wouldn't know what to do either."

She almost smiled. "*Jah*, you would. You always know." He was caught in her eyes for a moment, feeling her true admiration for him. It was something he'd hoped for but never thought he'd see. He pulled himself back to the problem at hand.

"I wish that were true, but with this, all I know is it needs to end."

Elsie looked up in alarm. "I'm afraid they'll do worse things."

"We can't let them continue to threaten you and vandalize others. What if someone gets hurt?"

Her dark brown eyes bore into his and held them for a moment. "That someone will be me."

Gideon cringed in frustration. "What do you mean?"

"I'm not sure of their motivation or anything about them, but the one thing I do know is that I'll pay the price for anything that doesn't go their way. They've made that clear."

He covered his face in his hands to hold back the unfamiliar anger that burned inside of him. Feelings of violence and revenge raged in him like never before. He didn't know how to hold back these detestable thoughts. But this was the one person he cared for more than any other, and she was in harm's way. *Lord, direct my path, my words and my actions. When I am weak, You are strong.*

Her expression showed her worry and concern. "Don't ever take on a burden like this alone again, Elsie. You have me now." And he would do whatever it took to keep her safe, even if it meant going against the Amish vow of no resistance.

⌒ Chapter Nine ⌒

ELSIE LET OUT the last of the milk cows and began to wipe down the teat cups. She had never seen Gideon so upset. That was the reason she hadn't told anyone about the incident with the Englishers. The Amish didn't know how to deal with oppression, at least not that she knew of. That brought to mind *Martyrs Mirror* and how relevant the situation was in her present world. This made her want to see Gideon and gave her an excuse to do so.

It would soon be time to prepare breakfast, and she didn't want her mamm to worry. Her mind drifted during milking and took longer to get the chore done. Should she tell her? She held the secret for so long she didn't know how to tell the truth about the situation. What a horrible web of deceit this had become.

Elsie finished up and closed the barn doors. She stared down at the ground as she walked, and after a few minutes she lifted her eyes to the white four-bedroom place she called home. There were a lot of good memories in the short time they'd lived in the house, making it their home once the others helped with the building and painting. Everything seemed hollow with Katie gone, and Elsie wanted to fill that void with the truth. She made her way up the stairs and into the kitchen ready to bare her soul once the meal was over and dishes were finished.

"Milking is done, Mamm." Elsie washed and made herself useful peeling potatoes for hash browns.

"Just in time." Mamm glanced over her shoulder and stopped mixing the eggs long enough to get a good look at Elsie. "What's on your mind?"

"Things I can't control, so I should stop thinking about them."

Elsie kept her emotions intact trying to find the courage to tell her mamm all she knew. If only Katie was here. She was the one so adamant about not telling anyone.

"I'm getting the jams ready for the market. Did you finish that quilt?" Mamm set the spoon down and took two steps to the skillet and turned the bacon. Her preoccupation gave Elsie the time to think through her words.

"*Nee*, I didn't get a chance to. I will, though." The peeler caught the side of her finger, and she grimaced at the sharp prick. She stuck her finger under the faucet and pressed on the cut.

"Are you all right?" Mamm went over and studied the injury. "It's a small cut, but those sometimes sting the most."

"I'm fine. I was careless." Elsie didn't meet her mamm's eyes. She wished for the day that she could do so with a clear conscience. It seemed worse now that Gideon knew. She somehow felt responsible for the damages since she knew the offenders, but her fear of them was stronger than her guilt.

Before she ate her meal Elsie prayed for wisdom then distracted herself by helping with the day's chores, sweeping, doing laundry, and cooking the noon meal. Her heart lifted as she worked.

Elsie twisted her hair into a tight bun then put on her white kapp. She took a handful of pins and secured the kapp. She was on her way out the door to see Gideon when her daed called for her to come see him.

"Why are you in such a hurry?" He folded his arms around his chest and gave her a teasing smile. He knew where she was going and who she was going to meet.

"I'm going to Rachel's to finish our quilt," Elsie bantered back. He frowned for a moment and then realized she was joking with him.

"Tell Gideon *hallo* for me." He grinned and turned back to the barn.

His playfulness made her smile as she walked over to Omar's home. Gideon often spent his lunchtime there and read *Martyrs Mirror* along with other books the minister gave him to study.

Gideon's passion to learn about their faith kept him committed to carve time out of his day as much as possible.

When Elsie got to the white building, the door opened, and there stood Omar, as if waiting for her. "*Gut* afternoon, Omar."

"Elsie, what brings you here?" He must have known why, but she'd play along. She didn't know if he would mind if the two of them were together. But Gideon wouldn't have asked her to come if he thought Omar wouldn't consent.

She smiled and shrugged "I would like to talk with Gideon. But to tell you the truth, I'm not sure what I'm getting myself into." She was referring to Gideon's search for knowledge. She knew Omar appreciated that in Gideon.

He chuckled as he walked with her to the den and stopped at the door. "How are you and your family?" He stood before her, his fingers twined.

"We're…adjusting." She knew he meant Katie, and although she appreciated his concern, she was more interested in the men they were choosing to go to the new community.

"God only gives us what we can bear. You and your family are strong, as is Katie. I feel certain you will all be together again." His eyes lit up when she smiled again.

"I hope you're right, Bishop Omar." She thought about the real reason she'd come and couldn't hold her tongue. "Have you heard who is leaving for the new community?"

He smiled. "You're eager to know Gideon's plans, I take it."

She felt her face heat and let out a breath to calm herself. "Well, *jah*, I am curious."

"I believe Gideon has a calling to ministry, Elsie. He feels that's true as well. If so, he may be called to go and do things that may be hard for his friends and family. We have many Amish still considering moving down here." He pulled on his beard and chuckled. "Although the northerners think we are making all kinds of money and getting enticed into temptations."

Elsie laughed with him. "Where would they get such an idea?"

"Oh, you know how people are. They get a piece and make it

into a whole." He took off his glasses and rubbed the arch of his nose.

"Maybe that's why so many want to move here." She grinned.

"Maybe so. They'll be sorely disappointed, though, won't they?" he said with lifted brow.

"*Jah*, the life down here isn't much different except for the heat." They both nodded, and he dabbed the back of his neck with a hanky as if saying the word made him hot. "Is Gideon in the next room?"

"*Jah*, go on in. Just try to drag one of those books away from him, especially that *Martyrs Mirror*."

"He's been telling me all about it. It is quite fascinating to study a book about our heritage and from so long ago." Elsie heard herself saying the words and felt she sounded like Gideon.

"I thought I heard your voice." Gideon stood in the doorway with his hands on either door frame, enhancing his lithe build. "Did you come to see me?"

"*Jah*, if you have a minute." She stood before he could answer and walked past him into the room he used for preparing the sermons and taking in parishioners who needed to talk to him privately.

She sat and put her hands on her lap, trying to stay focused on his studies but failing miserably. As much as she wanted to know if Gideon was leaving, she stopped herself from speaking. Even so, she couldn't squelch the thoughts. She wanted to tell him everything about those young men just to make him stay. "Is there anything in that book that can help us with our neighbors?"

Gideon didn't move for a moment, taking in her words, and then opened the book. He leaned forward, pointing to a paragraph. "Love is as strong as death and jealousy cruel as the grave. For here you see in a mirror, like our ancestors. Who can separate us from the love of Christ? Shall tribulation, distress, persecution, famine, nakedness, peril or sword?"

"Persecution?" Elsie closed her eyes and let out a sigh. "That's a Bible verse."

He nodded. "That we are to reflect."

"Gideon, I shouldn't have asked you not to tell anyone about those men." She fought the emotions that rose each time she thought of them.

Gideon stood and closed the door. He might be chastised for it later, but this was too private to let anyone overhear. "I'm hopeful we will get the opportunity to talk to these men. If not, we'll have to take some action of our own."

"What do you mean?"

He moved closer and stared at her intensely. "I originally thought it might mean breaking the vow of the Amish no resistance."

Elsie felt an alarm go off in her head. "No one is to break the laws our ancestors started years ago. The law against violence goes back to the Civil War when the Amish refused to fight." She didn't know what the consequences were, but she didn't want Gideon to face a shunning or, worse, being ostracized from her and the community. "You can't break the ways of our people."

"Unless it's to protect you. I would never forgive myself if anything happened. And it will only get worse with more Amish moving here. This needs to end before more settle in."

"*Jah*, I've thought of that too." She twiddled her thumbs. "Maybe they won't come back."

"I hope they do, so I can try to talk with them. And I'll go to Omar." Gideon leaned forward and spoke softly. "God has given us this task. He will walk us through it until His will is done."

"Your faith is strong, Gideon. I will try to be as strong as well." Elsie was glad to finally have someone to talk to about all that happened. She could trust him completely, and she trusted his opinion as to what she should do. She still owned the problem even though he was involved now. The feelings of helplessness against these men dissipated somewhat, and she knew it was because of Gideon by her side.

"I've talked with Minister Miller." He calmly pulled his chair up next to her, leaving her on edge as to what the decision was.

"I have offered to do what needs to be done either here or away. If Minister Miller requests me to go, it's not something I'll refuse." He smiled like a child with a new toy, obviously proud to be considered for the opportunity.

"I'll try to pray with an open mind." Elsie smiled, knowing she would need a lot of patience if she would have to share him with the new community.

"Maybe leading this group is a way to find out if I'm truly suited for the work." He was so humble about his standing in the community, but Elsie knew he would someday have a place, whether it was as deacon or minister. As she looked up into his shining eyes, she wondered what took her so long to come to him.

∽ Chapter Ten ∾

WHEN GIDEON FINISHED his morning chores, he went over to the Yoders. The heavy humidity and clear skies intensified the heat of the sun that shone down on his straw hat.

Solomon was under the weather, but Gideon hoped he would have the opportunity to talk with him privately. But Solomon could be ornery, especially if he was in pain. He insisted on instructing and giving direction to the group of men who would gather at his home to plant corn. Solomon had been in fits that the seeds were not in the ground yet. He could see spring budding from his window and was quite sure it happened overnight.

"The dogwoods are starting to bloom." Yonnie walked up behind Gideon and slapped him on the back. It was just hard enough to irritate him.

"You don't know your own strength." Gideon told him but with no hope he'd understand.

"See there." Yonnie pointed to the young leaves on the trees. His shaggy, curly hair fell into his eyes, and he brushed it away.

"Size of a squirrel's foot," Gideon said, wondering why he didn't notice. It was the sign they always waited for to know if the soil was warm enough to plant. They started planting a little earlier with some families due to the minister leaving and taking a couple of men who offered to go.

"You've haven't noticed a whole lot of anything lately, so I thought I'd point that out for ya." He shook his head, making his locks dance around his eyes again.

"I've been busy, and you need a haircut." He mussed Yonnie's hair, knowing that would stop the teasing.

Gideon eyed Elsie and suddenly didn't care what remark Yonnie was going to say next. Wisps of dark hair fell below her kapp that she fumbled with as she went out onto the porch. "Morning."

"*Gut* morning, Yonnie, Gideon. Mamm and I have made some breakfast if you're hungry." She gestured to the kitchen door, and Yonnie stepped right up.

"I can always eat." Once through the door Gideon could hear him greeting everyone with his booming voice.

"Do you want anything? My mammi made her blueberry pancakes." Her bright smile made him feel better. He was uncertain about talking with Solomon, and it lifted his spirits.

"No, thanks. My mamm didn't want any leftovers and decided I was the one to take care of that for her, so I've had my fill." He put a hand on his stomach.

Elsie smiled. "Did she feed you until you were stuffed?"

"Like the fatted calf." He grinned, and she did too. "I guess I should get to work."

"Thanks for helping plant today. It's made my daed very happy. Well, as happy as anything could."

"I'm sure he's wishing he was out there in the field."

"He says he's feeling better, but Mamm doesn't believe him." She put her hands on her hips as her daed came toward the porch. "Where are you going?" She took his arm as he shuffled across the white wood floor.

"If I can't help, I'm gonna at least watch. Isn't that right, Gideon?" He eased himself down into the rocking chair and let out a long breath.

"*Jah*, I'd be the same."

"I'll be buried in the land I've tilled. Want to make sure it's ready for me." He smiled at Elsie, but she just shook her head at him.

"You'll tell me if the pain flares up again, won't you, Daed?" She took a blanket that was folded on the back of the chair and laid it on his lap.

He pulled at it. "You fuss at me like I'm an old man."

"There's a morning chill." She put it around his shoulders, a bit more out of his reach.

Gideon chuckled. "I'm glad to see you're in *gut* spirits."

"And I'm glad to see you planting my corn, Gideon." When he leaned back, Gideon noticed his pale skin and shallow breaths.

"You take care now," Gideon said in a serious tone. "We'll take care of your field."

Solomon nodded and gazed out at the men readying the horses and deciding where each one would work and how many rows they each would plow.

Yonnie pushed open the screen door as he stuffed a rolled-up pancake into his mouth and brushed past both of them. "Hurry up, Lapp. I brought my best," he tried to say around the food in his mouth. Maggie and Tony were his two finest Clydesdales, each stronger than an ox.

"I'm right behind you." Gideon tipped his hat to Elsie and ran to catch up. He slapped down Yonnie's broad-brimmed hat. "Switch to your straw hat. It's almost summer."

Yonnie was about to protest but shut his mouth then mumbled the planting rotation under his breath. "Planting corn…hay…" He kept on until Gideon set him straight.

Yonnie slapped his thigh. "Why can't I get the southern rotation through my head?"

Gideon chuckled. "That's why you need me, my friend."

When they got to the field, Gideon dropped the plow and Yonnie steered the horses. The weather started to heat up, but Tony and Maggie stayed the course. Everyone had to adjust to the warm weather down south, including the livestock. Gideon settled back and let the horses do most of the work. They made the task seem effortless. The methodical movement of the plow cutting through the thick dirt dulled his senses.

They stopped for a break so the horses could drink, and the men were given tea or water. Then the women went in to finish the noon meal.

"*Um zu essen!*" Meredith called out for everyone to come and eat.

The women brought out plates of fried chicken, canned pears, sliced tomatoes, and pies. The young men started a game of baseball but were soon called back to work, leaving the younger children to carry on the game.

Gideon sat with the men, talking about the soil condition and estimating how much longer until they would be finished. When Elsie walked up to him, he couldn't help but ask her, "Did you make the pecan pie?"

She shook her head. "*Nee*, walnut, your favorite." Her eyes widened. "I put it in your buggy to take home. Be right back." She took quick steps to pick up speed. The pie sitting in the buggy all this time meant he might not get his favorite dessert. He'd just started to look for the pie when he heard what sounded like a drum.

"What's that?" Yonnie cranked his head around to zero in on the noise.

"Sounds like music." It was a strange noise for them, considering they didn't listen to music.

Others stared in the direction the sound came from, and soon a car appeared. Once the driver saw them in the field, he blared the music and drove faster. The horses' ears went back and their nostrils flared. Everyone turned to see what the commotion was as the blue car passed by, spitting out smoke from the exhaust.

Elsie. His buggy was an arm's throw away from the path that led to the main road the Englishers were driving by.

Gideon jumped up and ran down the lane. There was no sign of her. He clicked into high gear, pushing himself harder to get to her before they did.

A flash of black lured him over past her buggy. As he looked past the overgrown weeds beside the fence line, a blur of Elsie's dress caught his attention. The blond-haired one had her by the wrist, a grin spreading each time she pulled away. Another walked toward her, grabbed her kapp, and pulled it off. The long, steel pins gave way, but not without great pain, as Gideon knew.

He couldn't get his feet to move fast enough as he approached. Gideon went straight toward Elsie, with no hesitation, and yelled just loud enough to get their attention. "Let her alone." The voice did not sound like his. The deep yet wavering sound exposed his fear, and they fed on it.

"Come to save your girl, Amish man?" The blond one still had his hand on Elsie, making Gideon cringe.

He kept his eyes on each of them, then noticed movement in the backseat. He was more than outnumbered. Defeat zipped through his mind. But that wasn't an option. So he focused on Elsie and kept the others in the corner of his eye. He turned to the dark-haired one, the weaker of the two. "You will receive the same punishment he will—" Gideon nodded toward the blond one. "—unless you stop now."

Gideon knew their purpose was only to control, but he hoped they knew better than to go too far. These young men had been fed untruths about the Amish and their gluttony for land, an excuse to harass just for fun.

A thought went through his head, one he thought he'd never go through with, but this time...all it would take was one more hand on her. Brownie's hand wouldn't make it that far.

Elsie looked down at his left fist squeezing then opening. She hadn't said a word. By the look on her face he guessed she was in shock. "Gideon, *nee*."

Blondie yanked her closer to him. "Shut up."

Gideon's fist hit him on his left cheekbone, staying clear of Elsie. Blondie immediately dropped Elsie's arms and fell back against the car, causing those inside to rouse.

Gideon stood his ground, waiting for them to come at him. But instead Brownie grabbed his cohort off the trunk then shoved him into the car and ran to the other side. The car kicked out pebbles and dust, fishtailing down the road.

Gideon lifted Elsie up into his arms. Her rapid breathing pressed against his cheek until it slowed to a normal pace. "Are you all right?" He pulled back to see her pale face, with a soft pink slowly appearing—a good sign she was unharmed.

Although it went against their customs, Gideon only felt a shred of guilt for hitting that man. He had it coming; if it hadn't been Gideon, it would have been someone else. He wasn't about to let Elsie get hurt, even if there were repercussions.

"I'm fine." Elsie was slow to answer, her voice just above a whisper. When her shoulders stopped shaking, she looked behind him. Gideon slowly turned around. There behind him stood Omar with his hunting rifle. Gideon thought he'd scared those men on his own accord. Now he discovered he had another man with a gun who had done the job simply by showing up. He swallowed his pride and looked to Omar.

"Elsie, were you hurt?"

"*Nee*, just scared."

He put a hand on her shoulder to comfort her. "You're shaken."

"I'm fine." She didn't seem fine to Gideon, but he shouldn't expect her to. Her worst fear had reared its head and done to her what she'd hoped and prayed wouldn't happen. These men had used her for a bargaining chip, and she was the one who lost.

"Let's talk." Omar squeezed her shoulder but was talking to Gideon.

The walk back to the haus was quiet with a faint buzz of conversation on occasion. There would be plenty talk now that the incident happened in plain sight. But no one knew the whole story except for Gideon and Elsie and, soon enough, Omar.

Gideon looked back toward the road where the car had been. When he turned back, Omar nodded to him, frowning with question. Gideon motioned to the house, and Omar excused himself to those around him, stepping away from the picnic table, and followed behind him.

Elsie watched the interaction and stared at Gideon. Her chin began to quiver as she watched them walk up to the house. This was Gideon's chance to speak with him. He didn't want Elsie to be part of this conversation. She might deter him, and he didn't want to wait any longer; there wasn't a choice anymore.

The two men walked into the house and sat down in the chairs, but neither said a word for a few seconds.

"What happened out there, Gideon?"

"Those young men who drove by…"

"*Jah*; I wish they'd do their driving out of our community." Omar's stare was one of concern and great interest, almost too much for Gideon to handle.

"I know those young men." Gideon looked away, ashamed he hadn't come to him earlier. "They are the English who have done the vandalism."

Omar leaned forward. "How do you know this?"

He pushed out a harsh breath from his lips. "Elsie."

"Elsie?" Omar's brows knitted, causing lines to deepen between his eyes.

"They have been harassing her and Katie."

Omar moved back with force, a bewildered look across his face. 'Harassing them how?"

"By instructing them to tell us not to buy the land, to leave, and that we aren't wanted here, and making crude remarks." He kept his eyes downcast, waiting for Omar's next question.

"How long has this been going on?"

He forced himself to look into Omar's eyes, ashamed at how long Katie and especially Elsie had to deal with this alone. "Since before Katie left."

"How long is that, six or seven months now?" Omar shook his head. "Why didn't they tell someone?"

"Elsie didn't want the Amish men to be tempted into sin, so she hoped the English would stop without our involvement." When he heard the words out loud, Gideon realized his failing even more. "I should have come to you sooner."

Omar looked sharply at Gideon. "And are you the man she was worried would be tempted?"

"I guess I proved her right." Gideon paused. "I've learned that ignoring a problem doesn't make it go away; like a sore or an illness it festers and only gets worse."

Omar lifted a hand and shook his head. "What all have they done?"

"Vandalism, and harassment, as far as I know, but the worst was John Yoder's wheat field that caught fire. They'd never harmed anyone that I know of, until today." Gideon thought sure that would make him want to take action. "I'm the one who should have come to you."

"I knew of some infractions, but not that they possibly burned the field." Omar tugged on his beard and looked through his window at the road where the Englishers had been. "We are peaceful people, Gideon. All we can do is try and reason with them."

"I have talked with them, but it did no good."

"Why do they want us to go?"

"The land. They say we should go back up north. But I think it's an excuse; they like to bully."

"Boys, trying to act like men." He pursed his lips.

"So what do we do now?" Elsie appeared and stood by the door.

"It's not for you to fret over." Omar's eyes softened as he took a long look at her. "Child, you could have come to me. This was too heavy of a burden to bear alone."

"I didn't know what to do." She grabbed the end of her apron and started pulling at it.

"Secrets create self-doubt." He smiled warmly at her. "You should share this with your daed."

"So we do nothing to stop these young men?" Gideon knew what the answer was going to be, but now that Omar knew everything, there was a side of him that wanted to finish this in whatever way possible.

Omar leaned forward. "I know it can be hard to do, but it's our way. We do nothing." Omar sat back and twined his fingers.

"You mean like punching someone?"

Omar frowned. "I don't recall."

Elsie turned to Gideon, who lifted his brows at her. He

appreciated what Omar was doing, but he couldn't accept his pardon. Besides, there might have been others who saw what happened. "We are also to be honest, are we not?"

"I was the last one to the road, with my bad knee and all. I was glad to see that Elsie was all right. And it was a quiet walk back home."

Gideon and Elsie exchanged glances. "*Jah*," Elsie responded with one brow lifted.

Omar said one thing and did another. Whether it was right or wrong, he had final say in this conversation, and they had finally purged themselves in being alone involving this situation. But Gideon felt frustration stir up inside him. He tried to suppress it, knowing nothing was going to change. Omar was following their laws, and he had to abide by them. But Gideon wished he'd be called out for what he did instead of the constant turning the other cheek.

"When the authorities came after the fire, they encouraged us to let them do an investigation to make sure there was no foul play, but we told them it wasn't necessary."

He looked from one of them to the other. "They asked us if we knew how the fire started, and at that time we didn't." He pulled on his beard and paused just long enough to make them wait. "Now we do."

"So you want them to get caught?" Elsie asked.

"I want them to stop before someone gets hurt. The police can do that; we can't." Omar looked at her and then to Gideon. "Seriously hurt that is." He gave Elsie a sympathetic smile.

"That seems fair." As fair as it could possibly be in dealing with something like this. But Gideon was supportive of Omar's decision. He just hoped it worked before something worse happened.

Chapter Eleven

ELSIE WANTED TO get to the door before anyone in her family. The more they were together, the more questions. She dropped the carrot she was peeling and wiped her hands on her apron as she went down the hallway. She and Gideon were going to share a meal with Will and his wife, Ruby, and Elsie was grateful to have him along. Ruby was uncomfortable around anyone in her family, and Gideon seemed to have a way with everyone he met.

When she opened the door, she admired Gideon's smile that always lifted more to the left. With her mind on Jake all that time, Elsie could see how she might have taken Gideon for granted. Elsie had always thought Gideon was attractive, but she didn't bother to think of him any other way than the rock that he was. He had always been there for her family, but Elsie figured he was that way with most of the others as well. She thought he could be a minister one day. His ability to naturally serve and shepherd people made him an obvious choice. She didn't feel worthy of being a minister's wife.

His brows rose, and he smiled slightly. "May I come in?"

"Of course." Elsie backed away so he could step in, and they made their way back to the kitchen.

Mamm turned to him and smiled. "Gideon, I'm so glad you and Elsie are paying a visit to Will and Ruby." She turned back to the biscuits she was placing in the oven. "I was there the other day. They have the place...in order." Mamm's obvious worry over Ruby's housekeeping only made Ruby stop wanting to try. Give her a horse to train or shoe, and she was in her element.

Gideon nodded. "If we didn't see each other at church each

week, I'd never get a chance to talk with them. Even then it's difficult with so many around."

Her mamm frowned at her when she saw Elsie getting the kitchen in order so she could leave. Mamm turned back to Gideon with a straight face. "They don't seem to get out much, not even to visit us. Ain't that so, Elsie?"

"*Jah*, but they seem happy enough." Elsie hurried through the dinner cleanup, which was becoming a bad habit she didn't want to continue, but she found herself distracted when Gideon was around. The normal way of everyday life with each task being done with pride and pleasure was getting lost to social activities.

"I'm ready." Elsie wiped her hands and started out of the kitchen before Mamm found something she'd missed.

"You always seem to be in a hurry these days." Her mamm smiled and stepped closer to wipe off a bit of carrot on Elsie's dress. "Enjoy the visit."

Elsie caught her mamm glance over at Gideon and then to her. She hoped she wasn't getting the idea their relationship was anything more than supportive, although she thought Gideon felt more. As much as she admired him, Elsie didn't know if she knew how to walk alongside a man who had a calling into ministry.

He helped her into his buggy and went over to the other side. All the while Elsie kept her eyes on him, admiring his confident stride and tranquil smile. When he lifted his eyes to hers, she turned away, not wanting him to see her interest. "Are you comfortable? That side of the seat needs to be repaired. I need to tend to it before someone gets pinched or worse." He reached over and handed her a light blanket before she could reply. "Sit on this just in case."

"*Danke*." Elsie adjusted the blanket under her and thought about the evening ahead. It would be good to see her brother, and she hoped Ruby would be in a hospitable mood. She noticed her uneasiness when she came for Sunday meal. There were times Ruby seemed ready to leave as soon as she arrived. Elsie felt sure others would notice as well, but nothing had been said. Maybe tonight would be different.

Elsie was silent as they traveled down a narrow tree-shaded lane, and Gideon enjoyed the quiet. The locust singing in staccato was enough sound for him.

"It's nice of your daed to let us off on our own like this." She noticed he sat at the edge of the seat as far from her as he possibly could.

A rare few might take advantage of the situation, but Gideon was the least of those. He took his commitment to the church seriously, as did most others, never curious enough to experiment with *rumspringa* as some did. She had gone with Katie once to see a movie after she turned sixteen with her mamm and daed's reluctant permission. Katie wanted to dress like the English for the outing, but Elsie didn't want to go that far or leave the community to do something so silly, but she finally gave in to her sister's prodding.

"Elsie?"

His voice brought her back, and she finally answered, "He trusts you." Her smile told him she did too. She didn't need to say it.

"What were you thinking about?" His eyes hadn't left hers. The horse seemed to know the way.

"My daed. He's not been himself today."

"What do you mean?"

"He was complaining of more pain in his back."

Elsie was also thinking about her sister-in-law. She didn't want Ruby to know she was analyzing her, and even more so didn't want to talk about Katie. Elsie wanted this to be an enjoyable evening with her brother. His wit and sense of humor always kept the mood light, so she expected to have a good belly laugh or two before the end of the visit.

"He probably just needs some rest," Gideon suggested, and she agreed.

As they rolled into the driveway, Elsie's seat slipped to her right, setting her off balance. Gideon dropped the reins and grabbed her around the waist. She steadied herself and turned to Gideon, his face inches in front of her. "I'm so sorry, Elsie." He quickly pulled his arms away and reached for the leather reins. "I'll see if Will can help me fix it. Are you all right?"

"I'm fine." Elsie smoothed her dress and moved closer to Gideon. It hadn't given her enough of a scare to alarm her, but it did Gideon. She glanced over at the warped wood and leather drooping to the side. "But the seat isn't fine."

Gideon shook his head. "Crazy mule got riled up and started kicking up a storm right before I left. Hit the end of that seat a couple times, and that's all it took. Busted the wood base and ripped up the leather."

Elsie grinned, thinking of the sight. "Daed never took to having a mule for that very reason. They're stubborn animals."

Gideon glanced over at her. "I know a lot of people who are just as obstinate."

Elsie drew back. "Are you referring to me?"

He chuckled. "I don't know if it's so much stubbornness as not willing to let things go."

"*Jah*, but how do you let unjust actions go by?" She kept her eyes forward, not really wanting an answer. "Especially when the injustice affects other people."

"We have the choice to take the poison along with them...or not." He clucked at the horse to go around to the back of the barn and hitched him up. All the while Elsie pondered what he'd said. It wasn't fair of him to say such poignant words and leave her hanging in thought.

Will and Ruby's white clapboard home was newly built and painted by the men in the community. Elsie had only been inside a couple of times. She admired the healthy lavender and calendula flowers that grew in the garden with a small picket fence surrounding them.

Will opened the door before they had a chance to knock. Most of the time they would walk into a person's home and call out their greeting, but Ruby didn't seem comfortable enough for them to do that. Elsie was glad to see her brother before they had to make a choice.

"Gideon, *gut* to see you, my friend." He shook Gideon's hand with vigor and then enveloped Elsie in a huge hug. "It's about time you came to see me," he whispered in her ear with a slight seriousness in his tone, unusual for him.

His desire to have them come confused Elsie. Ruby hadn't invited them, not that they expected an invitation. Elsie had thought it best to wait until Ruby was settled in. "I didn't know when we should come."

"Any time is *gut*." He stepped back. "Come into our home. Ruby has been working hard on the meal."

Gideon waited for Elsie to walk in and followed her with Will a step behind them. Their home was of good size, but then Will always did everything big. He was a competitive one. Unlike most Amish he prided himself on stacking the most hay or bringing in a big crop. Mamm said it was that same pride that would make him falter, telling him, "No one should think their accomplishments are better than another." Will's answer was, "No two people can be the same. God made us all different, *jah*?"

As Elsie went through the family room and into the stark kitchen that hadn't a bit of color, knickknacks, or even calendar on the wall, It made her appreciate all the more her mamm's rack of spices and wooden hooks to hang hats and coats or handmade quilts. That's what made their house a home. Elsie took a quick glance around the kitchen floor and noticed the void of a rug. Thinking of all the hours she stood and prepared food with the comfort of a rug to warm her on cold days, Elsie couldn't imagine going without these simple yet much appreciated comforts.

When Elsie entered the kitchen, she saw Ruby's tiny, slim shape at the sink with drooping shoulders. Her dark hair was pulled to the side of her head with wooden combs that Will must have made for her. She stared at Elsie then Gideon without expression. "*Hallo*, Elsie, Gideon."

"Thank you for having us for dinner, Ruby." Gideon moved forward for what he would normally do, which was hug or shake hands, but Ruby didn't respond. The tension in the room began to heighten, so Elsie spoke to break the silence.

"Umm, how can I help?" Elsie moved forward to see where she could jump in to prepare the meal.

Ruby scanned the room as if flustered. "If you'd set the table, I'd appreciate it." She ran water over the green beans that should have been boiling by now, then reached for a potato and started to peel. Elsie noticed a roast in the oven, but it had no seasonings, carrots, or celery to add flavor. It would take some time to get everything prepared; this should have all been in the works by now and almost ready to serve.

Elsie didn't say a word about it; she just took the silverware on the counter and set the table. When she looked up at Ruby, she seemed so engulfed in her work Elsie didn't want to bother her, so she found some carrots and cut them up. When she'd finished, she walked over to the oven. "Would you like me to put this in with the roast?"

"*Jah*, please." Ruby continued to peel the potatoes, now a large number of them.

"We like lots of potatoes at our house too." Elsie hoped Ruby would get the hint and move onto something else. Ruby finished with the potato she held and wiped her hands on her apron, then went over to the beans that should have been in a pot, boiling after she cleaned them. Once those were in the works, Ruby glanced around the room and uncovered some freshly baked bread.

"Those look and smell wonderful." The light brown crust and heavenly aroma gave Elsie the opportunity to praise her baking skills.

Ruby beamed. "*Jah*, I can always count on the bread."

Elsie smiled, ready to encourage her with the rest of the meal when Will came barging in. His presence was as big as he was. "Smells *gut* in here." Only his eyes moved as he looked from the meat to the beans to the bread.

"Almost ready." Ruby covered the bread and checked on the meat, which would take some time to cook. She poked and prodded until Will stepped out.

Elsie didn't quite know what to do or say. *Did Ruby have a bad day? Did she always cook this way? And who was she to correct the newlywed?*

"Ruby, tell me how I can help." She meant this in a much broader sense than just cooking. Ruby always seemed out of sorts when she was with her family; maybe she was in general. Elsie didn't know her well enough to figure things out. She didn't know her own sister-in-law. Although no one said it aloud, her family had to feel that same unfamiliarity each time Ruby was around. She tried to think of times Ruby was with others in the community and if she acted distant to them as well. She couldn't remember. As with any group of people, some were more talk-ative and social than others. But if she didn't take notice, that must mean Ruby was more reserved or Elsie had been brooding over Jake and didn't spot it.

Ruby put a palm to her forehead then pointed to the beans. "If you can finish with those, I think I've got the rest."

"I don't mind helping." Elsie walked over to the boiling pot.

"It takes me awhile longer is all." The lift in Ruby's voice let Elsie know to work and not to talk. So that's what they did, and after one more visit from Will the meal was served.

Once Ruby and Elsie brought out the food, they sat together and silently prayed. "Amen," Will said, and they began to pass the food. There was more talk than eating, but it was good to be together. Elsie missed Will's stories, making the biggest tale out of the smallest experience. Ruby seemed to lighten once the meal was over and the dishes were cleaned and put away.

They settled in at the table once again to eat the apple pie Ruby made. After the meal they'd just finished, Elsie hesitated when she took her first bite. The sweetness of apples melted on her tongue with a hint of brown sugar, and the perfectly light crust blended with the rest. Elsie glanced over at Gideon, who had the same sense of wonder about him. Will finished his second piece and asked for a third. Ruby floated on a cloud as she served everyone another piece of the scrumptious pie.

Gideon and Will sat together in the family room while Elsie and Ruby washed the remaining dishes together with a completely different manner. "Ruby, that pie was so *gut*. I have to watch you make one."

Ruby shrugged, "You seem surprised." She looked up at Elsie as she handed her a plate to dry.

Not wanting to tell a lie, Elsie spoke the truth. "*Jah*, I suppose I am."

Ruby sighed. "Being one of eight girls and me being the youngest, my daed needed some of us to help do his work, and so I didn't learn to cook very well. That chore was always done by my older sisters."

"But your pie—?" Elsie tried to ask.

Ruby held up a hand and smiled. "I did learn to bake."

"My, *jah*, you did. You should take some of your pies to the bazaar next month. That truly was the best I've had."

Ruby's eyes held hers for a long moment. "Maybe I will."

"Okay then. Will you both be coming to Sunday dinner?" Elsie's family were disappointed that she and Will didn't come every Sunday to eat with them. Will came alone during the week every now and then, but Ruby didn't so often.

Ruby's posture straightened, and she averted her eyes. "It's a lot for just the two of us to take care of this place, but we'll try."

Elsie didn't understand this woman her brother married. But she wouldn't give up trying.

Chapter Twelve

GIDEON WASN'T SURE how the evening would transpire, but overall it had been an enjoyable meal and time with the newlyweds. As Elsie waved to them, he wondered how things went with Ruby, but he didn't want to bring up the touchy subject. He'd hoped the two had become better acquainted. Ruby hadn't said more than a few words to him the entire evening. Ruby's unease created tension; at least it seemed that way to him.

"Thanks for going with me, Gideon." Elsie gave him an appreciative smile. "You're *gut* at making people feel comfortable, even Ruby."

He looked over at her in surprise. "She hardly said a word to me."

"It was still more than most. This was the first time she ever really talked to me."

"Did everything go all right in the kitchen?" He'd been starving by the time the food came out and had wondered what the reason was.

"Ruby was one of eight sisters and didn't have any brothers, so she didn't learn to cook. She helped her dad with the chores instead."

Gideon cleared his throat, still guarded against making any comments that might not come out right. Amish women, especially his mamm, were proud of their cooking, even though pride was frowned upon. "*Ach*? That explains things a bit better."

She turned to him. "You thought the meal was fine then?"

"Not as *gut* as some, but then I come from a home of all boys who will eat whatever's set before them, so I'm not one to ask."

He thought he dodged that question quite well until he noticed Elsie was still staring at him.

"Your brother Will is a character with all his storytelling and always joking around." Gideon chuckled, thinking of one of his humorous tales. "Has he told you the one about the frog and the scorpion?"

"Only a hundred times." She shook her head and smiled.

Gideon was waiting for the right moment to tell Elsie he needed to decide if he should leave with Minister Miller. Because there was another going with the minister now, he felt he had more of a choice, but could he honestly tell himself he would be staying for the right reasons? His own community would need extra care while their minister was gone, but he needed to know he was making the decision with his head and not his heart. With Zeke delivering the sermon now, he might be needed here as there were some who didn't appreciate his ways. It would all be decided by a roll of the dice, their custom following the soldiers casting lots at the time of Christ's crucifixion.

"Elsie, I need to know you'll understand if I leave with the minister." He sighed and gained the courage to look at her. One gesture or word could change his mind if it came from her, so he prayed for discernment.

"I hoped you would stay." Her brows tightened in confusion and concern. Maybe he shouldn't rely on her giving him a subjective answer. He and Rachel were the only ones she seemed to confide in.

"I need you to support me in making the right decision."

Elsie nodded. "I will support you."

He couldn't read her tone, but he felt it was forced and not from the heart, which didn't help him with the decision. But he didn't feel comfortable leaving with those young men around.

The cicadas started their song as the light began to fade, and Elsie hummed a hymn with her mesmerizing voice. Gideon let Betsy the horse lead the way and relaxed to the rhythm of the plodding hooves. As he took in the night air, a faint noise brought him to attention, a noise like a purr or a rumble. Gideon glanced over at Elsie to see if she could hear it, but she seemed preoccupied with her humming.

The cicadas grew louder, another chorus drowning out the first. Gideon turned to his left at a large tree that seemed to be full of them. The noise got louder as Gideon looked behind him. A car skidded and came to a stop. Betsy whinnied then shot off into a full gallop. Gideon pulled hard on the reins, but the horse raced forward in fear. Elsie's sudden scream burst through the air, and then a loud *crack*! He whipped his head over to see her holding onto the sides of the buggy door. A splintered chunk of the broken bench fell off and flew onto the gravel road.

Gideon glanced over to see Elsie pulling herself back up into the middle of the bench right next to him. Betsy was more spooked than ever. If he couldn't stop her, he'd turn her. He leaned to the right and pulled on the reins. He hated to see the whites of the horse's eyes as he veered her toward the danger she was trying to escape. But one look at Elsie showed her fear of those men.

"Elsie!" He yelled until she turned her head. "Hold on to me."

He gave Betsy the reins and let the fright in her flow until they got up to the car. Elsie let out a long breath. "What happened?"

"The bench busted." Gideon was instantly upset with himself for not fixing it before she rode with him again.

He didn't remember jumping out of the buggy. Only when he was standing in front of the men did time slow down enough for him to gain his senses. Gideon wanted to be the barrier between them and Elsie even though he felt vulnerable out of his buggy. "What do you want with us?" His eyes locked on the one who seemed to be the leader, but the young man took his time answering. Then he turned back to Elsie to make sure she didn't get out of the buggy.

The young men chuckled, and one pointed at Elsie. "There seems to be a lot of accidents happening around here lately, Elsie."

She blanched at the sound of this man calling her by name. Gideon's courage tripled at the thought of Elsie being taunted by these men. "There are better ways to settle any problems you have with us."

The man closest to them put up his hands, mocking a surrendering gesture. "Do you really think we'll stand by and let you take all the farming land?" He cocked his head to the side with a slight grin.

"There's plenty of land for all if we only take what we need." Gideon's lip twitched with both anger and fear, realizing it would be difficult to reason with them.

"Not with all these newcomers moving down here." The tall dark-haired man, who seemed to be in charge, took a long hard look at him.

"Is that the only reason you don't want us here?"

"Don't need another. Ya'll know how important land is. That's why you moved here; not enough to hold all of ya up north." His voice grew louder as he spoke, his patience beginning to wane.

"Maybe we could come together and discuss this to get a better understanding—" The man held up his hand in Gideon's face. Gideon heard Elsie gasp behind him.

He motioned for Gideon to come closer, taunting him. Gideon leaned forward, just out of the man's reach. He could smell the tobacco on his hot breath. "You should heed my warning."

The conversation was going nowhere, and his first concern was Elsie. He needed to lower his pride and take Elsie and go. One of the other men, a younger blond man, began to mock him, but Gideon didn't listen to the words.

As he walked past them to his side of the buggy, he glanced into the vehicle and saw a youth in the backseat staring at him. He sat still as ice and kept his eyes on Gideon. He didn't know why they'd bring someone so young with them while they did their dirty work, but it appalled him to think they brought him along. He didn't respond, just lifted himself into the buggy and grabbed the reins.

When he sat down on the bench seat, he pulled Elsie close to him and tapped Betsy with the reins. Neither of them spoke for a long while. Thoughts of hatred ran through Gideon's mind. He shamed himself for them. Never knowing this kind of anger scared him enough to stop.

"Pray with me, Gideon." Elsie's eyes closed, and her hand clasped his arm.

He froze, his focus straight ahead and asked forgiveness for his wrath. No matter who was at fault, he would not let them bring him to that level again. These thoughts were as bad as words and actions. "Are you hurt?"

She opened her eyes and turned to him. "The bench scratched my leg, but I'm all right." She studied his face.

"I can't tell you how angry I am that this happened to you." He rubbed his jaw, wishing he could come back to his natural calm ways.

"The bench broke; it's not your fault." She turned away and let go of his arm.

Gideon furrowed his brow. "I heard a sound that spooked the horse. That's what caused you to fall. Granted, the bench needed repair, but other circumstances made it all happen."

"You don't know that for sure. And all I heard was the car." The rims of Elsie's eyes were red and watery.

"It's time to take action." Gideon heard her muffled cry. "I have to do something about this, Elsie." He had to tell someone before he left with Minister Miller, if he could leave. It would be harder than ever now.

"I can't, Gideon." She turned around and glanced at the car slowly driving away behind them.

"Then I will." He reached over and took her hand. Whatever qualms these men had instilled in her was something she couldn't let go. Maybe he was wrong to confront these men, but he had another reason to stand up to them. "Don't look back," he instructed her. But he was telling himself the same thing. He didn't want to look into the eyes of that terrified boy again.

Chapter Thirteen

ELSIE ROSE TO the sound of her daed's voice. She pulled on her robe quickly, all the while hearing his grumbling from down the hall.

"Ahh!" Her daed's cry was unheard of—he never showed any pain. She could hear shuffling and another loud grunt before she got to their room. Daed was doubled over, his hand over his chest and his face pinched.

"What is it?" Elsie feared the worst by the way he grabbed his chest. The deep red color of his cheeks alarmed her into action. With quick steps she grabbed his free hand and watched him wince.

"I'm not sure." Mamm reached under his armpit and steadied her hand on his back. "I've never seen him in such pain." She spoke calmly but wasn't. Her big strong daed fought through pain, but this was bigger than him. "Solomon, I'm going to lift you up now. You need to help me."

He nodded once, slightly, and grimaced again. Elsie didn't know what to do, but she wanted to help. "I'll help you, Mamm." She placed herself to match her mamm and waited for her signal.

"*Ens, zwei, drei.*" They sat him upright and put pillows behind him. Mamm stepped back when he wailed again. "Go to Rachel's and have them phone for an ambulance."

Elsie had more than twenty questions to ask, but she only nodded and ran out of the room. Her daed's groan made her move quickly to her room. She pulled on her dress but skipped the apron and kapp. She then grabbed her work boots and stomped out the door. The door slammed shut behind her, making her jump. She wished the boys would sleep through this, but with her racket and Daed's outbursts, they would be up soon enough.

She wanted Gideon to be with her. This was the day the deacons, elders, and Minister Miller were meeting at Omar's to discuss the needs of the newcomers. Gideon also planned to talk to Omar about the Englishers. Word would eventually get to him that her daed was ill, but it couldn't be soon enough for Elsie.

Rachel's place was not the nearest farm but second next, but more importantly they had the community phone. She would be glad to see her since Elsie kept to herself so much lately. Elsie couldn't get Angus out of the barn fast enough. She worked as quickly as she could to place his halter on and then jumped on him bareback.

Angus ran like a fire was under him. Sensing his rider's urgency, the horse tucked his head and ran full speed. Elsie's dress flapped in the wind, her hair whipping against her cheeks and back. She didn't know what time it was but hoped someone would be out for her to call to along her way to Rachel's. The first of two farms between them showed a dim light in the barn. Someone was milking, so it must be around four o'clock.

"*Hallo!*" Her yell screeched through the air, rousing the occupant in the barn.

"What in tarnation—" The old man pulled on his suspenders over his shoulders then flipped the brim of his hat up to get a better look at the crazy rider who came barging up to his peaceful barn.

"It's Elsie Yoder. My daed needs help."

"Elsie?" Too stubborn to wear glasses, Ira squinted so he could see her. "Well, what's wrong with him?"

"He's in a lot of pain. I'm going to the Kings' place to call an ambulance." Elsie choked out the words as she tried to catch her breath.

Ira wrinkled his stubbly nose and shooed her away. "Okay then, I'll take care of things on this end. You go on now."

With that she turned around and galloped back out onto the

road, jumping a white fence along the way. The pounding of Angus's hooves increased with each stride he took. By telling one person, the news would spread and help would be on the way.

Although it was a short distance, it felt longer than ever. She rode Angus right up to the house and jumped off, not bothering to hitch him to the post. Rachel's daed opened the door and walked out when he saw Elsie.

"What's wrong, Elsie?" Rachel's daed put a hand on her shoulder, his dark eyes holding on hers.

"It's my daed." She blew out a breath to compose herself and force back the tears. "He needs a doctor." Elsie leaned against Angus as Rachel's daed ran to the house. At that same instant Rachel came running to her.

"What happened?" she asked as she enveloped Elsie in a hug.

"He's in such awful pain." Elsie let herself cry into her friend's arms. "He's got me scared, Rachel." She shivered against the cool summer air. The sun was far from rising.

"How's your mamm and the boys?" Rachel tucked her arm with Elsie's and guided her to the house.

"The boys weren't up when I left, but I'm sure they are now. And the look in Mamm's eyes...she was scared too." Elsie had only seen this expression on her face one other time, and that was when Adam fell out of the hayloft door. He'd landed in the wagon that held a thin lining of hay, but that wasn't enough to break the fall. To this day her daed thought that incident made Adam a little slow. Mamm insisted he was just shy, that his only injury was a foggy head. Elsie saw that same fear in her mamm's face when Daed cried out.

Rachel guided her inside the house, and they listened as Rachel's daed got off the phone. Rachel's four brothers slowly came out one by one to see what the ruckus was about. One went to the kitchen to make a pot of coffee, knowing when the phone was in need, so was one of their people. Another went in with Rachel's daed when he hung up the phone. The youngest of the brood gave Elsie a hug, waiting to be filled in on what was happening. Elsie grew up with these young men in Virginia, and they were as much her brothers as Adam and Aaron were.

"I'll take you back in the buggy if you'd like some company." Rachel's brother offered. His attention to her long flowing hair down her back reminded Elsie that her head wasn't covered.

Rachel watched her toy with it and started for her room. "I'll get you some pins."

The oldest brother went over and gave his brother a stare. "You didn't have to embarrass her like that. You know she can't go with you alone in the buggy."

The younger brother wrinkled his brow. "Gideon takes her in his buggy."

Elsie turned a darker shade of red and turned toward Rachel's room as she was coming out. Were people talking about them?

"I'll go with her." Rachel went to the barn as the boys and her daed offered Elsie prayers and said they would come check on Solomon later in the day.

Their mamm passed away giving birth, so they were accustomed to doing a lot for themselves and pulled together more than some simply because they had to. Rachel, being the only girl, was expected to just do one person's job, but much of the household work fell onto her anyway. Elsie felt the extra load once Katie left and couldn't imagine the work Rachel had to do.

"I don't want to wait to hitch up the buggy." Elsie had no patience and needed to get Angus home, so she didn't feel she was being rude. "If the ambulance gets there before me, the boys will be alone."

"I figured you wouldn't. You go on ahead. I'll be there soon."

"I never thought I'd be so glad to use a phone. Did they say they'd call back when they know what's wrong?" Elsie's voice cracked as the emotions wrapped around her chest.

"My daed won't leave the house until they do. And one of the boys will come to the house with any news." Rachel grabbed Elsie's hand and squeezed. "There's a lot of common things that can be wrong. Don't think the worst. Think the best."

The ride home calmed her nerves and gave her some alone time to ask God for healing and for the good doctors to have wisdom while tending her daed. She'd never been in a hospital, and the only doctor she'd seen was the one in their old community. Others said the care was good and the hospital doctors understood their ways for the most part.

When she got home, she put Angus out to pasture and ran quickly to the house. Adam and Aaron were in the kitchen, trying to wash the dishes. "The car came to get Daed," Adam blurted out as soon as he saw her.

"The ambulance," Aaron corrected him.

"That's *gut*. They'll take him to doctors who will help him feel better." Elsie gathered the remnants of food that they used, making an interesting breakfast for themselves. "Carrots and cheese?"

"Mamm said to wait for you, but we got hungry." Aaron watched her clean up the mess.

Elsie managed a grin as she studied them. Their somber expressions urged her to let them milk with her. They liked the chore, and it might help keep their mind off things, and it was a chore that had to be done. "Would you boys like to help with the milking?"

Their eyes lit up. What was work for older boys was a treat for them. "I'll get my boots." Aaron was in the mudroom in a flash, with Adam close behind. But then Adam usually was following in his brother's footsteps.

Although he was the older, only by a few minutes, he was slower than his little brother. Elsie had a tender place for him in her heart. She watched him struggle with his work boots and start to cry with frustration when his brother ran out the door.

Elsie bent down beside him and gestured for him to sit on the wood floor. "Getting upset only makes you more frustrated." She smiled when he wiped his eyes with his sleeve and stuck out his bottom lip, trying not to cry. "See there, it's done."

He kicked his boots together, digesting her words, and after a couple of seconds got the idea he was done and stood to go. He stopped at the door and looked back at her. "I never get there first."

She smiled. "It's not about who is first; it just matters that you get there." His frown turned upside down, and he pushed open the back door that led to the barn. Elsie was close behind but didn't want to get there before him. Although the Amish never encouraged status among one another, Elsie didn't think it hurt anything to let a little boy get to the barn before her.

The milk truck tanker came down the dirt path, startling Elsie. She'd lost all track of time. They would normally be done with milking long before Jerry came to pump the milk into the storage tank.

Elsie went to the barn and got the boys started as quickly as she could. It would take some time to attach the suction pumps to almost twenty cows. "Boys, we need to hurry. Let me show you a trick or two so we can get this done faster."

Aaron caught on fairly quickly once he got the hang of it. Adam didn't let his slow actions perturb him. When he got stuck, he'd watch Aaron and figure what step he was on. "How's this?" Adam asked after finally attaching the cups.

"Very *gut*." Elsie praised him, although he missed an important step. "Did you wipe down the teats first?"

He shook his head. "But I won't forget now."

Elsie nodded and grabbed a handful of newspapers for him to use. "I know you won't. We learn from our mistakes." She heard the barn door open and spoke without looking up. "Morning, Jerry. We're running behind today. You may want—" When she turned to see him, a taller figure stood in his place. This man was unrecognizable with the sun coming up behind him. He was a shadow, still and mute, watching them from a distance.

Elsie's heart began to bang in her chest, concerned that this was one of the men who harassed her. Her first instinct was to protect the boys, but she didn't want to scare them. "Where's

Jerry?" She took slow steps to put herself between this man and the boys.

"I'm his replacement." The man stood stock-still. Was he nervous? Waiting for her to make a move?

"What happened to him?" Trying to keep her voice calm and him distracted might be her only chance to keep him at bay.

"Got a different route closer to home is what I hear." His head moved toward the boys, making the blood rush from her face. She wouldn't put anything past these men with all the stunts they'd done. What they didn't seem to understand was that although the Amish were gentle people, they would be hard pressed to leave their land. Elsie remembered Gideon's words and was willing to take the brunt of that even though these moments scared her to death. But how long could she hold on to that thought?

"The company would have told you if they could have gotten ahold of someone. But from what I hear, that's a hard thing to do." He spoke with no malice in his words, making Elsie question her suspicions, but she didn't want to let down her guard yet.

"Where are you from?" She let out a breath, along with some of the fear, and breathed a little easier.

"I'm new to this area. My family is up north." He stepped to the side away from the sun to show his face. "I didn't mean to alarm you, ma'am. I can call my supervisor and have him tell you about the change."

His strong cheekbones and firm build intimidated her, but now she saw the baby face of a young man not much older than her. His sun-kissed light brown hair and large blue eyes caused her to stare. "*Dass tut mir leid.*" Elsie put a hand to her forehead, flustered and embarrassed. "I mean, I'm sorry. I thought you were someone else."

"Perfectly understandable." He shoved his hands in his pockets and smiled. "Did you call me a bad name?"

She laughed, a little too hard, but it released her nervous energy. "*Nee*, I said I'm sorry, which I really am." Now with the fear gone, irritation took its place at how those men could make her panic without even being nearby. "Please, give me a minute to help the boys finish." She was pleased to see they had all the pumps on and working. "We're not usually late, but we had a family emergency." Her voice cracked a bit going back to thoughts of her daed.

"Well, let me help then." He took careful steps over to her, maybe still trying to earn her trust.

"Have you ever milked before?"

"By hand mostly, but I've learned this system as well." He turned to Adam, who was staring, in fact, both boys were, waiting for Elsie to give word everything was all right. "Hello, I'm Timothy. You can call me Tim."

Adam remained silent, but Aaron stuck out his hand to pump Timothy's hand in the Amish way. Timothy followed his lead then turned to Adam, who seemed to ease a bit after seeing his brother's example. "I'd like to call you Timothy," Adam informed him.

"Well, that's fine with me. I'll answer to either." Timothy went to the far end and waited with them until the first heifer ran dry. Once one did, the others followed close behind, until they'd finished the task.

Adam leaned into Timothy, who sat on a milking stool. "Forgot to tell ya, old Ginger is a kicker. We use a boot if she's feeling ornery."

Timothy grinned. "Good to know. But I kick back, and they tend to stop on their own." Adam's jaw dropped and Timothy winked. Adam caught onto his humor and chuckled.

Elsie appreciated the interaction Timothy gave the boys. It not only made time go faster, but it kept her mind occupied with other thoughts besides her daed. Once the milk started pumping into the tanker, the boys went off to the house to eat a decent meal as Elsie promised them. "I don't suppose you have time for breakfast. It's the least I can do for all of your help."

He looked up at her with kind eyes. "I wish I could. I grew up on a farm and have heard the food around here is just as good."

He wiped his hands on his jeans. "I've got to make up some time though."

"How silly of me, of course." Now she felt selfish for offering. She'd taken his time and hard work to get their milking done. "I should have let you go to another farm and come back. I wasn't thinking."

"Do you mind me asking what emergency you were speaking of?" His sincere tone gave her a certain trust enough to confide in him.

"My daed woke in the middle of the night in a lot of pain. The ambulance took him and my mamm to the hospital." That's all she could say without emotions welling up again.

"You mean your dad, right?"

She could only nod. "I'm sorry to hear that." He paused and studied her. "Would it help if I told the others on my route about what happened? I know how you all help each other."

Elsie knew of the growing fascination the secular world had with the Amish, but she didn't get that sense from Timothy. He seemed to know their ways though. The deacons would be making visits to ask folks what they could give to help with the medical expenses. "I don't know how people get by that don't live that way."

"It's sorta the way I grew up in the country, so I get it more than most. And I agree with you. Although we lived miles away, we still knew what was going on with each other." He stepped away, and she realized she was keeping him again. His comfortable ways made it easy to get caught up in conversation.

"Thank you, Timothy, for everything, really. I promise next time we'll be ready for you." She hated to see him go. He'd been so helpful and encouraging when she needed it most.

Chapter Fourteen

WHEN ELSIE WENT into the kitchen, Annie and Beverly Zook were cleaning up the dishes. Elsie felt the tears rise once again this morning and took a deep breath before greeting them. "Any word yet?"

Annie looked up from the sink with her large brown eyes. "*Nee*, not yet. But I'm sure we'll hear soon." Annie had strength when others didn't. Elsie thought she was one of the strongest people she was blessed to know, and she prayed for the peace Annie had.

"You know how long it takes those English doctors to run their tests and all," Beverly offered as she took a plate from Annie and wiped it dry.

"So I've heard." Elsie wasn't comforted. No news was better than bad, but it would be nice to hear Mamm's voice right about now. She noticed Rachel with the boys in the other room. "I was wondering where you were."

"I got here soon after you. But I ran into Ruby and asked her to come over here with me." Rachel shrugged. "And she did." She grinned with satisfaction, knowing what a great feat that was. Maybe dinner the other night with her made some sort of difference between them.

"Where is she?" Just as Elsie asked, Ruby came downstairs with some dirty laundry. "Ruby, thanks for coming over."

She wiped a dark strand of hair off her forehead and stuck the bundle of clothes under her arm. "I heard about your daed. I was almost to the neighbor's house to find out more when Rachel rode by and told me." She squeezed Elsie's hand. "Will is on his way."

Elsie's bottom lip trembled as tears quietly ran down her

109

cheeks. She wiped them away when Rachel stood and put her arm around her. When Adam and Aaron came thundering down the stairs, Elsie pulled herself together and told them to slow down. "What's the hurry?"

"Ruby told us if we helped her clean, we could have a piece of her berry pie," Aaron announced, as if he'd never eaten pie before. Adam grinned and followed Aaron to the kitchen. No one else felt like eating, so they kept busy doing what they could around the house and received visitors who came to bring a dish for dinner or a pastry for the family.

"I hope that's all right." Ruby walked up beside Elsie and slowly turned from one side of the kitchen to the other. The counters were full of casseroles, bread pudding, and a variety of other dishes.

"Of course, and I hope you bring another one of your pies, Ruby." Elsie meant it, but she also wanted Ruby to feel better about working in the kitchen.

Time seemed to stop as they all sat in the kitchen and spilled over into to the entry room. A second pot of coffee was made just as a car pulled in. Elsie stood and waited for Mamm to come in and tell her about her daed. Mamm greeted a couple who were leaving after sharing a cup of coffee and leaving a couple loaves of bread. Mamm thanked them but didn't smile when she explained there was no news yet.

When she went into the kitchen, her gaze went straight to Elsie. They embraced and sat closely at the kitchen table while the others made plates of food and stored much more for future meals and visitors.

"It's not *gut*, is it?" Elsie sucked in a breath to prepare herself.

"The doctors say it's his gallbladder. Once it passes, he's on the mend. I need to go back and stay with him. I wanted to tell you myself and pack a few things for your daed and me to spend the night."

"Thank God. So when will he be able to come home?"

"Soon I hope. He's complaining to me he wants to come home,

so that much is *gut*. He's worried about getting the work done."
Mamm gave Elsie a tired smile and stood to go upstairs. "Help
me pack, will you?"

"*Jah*, sure." But she didn't want to help her mamm. Elsie didn't
want her to leave or for Daed to be gone. As she followed her
mamm, Elsie thought of all the extra responsibilities she would
have. The boys would need three meals a day, and then there
was the milking, feeding, and care of the animals. The goats and
lambs would birth soon, and then there were Mamm's chores
that she now would need to combine with hers. Her mind began
to spin then stopped when she realized Mamm was calling to her.

"Sorry, Mamm. I didn't hear a thing you said." She didn't
want to hear the long list that she already knew by heart. There
was nothing that could be done later or could wait; a farm their
size couldn't run that way.

"What were you thinking about so intently?" Mamm's brow
wrinkled with concern, and Elsie felt badly for giving her anything else to think about.

"I'll take care of everything while you're gone." Elsie gulped,
saying what she felt she couldn't do. Will might be able to help,
but he had his own farm to work, with no help of his own. "I
might need a hand though." She thought of Gideon, knowing she
could count on him.

"Elsie, do you remember when the Lambrights' barn burned
down? And the Hershbergers were in a bad way when their crop
didn't produce what they needed one harvest?" Mamm turned
and finished packing then took one bag and handed Elsie another.

"*Jah*, why?"

"You won't be running this farm alone." Mamm finally smiled,
making the wrinkles in the corner of her eyes fan out. And Elsie
knew she was right.

When they walked into the kitchen, Mose was sitting at the
table with Yonnie and Will. The boys sat with them wide-eyed as
they spoke of the weather and their crops. Rachel's daed came in
the door and joined them. Elsie felt a huge void because Gideon

wasn't there. She wished she hadn't given him her blessing to leave. She needed him here now.

Mamm grinned at Elsie. "You were always on the helping end. This is what it's like to be on the receiving side."

When Elsie looked at the table with every chair filled and some men standing, her eyes caught on Mose, who was staring right at her. Those blue eyes would always remind her of Jake, and then the thoughts of him would capture her mind. And then there was Katie, unaware that her daed was in a hospital. She wondered if Katie kept in touch with the community, but Elsie didn't know how, nor would her daed want to know. He felt abandoned and shamed that she left, not married, but with a young man. But Elsie thought Mamm would want to know of her whereabouts about now. "Should we try to contact Katie?"

Mamm stopped on the porch and stared at Elsie. "Your daed has forbidden it."

"*Jah*, I know." She frowned down at her black, soiled boots and questioned herself. "But doesn't this change things?" Elsie was surprised in what she was asking her mamm. As upset as she was with her sister, Elsie knew family came first, especially in crisis.

"Maybe, I don't know." Mamm's eyes teared as she hugged the boys and then got into the car of an English neighbor who helped them now and then with transportation. "You take care of each other."

Her mamm didn't say yes, but Elsie didn't hear a definite no either. She would talk with Mose as to what he thought. Maybe she was wrong, but if she was right, she would never forgive herself for not giving Katie the chance to know that her daed was ill.

The women prepared a spread of potato soup, dilly carrots, and snap peas for a midafternoon meal. They gathered bread and desserts that visitors brought and set them on the counter for people to eat and come back for more. Elsie enjoyed the conversation and the busyness to keep her mind off things.

When she finally got the chance to fix herself a plate, she searched for Mose and sat next to him. They sat on either side of the table and spoke quietly so no one could hear. "Any word from Jake?" She took a sip of the creamy soup even though she had no appetite. Concerns about her daed and the slightest thought of Jake and Katie coming back made her stomach queasy.

"*Nee*, have you?" He stuck his fork into the flaky crust of an apple pie.

She shook her head. "They can't stay forever, can they?" Maybe that thought was not on Jake's or Katie's mind. Perhaps they were living a happy life on their own, not missing them at all.

"I'm beginning to wonder." He set the fork down and looked straight at her with all seriousness. "Do you think they know what's going on here? Like this?" He nodded his head toward the commotion caused by her daed's bad health. "I wonder if they keep in contact with anyone here."

She frowned. "If they want to communicate with someone, it should be us; they're our family." Elsie couldn't hide the bite of anger in her words.

"They may turn to someone else for fear of not being accepted by us. But I would think Katie would want to know about your daed."

Elsie leaned forward in appreciation of his words. "I asked my mamm if she thought we should try to let her know."

His eyes brightened, and Elsie knew he had the same longing that she did. "And what did she say?"

"She didn't say yes, but she didn't say no either." Elsie cringed, regretting bringing Katie into the picture and wishing she would have waited for Gideon. "I shouldn't have asked her; she has too much on her mind."

He put his hand on hers, and she met his eyes. "You should give her a chance to make her own decision."

"Making her own decisions is what got her where she is now," Elsie said with spite. "But yes, I think she should at least be informed and leave it at that."

"Do you want me to take you to Rachel's?"

"*Jah*, I suppose so." They both looked around the room until they spotted Rachel. When Mose gestured to her, she came over and sat with them.

"You two seem to be intent on something." She gave them a sidelong glance and waited for them to tell her what was going on.

"I need to use the phone at your daed's." Elsie wasn't sure how much she wanted Rachel to know. She and Mose had decided what to do, and she didn't want a lot of other opinions to confuse her.

"I'd like to go too," Mose responded quickly, as if he'd lose the opportunity if he didn't claim his place.

Rachel nodded to confirm his request. "Let's tell Annie, and I'll go with you." She didn't ask any questions, which Elsie appreciated, but she wasn't sure Rachel would agree with what they were doing.

Elsie told Annie and the boys she was leaving. "Can you keep an eye on Adam and Aaron for me?" She wrung her hands while she waited for Annie's answer, even though she knew what her response would be. But Annie studied her for a moment before she answered.

"Of course." Annie clasped her hands over Elsie's, and her hands went idle. "Whatever it is that's holding you captive, stop and pray it away."

Annie had filled the hole after Katie left, and Elsie didn't know what she would have done without her. Annie had left and gone into the secular world and returned, which gave Elsie hope. But Katie was nothing like Annie, chasing after the things of the world whereas Annie went to find a mother she never knew she had.

"Words of wisdom." Elsie found a smile and squeezed her hand. "*Danke* for taking care of the boys."

"No worries. Do what you need to, Elsie. Only you know in your heart what that is."

Elsie gave her a thoughtful grin and joined the others in Mose's buggy. She was in silent thought during the ride to Rachel's haus. As they walked up to her haus, though, she wasted no time explaining why they were there. "Rachel, Mose and I have decided to try and let Katie know about Daed." Elsie watched Rachel's face as she told her.

She pursed her lip and nodded once. "You sound set on that."

"We are, although we're not sure how to get hold of her."

"My daed might know." Rachel seemed a bit concerned, but Elsie had come this far, she wasn't going to change her mind now. The sound of the wheels crunching gravel was all that was heard for a short while. "You don't agree with our decision?"

"I don't know what to think. But it's not my decision to make." She turned toward Elsie. "It's yours."

Elsie caught her meaning but didn't agree. This would affect Mose and his family as well.

Rachel's daed, Henry, came from the barn and gave Elsie a gentle hug. "You want to try the hospital?"

"*Nee*, actually I'd like to reach Katie."

"And Jake," Mose added.

He took a step back and rubbed his face. "Does your daed know about this?"

"*Nee.*" Mose shook his head.

"I asked my mamm." Elsie felt that was enough information. If she was in Katie's shoes, she would want to know, so she would do the same for her.

"Well, I think you should ask your folks, Mose." Henry let out a breath. "But I'm not gonna be the one to say no. I'm sure Katie would want to know, but I'm not so sure I agree with you talking with Jake. He doesn't have a daed who's in a bad way."

Mose remained silent for a moment then nodded. "It's more important that Katie gets the news. I'll wait on Jake."

Elsie gave him a brief glance, appreciating his understanding, and took the phone after Henry dialed. When a woman answered, Elsie became flustered, and Mose touched her shoulder to calm her. "*Hallo*, I'm trying to reach Katie Yoder."

"There's no one here by that name. Who's calling?"

Her cheeks heated in disappointment. "I'm sorry." Rachel shook her head, and Mose smiled at her nervousness. "My name is Elsie Yoder."

"You must be one of those Amish people." The woman didn't sound either irritated or overly excited at the realization.

"*Jah*, I'm looking for my sister to tell her our daed is ill."

"Well, like I said, there's no Katie Yoder here."

Elsie's heart sunk, thinking that she was so close to actually talking to her sister after all this time. "I'm sorry to have bothered you."

"But there is a Katie *Fisher.*"

Chapter Fifteen

GIDEON TETHERED HIS buggy and took quick steps to Rachel's haus just as Elsie was handing the phone to Rachel's daed. He watched Elsie make her way to the couch and sit down. She hadn't even acknowledged him, just staring blankly in front of her. "Is everyone all right?" He scanned the room to see Rachel's daed, Mose, Will, and Rachel. "Are the boys here?" He didn't know how candid he could be.

"Gideon." Elsie's eyes were large, bewildered as she stared at Gideon. "They're with Ruby and Annie."

The tension in the air consumed him. He remained standing, ready for more bad news. "What's wrong?"

"I called to tell Katie about Daed." Elsie stared into his eyes, waiting for his response.

"Who decided this?"

She started to look at Mose but stopped and turned back to Gideon. "I did." Gideon didn't believe she made the decision alone, but that could be discussed later.

"The woman who answered told me there was a Katie Fisher staying there." She fumbled over the last word and took in a breath.

Gideon couldn't imagine what this was doing to Elsie. Her pale face and sadness around her eyes made it obvious, but what she was feeling internally must be breaking her apart. He sat down next to her, across from Mose and Rachel. Rachel's daed asked his boys to go out and do some chores so they could have privacy, then he stood by Elsie. "Are Katie and Jake married?"

Elsie's eyes dropped down to her hands, folded on her lap.

Gideon knew she was trying not to twiddle as she always did when she was upset or nervous. "I don't know."

"Or were they only saying they are to be able to find a place that would take them in." Will offered but shrugged as if he really had no idea.

Mose didn't take his eyes off Gideon when he spoke, maybe to confirm the thoughts he told Gideon about the possibility they were married. "I don't know if it matters out there."

"Either is a possibility." Gideon felt helpless that he wasn't familiar with the world outside their community. He questioned if Elsie should have tried to make contact for this very reason. When he saw Elsie wrap her arms over her stomach, trying to comfort herself, Gideon was glad he was there.

She touched Gideon's hand. "I left the house without telling you where I was going, bent on making that phone call that I now regret. The more I know, the worse I feel."

"It's okay. I'm sorry I couldn't get here sooner." Gideon noticed all of their eyes were on Elsie, and he tried to bring their attention back to the issue at hand. "How did you know where to find her?"

Henry's solemn face showed his discomfort with the question. "I'm put in a difficult position some times because I have this phone." He moved away from Elsie and sat in his rocking chair. "Katie called awhile after she left and asked me to let her know if anything happened concerning her family. I told her I couldn't do that, but I'd take her number in case any of you wanted to reach her." He rubbed the back of his neck and studied Elsie's face.

"I'm sorry you had to make a decision about that." Will sighed. "I'm surprised she called and asked you to do that. I doubt she thinks about us or misses us." His words brought tears to Elsie's eyes.

"Too bad she wasn't there when you called." Rachel said it almost as a question more than a statement.

"Maybe it's for the best. She's been told about daed, and the decision is hers as to what she wants to do from here." Elsie pursed her lip, feeling that she'd done her part.

Gideon moved his eyes slowly back to Elsie wondering if that was a wise choice. "So she is going to find out from the person who runs the boardinghouse?"

"Maybe not the best way to be told, but this way the decision is hers." Elsie looked at him with new confidence, and he decided he shouldn't give his opinion. He didn't know what this felt like for her. No one did, except Mose.

"Well, I'm glad you made the call for my own benefit. I miss my *bruder* no matter how wrong he was to leave." Mose's eyes were only on Elsie. "And I hope they come back."

"Sometimes something like this is what it takes." Rachel smiled at Elsie to show her support. "God only knows."

"How is your daed?" Gideon had forgotten to ask about the most important reason he left the meetings and came to see Elsie.

"He's recovering. It's his gallbladder." Elsie forced a smile.

Gideon didn't appreciate the way Mose stared at her. The fact their siblings both left had created some sort of bond between them, but Gideon had no patience for it at the moment. "When will he come home?"

"In a day or two maybe, if the doctor says he's healed well enough." She looked out the window, distracted. "I'll need some help around here for a while."

"Done, whatever you need." Mose said it so fast Gideon didn't have a chance to answer quickly enough.

Gideon's mind went straight to her safety, not the chores. She and the boys were his first concern. "You and the boys shouldn't be home alone. I'll be around to make sure you're safe."

Mose stared at Gideon. Maybe he was being too forward to make such an offer, but with her daed ill it gave Gideon the leeway he needed. "With your daed's permission, of course."

Rachel stood. "If I could leave my brothers alone for any length of time, I would come. You know how helpless they are without me. But I'll come by to check on you. As a matter of fact, I should start making the evening meal. But I'll come over and check on you later, Elsie."

"Don't worry about me. But it would be nice to have your company. Too many thoughts go through my head if I'm not visiting or working." Elsie hugged her friend, and they went to the door.

Mose stood too and walked toward Gideon as the others made their way out. "Do you feel it's proper to be with Elsie alone?"

"There are certain circumstances that require someone to be with her, even more so with her parents being away."

Mose kept his stare.

"I'll let you know what that is after I talk with Elsie about it." With that Gideon took a step toward the back door, but Mose caught his arm.

"I'm not sure what's going on exactly, but as far as I know, Elsie can make up her own mind about what needs to be done and who she should have with her." Mose stood almost equal to Gideon's height, and there was a certain defensiveness he showed more than just Gideon.

"Let's not make this about you and me. Let's think of what's best for Elsie." Gideon felt it was a good time to walk away before the conversation became heated.

"Do you plan to court Elsie?" Mose spoke loud enough for Rachel and Elsie to look over at him.

Gideon smiled at them and turned to Mose, speaking as quietly as he could, "My intentions are not clear right now. I doubt yours are either."

"*Jah*, they are. To help the Yoders with the problems at hand. Anything else can wait." Mose put on his straw hat and pushed past Gideon.

Gideon watched him walk away, tipping his hat to Rachel and Elsie, and then walk out the door. He felt small after hearing Mose's response, but he couldn't seem to keep his feelings for Elsie out of the way when making decisions. When he had the opportunity to talk with Elsie's daed, he would ask him what he wanted done. But that would mean telling him about the English men whether Elsie wanted him to or not.

⌒ Chapter Sixteen ⌒

ELSIE LOOKED HIGH and low for her two brothers. She checked every room in the haus, but there was no sign of them. After making their beds, sweeping, collecting eggs, feeding the livestock, and milking with Timothy, the boys had been dragging during breakfast.

She had excused them from the table and told them to rest until midday when she had lunch ready and the afternoon chores would need to be done. They usually had at least one if not more of their neighbors come to help out, but this morning only her one-legged neighbor came by, and he talked more than he worked. But she didn't mind; his stories were always a good distraction and made the chores go by quicker.

Once he left, Elsie went to Daed's woodworking area in the back of the barn. It was quiet now, no tapping of a hammer or sounds of a saw. She swept up the wood shavings and put some tools away. Just being in this room made her feel a little closer to him.

After making a complete circle around the house, she went outside to search. How she wished she had someone to help her figure out where they could be. She tried to think like two five-year-old boys, but she'd run out of ideas. There was no noise in the barn once the milk cows had all been turned out. The horses were grazing in the pasture, pigs were squealing over their slop, and the chicks the boys became fond of were quiet in their nest.

"Elsie." Gideon's voice created a rush of relief. Even though he'd done nothing yet and only said one word, Elsie knew she had the help she needed.

"Thank goodness you're here. I can't find the boys. I've looked everywhere I can think of, both inside and out, but—"

Gideon took her hands in his. "Slow down. You haven't looked everywhere or you would have found them. You searched thoroughly in the house?"

"*Jah*, and I've been searching around the barnyard and can't think of where they could be out here that I wouldn't hear them. We've finished the morning chores, so they'd be playing...or sleeping. They were really worn out this morning after milking."

"Hmm, I have a thought. Come with me." He went over to the side of the barn where the large tree with the nest of chicks stood tall.

"I already checked there." Elsie felt an urgency that was making her inpatient. She wanted Gideon to fix this. That's what he did for goodness' sake; he was a fixer. He turned and headed to the tall barn doors and opened one side.

"We were in here right before breakfast. They wouldn't be in here; the milking is done." She was so sure that she didn't follow him into the barn to where the stalls were.

He walked to the farthest stall next to the open back barn door overlooking the back pastures and then stopped. Elsie quickly came up to stand beside him in the stall. She was so relieved she almost wept. Adam, Aaron, and the foal were asleep lying in a fresh bed of straw. The boys' soiled clothes and dirty faces were a sight, but their heavy eyelids and breathing showed how content they were. The brown foal rested right next to them on the soft, yellow, straw bedding.

The mare turned to Gideon and Elsie with a stance of protection over the three little bodies in her care. "It's okay, girl." Gideon stroked her strong thigh, and she gave him a soft whinny in return. Her stare focusing out the window was a perfect example of a mamm's sacrifice for her young. Elsie would remember to let her out for a good romp around the pasture after the little ones woke up.

"They seem so comfortable it makes me want to lie right down there with them." He looked over at Elsie. "You can breathe now." His smile lit up his handsome face.

She laughed giddily and thanked him. "They do seem to be content, all three of them." They both watched the boys and their equine friend in their peaceful slumber for a moment until Gideon motioned for her to step outside with him.

"How did you think of them being in there?" Elsie kicked herself for not checking the barn.

"I bonded with a premature colt that required a lot of attention when I was young. He needed milk every couple hours a day, couldn't take large amounts at a time." He turned away in thought, as if he was there again. "That little fella followed me around every chance he got."

"What happened to him?"

"He was a hardworking horse, and my dead was offered a good deal of money from an Englisher for him. I cried like a baby, so Daed made a compromise, that he'd sell him to someone in the community so I could still see him every now and then."

"And did you?"

"For a while, until I became interested in other things." He shook his head fondly. "I can remember sleeping with him like those two are; that's what made me think of it."

"*Danke*, Gideon. I honestly don't know what I'd do without you." And she didn't want to find out. She was grateful to have Gideon there with her.

"You don't need to thank me." He stuck his hands in his pockets. "Did Katie ever call back?"

Her head lifted, and she took a quick glance at him. "*Nee*, she hasn't." There was a long pause. She had nothing more to say. The only way to deal with the pain was to try not to think of her. She didn't exist in Elsie's world any longer. That's the only way she could deal with the rejection.

"Did you tell your daed and mamm that you called her?" He looked up into the sun and held up a hand to block the bright rays.

"I didn't see any reason unless she called me." As much as Elsie wanted Katie to call, there was a part of her that didn't. There were too many things that may have happened that she didn't want to know. It wouldn't be the same as before she left.

He nodded and then zeroed in on the fence line. "What needs to be done?"

"Everything is taken care of. A lot of people have come to help, and Will has been doing most of the work that daed usually does. And we have more food than we can eat in a month."

"I'd like to tackle that torn-up fence. It's only a matter of time before it breaks completely." He looked toward the toolshed. "Can I grab a hammer and some nails?"

"Help yourself. I'll start on lunch." She would rather be helping him patch up that fence. If Mamm were here, she would be able to. Elsie was appreciative of all that her parents did to keep the farm running and hoped they'd be back soon. Help from the community was more than they needed, as usual for their people, but Elsie wanted her family back together.

Elsie had almost reached the door when Gideon spoke. "If you can't find me later, you know where I'll be." He grinned and pointed to the barn.

She turned around and laughed. "Not you too?" She teased and pushed open the screen door. It closed with a *slap*, and Elsie found herself in the kitchen, alone. How she missed the time when it was Katie and Mamm with her, all cooking, cleaning, and doing the work together. This was the first time she didn't have someone with her.

A sense of loneliness came over her, and her tears welled again. She willed them away and got to work. That was the best medicine, as her mammi used to say. With that thought she missed her mammi now too. She only had one set of living grandparents and felt deprived because of it.

Elsie decided on chicken potpie and got to work. She had just gotten the meat out to slice when she heard a knock at the door. Most hollered and walked in, with a few exceptions, so Elsie was curious as to who it was. She wiped her hands with a towel and went to the back door. "Ruby!" She couldn't hold back her surprise.

"I came by to give the boys the pie they liked the other day." She held a basket with a cloth covering the pastry.

"It smells wonderful. The boys will be thrilled." They went into the kitchen together, and Elsie instantly felt better to have Ruby with her. "I'm making chicken potpies. Would you like to make the crust?"

Ruby's eyes lit up. "Well...sure."

The time went much faster once she focused on cooking and not on how she was feeling every minute. While making the crust, Ruby watched and learned how Elsie made the chicken potpies. When they were in the oven, they warmed one of the loaves of bread Beverly Zook brought them and set the table.

The back door opened, and in came Aaron and Adam. Adam had a few pieces of hay still stuck in his hair, so she sent him back outside with his brother to clean each other off. "Are you two hungry?"

"Starving." Aaron sat at the table, with Adam close behind. "Ruby made you some peach pie."

Adam and Aaron looked at each other and then at the napkin covering the pie. "Hurry up and eat," Aaron told his brother. Ruby and Elsie chuckled, and then Elsie got serious.

"You two scared the life out of me. I didn't have any idea where you went to. If it wasn't for Gideon, I don't know when I would have found you."

"Gideon's here?" Adam's eyes widened, as did Aaron's.

"*Jah*, he's working on the fence line."

Aaron jumped off his chair and ran out the back door. Adam stared at the pie on the counter and then the back door, debating. Then he took off after his brother.

Elsie was about to holler at them to come back but decided their stomachs would bring them home. Not much later all three of them walked in together.

BETH SHRIVER

"Ruby, the boys said you were here. More importantly, that your pie was here." The boys started for the table, but Gideon put up his hand. "Wash up first."

It was nice to have someone helping her with the boys. They were so young and full of energy that they made her tired. She wondered how her mamm did such a good job and seemed to have energy to spare. "I'm so glad you came over today, Ruby."

"I didn't mind the work. It's good to stay busy." She folded the napkin and took the basket she brought the pie in. "I should go. Will's probably getting hungry. But *danke* for showing me how to make those chicken pies. Will is going to be surprised."

"Take one with you. We made extras." Elsie took one off the counter that was ready to go in the cooler and placed it in Ruby's basket.

"*Danke*, Elsie."

Elsie couldn't have been happier to have spent time with her sister-in-law. She and her mamm could cook a meal with little instruction, but with Ruby there was a lot of interaction, which was a nice change. Maybe it was because of them being close in age…like a sister.

The boys dove into the chicken pies, and Gideon had another. Elsie decided to cook this time instead of heating up one of the meals from her neighbors because he was there. He didn't let her down and raved about the food. The boys finished quickly but stayed at the table until Gideon stood. "I'm almost done with one section but then found another, so I'll be awhile."

"Do you have the time, Gideon? If not, I understand."

He wiped his lips with a napkin and plopped it on his plate. "I wouldn't want to see that little foal get through that fence. I'll feel better if I know he's safe."

The boys went with him to "help," and Elsie cleaned up after the meal. She had made three extra chicken potpies, so she thought she'd deliver one to a family in the community whose mamm was ill. But that would wait until Daed and Mamm would be home and the boys could stay home with them.

Elsie took a break once the kitchen was spotless. She thought she'd take the boys a snack of baked pretzels and iced tea. Then it would be about the time the doctor would call or Mamm would come home for a while. Each day she hoped the news would be that Daed was coming home. Three nights had passed, and Elsie began to worry there was something she wasn't being told. The daily report had always been positive, but if so, why wasn't he released from the hospital?

Adam ran to her when he noticed the food and drinks. "Thanks, Elsie." He started to grab for a snack, but she stopped him.

"Guests first, Adam."

He frowned and walked back to the others with her. "Now?"

She nodded, and he handed Gideon and Aaron a pretzel, and then to her delighted surprise he handed one to her before taking one for himself. She loved his big heart and accepted his gesture.

They had just settled in when Rachel rode up the driveway on her favorite horse, Charles. Elsie waved with apprehension, wishing Rachel would kick her lazy horse into action.

"Afternoon, Rachel." Elsie tried to hold herself back from rushing their greetings, but it didn't last long. "Do you have news?"

"*Jah*, the doctor said there was an infection, so they are keeping him longer until it's gone. They say he should come home soon."

That wasn't what Elsie wanted to hear. She wanted him home now, but at least he was healing. "So he's okay?"

"The doctor said it's better to have him heal in the hospital. They say the Amish go back to work too soon." She smiled, and Elsie didn't know if she was just trying to make her feel better or if that was true.

As Elsie pulled away, she noticed Gideon staring at the road. She turned to see Mose driving a horse with the wagon her daed wanted repaired. Elsie had almost forgotten about it, but she knew her daed would appreciate getting it back. But the timing couldn't be worse. There was an ever-heightening tension whenever the two young men were together, making Elsie more than uncomfortable.

Rachel seemed to notice as well and shifted her weight from one foot to the next as Mose walked up. His confident ways always made him appear he was in control of any situation. Gideon had confidence as well, but in a more humble way.

"Afternoon, Mose."

He nodded to Gideon and smiled at Rachel. "Elsie, tell your daed I'm sorry it took me so long to get this trailer back to him. There was a few other things wrong with it, and I had to go into town to get a couple parts." He pointed to the trailer and cringed. "This is an old wagon, hard to find parts for it."

"*Danke*, Mose. I'm sure daed will appreciate all the effort you went to."

He shook his head. "I feel badly I didn't get it back to him sooner."

"He'll get payment to you when he gets to feeling better."

"Don't worry about it. It's the least I can do with him laid up and all." Mose stuck his hands in his pockets and sheepishly smiled. It was one of the few times she'd seen him so humble. She couldn't help but find that attractive in him.

"Well, that's awful kind of you. I'm sure he'll want to thank you in person, but right now Mamm has him stuck in bed until he's healed."

"When will that be? Do you know yet?"

"Mamm said when the doctor says so and not a day before."

Gideon hadn't said a word, just fiddled with the tool in his hand as if waiting for Mose to go. "Thanks for dropping off the wagon, Mose."

Elsie let out a breath, glad he'd finally spoken. It was almost rude the way he was acting. It made Elsie wonder what was between them. But by the way they looked at each other and then at her, Elsie was pretty sure what she suspected was true.

Chapter Seventeen

ELSIE PLACED A cup of tea on the tray along with a bowl of Rich Man's Rivvel soup that consisted of chicken broth, corn, flour, eggs, and a dash of salt. She tried to balance the tray so the soup didn't spill as she went up the creaky stairs. She usually looked forward to the outing, but today she wasn't. Those young men surely lived in town, but were they bold enough to cause a scene in public? She didn't think there was anything they wouldn't do. Had the people in town heard of the things they'd done? The police became involved when the wheat field caught on fire, but that was the only time the people in town were involved. They would never know if it was deliberate now that the field had been tilled and reseeded.

Her daed's head hung to the side, and he softly snored as he slept in his double-sized birchwood bed. She hated to wake him, but he needed to eat, and the soup would go down easy.

She was about to set the tray on the wooden dresser when she heard him stir. Her boots tapping against the floor woke him, and he tried to sit up in bed. "Daed, let me help you."

He grumbled then pushed down with his large hands on either side of him and pulled himself up. Elsie tried to help, but he had too much girth for her to be able to do much for him. "You don't need to fuss over me." He pivoted to the side and put his feet on the floor. "I'm fine."

"Where do you think you're going?" Mamm appeared at the bedroom door and put her hands on her hips.

"I'm going into town to the farmer's market like we always do, as a family." He stood and seemed to be stable, but Mamm didn't care how well he thought he was.

"We will do just fine without you. Stay here and mend." She gently pushed him back on the bed. He eyed her and was about to protest when she chimed in again. "You need to get healthy so you can help plant the Lapps' field." Mamm always knew what to say to Daed when he was being stubborn. They both knew he wouldn't be able to do much at the planting but would want to be there anyway. With that he slipped back into bed and sighed.

"I'll bring you some lunch for later so you don't have to walk downstairs, Daed." Elsie offered as her two brothers came jumping into the room.

"We get to go to the mud sales today!" Adam shouted with excitement.

"They don't call it that here. It's called the market." Aaron tugged on Mamm's dress. "Can I take the horse I carved to sell?"

"*Jah*, Aaron. Now go eat your breakfast so we can get an early start." Mamm gave Daed a kiss on the head and started for the door. "Don't you do too much today."

"Humph," was his only reply.

"I'll put one of Mamm's sugar cookies in with your lunch," Elsie whispered. That made him smile a little.

They hurried the boys through their meal and packed the buggy full of goods and food to sell. The Lapps offered to transport the Yoders' livestock and furniture Daed made. They brought only samples due to the room each piece took in the wagons. In Virginia they made a pretty decent living selling their goods. The drive took two hours to the area where up to thirty markets in the vicinity sold a large range of goods. The idea was still in process here. The fewer Amish and the distance from the different communities in this large state made it difficult to have one big market, unless they joined in with the Texas farmers.

The boys chose Chester, a sturdy steed that could handle the distance. Elsie stared absently at his black behind as he clip-clopped down the highway. She averted her gaze to a field of blue-bonnets peeking through a pasture of wild grass and the green buds on the large trees by the road. By next month everything would be in full bloom. There was still a nip in the air that could be easily remedied with the black shawl Elsie brought.

Once they got into town, heads started turning. The English were still getting used to the Amish coming into town in droves once a month for the market. Many of them couldn't wait for the weekends the Amish came and were regulars who bought their favorites each time. The positive thoughts made her feel better about coming into town. Even if those boys did show up, what could they do at a busy market full of people?

"They still stare at us like we're strange." Elsie stared back at them, searching for a face in the crowd that was an unwelcome reminder of those boys.

"It's different than up north where the Amish were already settled. Here they are still getting used to us. But you know this." Mamm glanced over at her then back to driving the buggy. "Why is it bothering you today?"

The weight of her secret was lifted after talking with Omar. She wanted that same relief by telling her mamm. But she feared telling her daed. Although he was a gentle man, he had little patience for dishonesty or betrayal—both of which his daughters had done, Elsie for not telling them about the English boys and Katie's choice to leave with Jake.

"I am worried I might see the English boys who have been coming to our community." Elsie looked straight ahead, but she could see her mother snap her head back over to her.

"Why would you worry about those boys?"

Elsie could hear the hesitation in Mamm's question, as if she knew the answer would be something bad, one more thing for her to worry about. She felt the same guilt when she told Gideon, knowing the pain it caused people to hear about what had gone on without any idea it had been happening.

"Because I talked to them when they were in our community." Elsie took a moment to choose her words. Mamm didn't need to know the worst of it, only that there had been contact.

"What did they say to you?"

"They mocked me and told me we should go back to where we came." She bravely stared into her mamm's eyes. "They are the ones who did the vandalism, at least some of it if not all."

Mamm's mouth opened, but she didn't speak for a moment, digesting the information. "Who knows about this?"

"Gideon, Omar, and Katie."

Mamm jolted back a little and frowned. "Is that another reason she left?"

Elsie shook her head. "No, she wasn't as scared of them like I am. She left to have more freedom and for Jake."

"How long has this gone on?"

"A few days before Katie left." Shame and guilt plagued her. How many times had she told herself that it would stop? That they would go away and not come back? Her denial had been risky; she could see that more clearly now.

They were silent as they rode through the small city, but Elsie knew the conversation wasn't over. They had work to do, so this would have to wait.

The small sign with the name Beeville got the boys excited. They passed the opera house and post office then knew they were close. When they got to the edge of town, they went to the back of the parking lot that was filled with buggies then stopped by a corral that was set up for the horses. They carried in their goods and went inside a large building to set up. Elsie and her family brought tables, stands, and shelves to arrange their stand of quilts, baked goods, dolls, and tools. Elsie wished she and Rachel had finished that quilt now. The English paid hundreds of dollars for one they took a liking to, saying the quality couldn't be compared to any others they saw in stores. Elsie planned to visit a store and see for herself.

The customers trickled in, and soon there were crowds. The pies were selling, and people seemed to like the variety. Pear and gooseneck were the first to go. Many of the townspeople said those were kinds they'd never tried. The others sold almost as quickly—rhubarb, cherry, peach, and huckleberry. The walnut, pecan, and pumpkin pies they would bring in the fall.

An older lady admired one of the quilts Mamm sewed and one Elsie made. She studied the stitching, nodding to herself. Her hair seemed to be a bluish color, but Elsie overlooked the strange hue and began to explain their names.

"Do you name the patterns?" She examined the quilt up and down.

"*Jah*, that one's called Log Cabin. It's more rustic." The gray, white, and brown gave it a homey appeal.

"I like that one." She pointed to one her mamm made. The woman gave her a considerable amount of money for the quilt. Mamm learned from others to start high and bargain down.

"*Danke*." Elsie smiled.

"I looked up some Amish words so I'd know what to say. *Wilkom*." She lifted her shoulders with excitement.

Elsie couldn't help but smile at this eager, precious lady who was trying to connect with her. This was a good reminder of how hospitable the Texans were, not all like that group of young men with too much time on their hands. Other than those recent incidents, all the people down south had been helpful and friendly.

"Very *gut*." Elsie grinned, and the lady turned to walk away. 'Enjoy your quilt."

Mamm came back from wandering around the market with the boys and noticed the one missing quilt. "It sold?"

"*Jah*, to a sweet older lady." Elsie hoped hers would sell too. It was encouraging when someone appreciated her work, and it made her want to spend more time doing it when she got a sale.

A young family stopped and looked at the dolls she'd made. The little Amish boys and girls dressed in their traditional clothing were usually big sellers. Elsie put different colors of shirts to make them individual as the English seemed to appreciate the different hues.

Elsie watched and waited for the common question. The mamm held a girl doll and asked, "Why don't they have faces?"

"In the book of Exodus graven images are forsaken." She smiled as she said it. People seemed to appreciate what she was saying better when she did.

The oldest child, about the twin's age, said, "I don't want a doll with a naked face."

But the little girl held one and wouldn't let go. "I do, and I'm going to name her your name." She pointed at Elsie.

Elsie was a little flattered and folded her hands together. "My name is Elsie, and I'd be honored for your doll to have my name."

"I'll take two." The mother pulled out her purse and reached for the boy Amish doll. "I don't want Elsie to get lonely."

"*Danke* for your purchase." Elsie watched the mamm's face as she figured out what she was saying. When she walked away, Elsie almost felt at home. It had been over a year now, and she needed to think of Texas that way. There were obstacles, but she would deal with them a lot better if she appreciated her new homeland.

Aaron looked back at their booth. Elsie glanced over with him. A boy was holding the wooden horse he'd carved. She nodded her head toward the boy, and Aaron approached him.

"Do you like it?" Aaron asked without hesitation. "I made it."

The boy's brows lifted. "You did?" Then he glanced up at his mamm. "Why can't I make one?"

She shook her head. "You aren't allowed to use knives. But I'll buy that for you if you like." The boy seemed to agree with the compromise and held the horse while his mamm paid.

"*Danke.*" Aaron turned and showed Mamm the money he'd earned. "Can I go get something with it?"

"Save a lot and spend a little." She told him, and then in a quiet tone she added, "And get a little something for your brother."

"I'll take them, Mamm." Elsie held Adam's hand as Aaron looked at all the goods he could buy. She could see how money might become a problem for the English. There were so many temptations, and this was only one market. She knew there were huge malls that had so much more than this.

The food seemed to be most intriguing for the boys. There

were cheese and meat stands, and something new to her was the rice cakes; there were also a deli, cakes, pretzels, and meatball sandwiches. The boys decided on the rice cakes and weren't disappointed. Elsie took a bite and liked the taste. It was nice to eat something someone else made.

On their way back to their booth they passed the livestock arena where horses, goats, lambs, and horses were auctioned off. When they stepped outside, the boys spotted Gideon with his family selling their outdoor furniture, and Daed's as well. The boys ran over and hugged on Gideon. The affection the boys gave him touched her, and for a brief moment she wished she could do the same, causing her cheeks to warm.

"Good turnout?" She asked to any of the Lapps who were around.

"Um, *gut*," his brother Joseph answered.

Gideon's daed was a quiet, gentle man and, unlike her own daed, a man of few words. His mamm was helping a customer, as were his brothers.

"Aaron sold his horse," Elsie told Gideon with a smile as she sat in one of the porch swings they were selling.

Gideon sat next to her and smiled. "So that's what the extra excitement is about." He watched the boys go from a shed to the playhouse and then to one of the swings. "*Gut* for him. He's an official entrepreneur."

"Aaron treated us to rice cakes with some of his earnings."

He frowned.

"*Nee*, they were *gut*. You should try one," she urged him and walked with him to the stand.

Gideon's daed knew how to handle boys and the twins took him seriously, but they also enjoyed being with Gideon's brothers.

When they got to the stand, Elsie talked him into buying a rice cake, and when he took the first bite, his squinty eyes said it all. "I told you they were *gut*."

When they started the walk back to the Lapps' booth, Gideon stopped. Elsie stood next to him and followed his gaze to a young man. "Who is that? Do you know him?" She didn't recognize the English teenager as one who had been on their property. He was smaller than those young men, maybe younger, but what caught Elsie's attention was his gaunt, sad face and skinny frame.

"*Jah*, I do," Gideon finally answered after a long stare. He stood and took a step toward the young man. As soon as the boy saw Gideon, his eyes seemed to click with recognition. As Gideon got closer, the boy's eyes grew wider. He took off, making his way through the crowds with Gideon close behind him.

Elsie tried to follow but fell way behind. As she darted around the crowds of people, she wondered about Gideon's strange behavior. His intensity surprised and worried her. Did the young man take something from their booth? Maybe he was one of the Englishers, and she didn't recognize him. She tried to ignore them each time they came around, and she couldn't always get a good look at all of them.

When she finally found him, Gideon had the boy cornered in a hallway by the bathrooms, obviously upset. The boy stared up at Gideon with wild eyes then turned to her and dropped his head. She looked away, not wanting her stare to intensify the embarrassment he seemed to feel. Gideon motioned for her to stay put, out of reach but close enough to hear the conversation.

"I'm not going to harm you." Gideon's face was flushed, and his gaze locked on this young man. "I want to help you."

The boy moved the mop of dark, shaggy hair from his eyes and frowned. "Why?"

"I saw your face that day. The day you were with the others. You didn't want to be there, did you?"

He scoffed, but his eyes stayed fixed on Gideon, almost as if he wanted him to go on but couldn't show it. "How would you know?"

"I could see it in your eyes. You were scared."

He tried to take a step forward, but Gideon blocked his way. "I was not afraid of an Amish guy and his girlfriend."

Elsie blushed, wishing she could stop the crimson color

creeping up her neck. She could see why some in the community might make the assumption, but for all this young man knew, she could be Gideon's sister. That made her uncomfortable, and she began to rethink her actions. Gideon's community was more flexible than Elsie's was back in Virginia. But since moving here, that changed, and her group was becoming more relaxed with their rules, maybe too much so. Even more concerning was if their actions portrayed a commitment between them.

They were quiet during her thoughts. Gideon's fists were dropped to his sides, opening and shutting as if to calm him after the boy's last comment. "A young man should speak respectfully of a young woman."

The boy shook his head. Elsie wondered why Gideon was trying so hard to reach someone who had no interest in what he was saying.

"Just like you treat your mother with respect." Gideon waited for a response, but the boy didn't seem like he was going to answer. So Gideon stood there and waited. He was at least four inches taller and had more muscle by far than the young man did. But Elsie still wasn't sure why Gideon was so interested in this boy. He wasn't the one who seemed to cause the problems.

He finally nodded, and Gideon let out a breath—as if they had reached an agreement that Elsie couldn't identify. "I'm Gideon. What's your name?"

The boy scoffed. "How about...James Dean."

Gideon frowned. "Why were you with those other guys?"

"You aren't gonna leave me alone, are ya?" The boy's face flushed, and he bit his bottom lip. "It was an initiation they make you do to hang out with them."

"Picking on innocent people? How hard is that?" Gideon's chin tightened. "Was it worth it?"

He shrugged. "There's more. I'm the grunt now."

Gideon dropped his guard. His shoulders lowered and his chest moved quickly. "What are you going to do?"

"I don't know, man. But if they see me talking to you, we'll both pay for it." He scanned the area and took a testing step away.

"Tell me your name. Mine is Gideon." Gideon moved, as if giving him the room to go.

"Then will you leave me alone? It's Nick." As soon as he saw the opportunity, he took two steps and took off running again. Gideon watched him go and Elsie watched Gideon.

They walked back to the Lapps' booth in silence. Gideon sat down on a porch swing he'd help make, and she sat next to him. She wasn't sure what to make of the situation, so she waited for Gideon to explain.

"Do you remember seeing that boy?" Gideon pushed his feet forward, easing into the rhythm of the swing.

"*Nee*. When did you see him?" She looked sideways at him, but he kept his head down.

"He was in the back of the car that day the bench broke in the buggy."

"Why did you follow him?"

"I wanted to talk with him. He looked so scared that time I saw him. I could tell he didn't want to be there." Gideon put his elbows on his knees and folded his hands.

"You probably scared him to death chasing him like that."

"I just wanted to find out about him and hoped he would care that I was angry with him for the way they treated us that day." Gideon nodded his head as if trying to convince himself. "I think he did, even though he didn't show it."

"I hope he doesn't do any more of those awful things to others." Elsie couldn't believe what she was hearing. "Why would people make someone do such a thing?"

"Sounds like we were one of many."

"Why would anyone want to be in such a group?" Elsie folded her arms over her chest, angry at these hateful customs the English boys had.

"I hope this kid figured that out when he saw the way we were treated, and that he follows through in trying to get out of it."

"What do you mean, trying? Can't he just ignore them?"

"Doesn't sound like it." He looked over at Elsie to see if she understood.

She moved back in the swing. "That's awful." She met his stare. "As frustrated as you were about not being able to retaliate against them, this shows us exactly why we shouldn't. Violence only leads to more violence, and hate only brings more hate."

Gideon's face clouded with emotion, and he looked away. "I hope this young man finds that out. I wish I could do something to help him stay away from it."

She took his hand in hers and felt the blood beating in his wrist. His concern for this boy reminded her to pray for God to protect them from their adversaries. "You can. Pray."

Chapter Eighteen

GIDEON NOTICED THE sign had finally been put up at the entrance of their community, *Meadowlark Valley*. It was meant as a pun due to Texas's flat land, but the small hills around the outskirts of all the farms gave off the "valley" effect.

Gideon drove his mamm to the community grocery store, not that she couldn't drive the buggy herself, though. Living with five sons and her husband brought out both the toughness as well as the softness about her. Gideon admired both. She was stern when she had to be and was there to console and encourage when any of them needed it.

"Looks crowded." He brought the horse to a halt and tethered the reins on an old fashioned hitching post, much like the one that was recently put up in town specifically for the Amish. The store was a log cabin with a full porch and rocking chairs that were mostly occupied by tourists.

"I don't like to come on a Saturday, but I couldn't get my tulip bulbs bundled up in time yesterday. Your brother had a young lady over last night and didn't give me much warning."

Gideon tucked his chin under in surprise. "Why didn't I know about this?"

His mamm stopped unpacking the bulbs long enough to get his attention. "You're busy, son."

They took the crates packed with her multicolored tulip bulbs until their arms were full. "That's true, but I'd like to know about occasions like that. I would have made time."

"When, with all the chores you do, visits you make, and

141

spending time with Elsie." She wiped the dirt away as much as she could and started to walk to the store.

Gideon pushed a chunk of dried mud off one of the bulbs and asked himself if he was using his time wisely. He'd helped a young family whose baby was born prematurely and didn't have a favorable prognosis from the doctors. Then there was the widow who lost her husband but was doing well with the assistance of her son. He spent time with his dawdi and mammi every week. There were always the deacons who informed him of the community's needs and his studies. And then there was Elsie.

"Are you coming?" his mamm called as she stood by the door.

He took quick steps until he was next to her. "Do you feel I'm neglecting my own family?"

She reached for the door but stopped at his words. "*Nee*, you have a calling, son. I don't know what for exactly, maybe not a minister or deacon, but someone who sees the needs of the community and has the compassion to act on it." She put a hand up to his cheek. "And it will soon be time for courting. You'll need to make time for that so you don't have another year of being alone."

Gideon was taken off guard. He wasn't one of the young men who courted his first year and married, but there were others older than he that hadn't yet either. And Elsie was younger; this was the first season her daed considered her old enough to court. "What do you mean alone?"

"There comes a time when family isn't enough and you need your soul companion." She smiled, and her dark eyes shone. "You've found her. Now take that same spontaneous action you do for others and do it for yourself." She dropped her hand and opened the door, entering into the bustle of the room while Gideon stood in place taking in her thought-provoking advice.

He walked into the small store that wasn't big enough for the owners who ran the place. The growth kept them busy, leaving the farm pretty much up to their grown children. Annie and John Yoder's bed-and-breakfast and the Byler's store complemented one another in exchanging business.

The tourists were out in droves, so he decided to go over to see if John was around. He had become somewhat of a big brother to Gideon, and since all of this business with Elsie had started up, he'd been leaning on John more than ever.

He didn't make it into the haus before finding John brushing down his pride and joy, a bay stud that looked to be about eighteen hands. "Good-looking horse."

John startled, which made the energetic equine start as well. "Gideon, you caught me." He grinned, having been found out by his friend who could relate completely. The Englishers loved their cars, and the Amish felt the same about a well-bred horse. "What brings you here?"

Gideon felt awkward but only for a second. He was assuming John knew he wanted to bend his ear about Elsie, in which case he'd be right, but he didn't want to become an unwelcome guest.

They walked together to a round pen. "You got Elsie on your mind?" John's grin told Gideon he was there to listen. He took off the horse's halter and guided him in the large area. The horse kicked up his hooves and swung his head from side to side. John hung his arms over the fence, and they both watched him in silence.

"So what's it like, a wife and two kids..."

"And one on the way." John didn't look at him, just smiled and waited for the slap on his back, which Gideon did with a chuckle.

"Congratulations. Want a girl this time?"

"As long as the baby's healthy, it makes no difference to me."

"Well said."

"It'll be you soon enough." John turned to him. "You having some troubles?"

"I'm ready. I just hope she is as ready as I am." That's what it was, what had been nagging at him. From the beginning of their relationship he was trying to make sure Jake was out of the running and he was in. It wasn't until this moment he felt their feeling for one another could be mutual.

John kept his focus on the horse, but Gideon knew he was

processing what to say. He was never in a hurry and spoke from the heart. "I'm glad you came over, Gideon, because somebody has to get it into your thick head that it's time to settle down."

Gideon's heart jumped. "I don't want to rush anything if she's not ready."

"How do you know that?" John was bold and confident, much like Gideon but even more so. Except he was not so much when it came to Elsie.

"*Nee*, I get mixed signals. I don't know if she thinks anything more of me than a helper and someone to listen."

John grinned. "Well, you could come right out and ask her."

Gideon didn't want to take the chance she'd say what he didn't want to hear. It was safer leaving things be. "I suppose I will sooner or later."

They talked on until Gideon turned to go and John walked him out. "Sky is calm today, just a little breeze and sun to grow the crop."

John was like a walking weatherman, but he was usually right on the nose. "Good to know." Gideon took the promising weather along with John's advice to ask and not to wait. But he didn't have John's grit.

As he got closer to the store, he took note of what the tourists were buying. They sold a little bit of everything but specialized in the roots market. They had basic supplies, but the tourists in town would come on the weekends for the fresh fruit and home-made cheese.

Gideon was still in a daze when Solomon slapped him on the back. "Solomon!"

Solomon's eyebrows shot up. "Why are you so surprised? Didn't you expect me to be shopping?" He belted out one of his laughs.

Gideon snapped out of it and knew this meeting wasn't a coincidence. "*Nee*, but I'm not surprised to see that deer jerky in your hand."

Solomon glanced down at his weakness. "Don't like to shoot

'em but do like to eat 'em." He lifted his left cheek into a half grin. He looked around the room. "Are you here alone?"

Why was everyone asking him about being alone? He was never by himself now that he thought about it. Except for maybe a buggy drive to make a visit or to pick someone up. But he knew exactly what his mamm and Solomon were referring to, and he needed to get past the issues involving the English boys and move on to his relationship with Elsie.

"I'm helping my mamm." Gideon waved over to her, and she waved back at them. This was his chance to clear the air and get the heavy load off his chest.

Solomon nodded his acknowledgment. "I heard some Englishers were driving in the area again. What brings them here without so much as a greeting?"

Gideon was so shocked to hear Solomon address what he was about to that he waited too long and Solomon spoke again.

"I hope it's just that they're curious and not causing trouble. I can't figure if they want to know about us or to do us harm. They seem to be curious. I wonder what they find so interesting." Solomon pulled on his beard as he babbled on. Gideon took in every word as his mind went through what he needed to say.

"Solomon, can we talk outside?" He turned to go before Solomon had a chance to answer. Solomon was unusually quiet as they walked down the three stairs and to the side of the store as if feeling the seriousness of the moment.

"Gideon, I don't know that I can stand hearing anything bad, especially about Elsie." He paused. "She's doing well, *jah*?"

Gideon's heart swelled with empathy for this daed, but he had to tell him. The fact that he brought up the subject told Gideon that he may already know something already. After a quick prayer Gideon was given another matter to talk with Solomon about. He thanked God for the insight.

"Solomon, Elsie and I haven't been honest with you."

Solomon tried to speak, but Gideon held up a hand as it was hard to keep this man from talking.

"The English you were talking about have approached both Katie and Elsie." He let that soak in before continuing, watching Solomon's eyes grow into saucers and a reddish color seep up his chest. "They've continued to harass Elsie after Katie left. I've spoken with them and talked with Omar about the—"

Solomon interrupted, "Were they harmed?"

"*Nee*, they scared them because they are so forward and like to taunt. Bullies basically, vandals."

Solomon rubbed his stubbly face and let out a long breath. "Elsie shouldn't have been alone to deal with those boys." His voice was rising with every word he said, enough to gain the attention of a couple of tourists leaving the store.

"We don't know exactly what they have done or why," Gideon said with a hushed tone, trying to quiet the conversation and bring it back into focus. "We hope they've stopped. But you should have been told when this first started. It put Elsie in a difficult situation."

Solomon stared at Gideon as his eyes glazed over. He took a long while before answering. "Elsie may have been the one who kept it a secret, but she wasn't the one who made it so." He took in short amounts of air through his nose and let it out as if to control himself. "Elsie wouldn't lie to me unless she was made to."

Anyone who knew the two girls might come to that conclusion, but it was not for them to judge, unless Solomon knew something he wasn't telling him. "I understand your disappointment, Solomon, but anger won't help what's already passed."

Solomon's breathing slowed, and he lifted his eyes upward. "I hope you never have a prodigal child who doesn't come back to you, Gideon. And unless you do, you can't begin to understand what it does to a parent's heart."

He was being corrected, rightly so. It wasn't the first time, and he was sure he'd be told many things about parenting before he had any children of his own. But this was about Elsie. Solomon should give him credit for knowing at least one of his daughter's ways.

"*Nee*, I don't know. I hope to never find out with my own children. But I am experiencing it through yours."

Solomon nodded in a conceding manner. His eyes narrowed and head lowered. "You know I give you my gratitude for all you've done for our family. But I expect even more."

Gideon examined his relationships with the Yoder family members and wondered what he was missing that Solomon wanted him to do. "What is it, Solomon?"

He stared at Gideon long and hard, to the point Gideon thought he may have done something wrong. "Take care of my Elsie."

Gideon saw the opportunity to talk with him about the second matter he had on his mind. "I plan to with your permission. That is, I'd like to court her."

Solomon's sensitive side revealed itself in hearing the words. He wiped his eyes and gave Gideon one of his affectionate slaps on the back. "Praise God!" was all he could say.

Solomon turned abruptly to walk away as Gideon rubbed the sting on his back with appreciation. He felt he had been given a huge task, but it wasn't anything he hadn't already been willing to do. Gideon had every intention of courting Elsie if she'd let him. He hoped her feelings for Jake were honestly gone. But she seemed to be more hurt about Katie than Jake, which gave Gideon confidence.

His mamm and Meredith came out of the store and said their good-byes. Meredith smiled at Gideon as she walked over. "I saw you talking to Solomon and then you both disappeared. Is he out here?" She looked around but didn't see him.

"*Jah*, he's ready to go home, I think." Gideon pointed to their large buggy, enough for the whole family to ride in. "I may have upset him. If I did, I apologize."

Meredith pursed her lips. "I can't imagine you upsetting anyone, Gideon, especially Solomon." She stopped and put a hand on his arm. "Elsie told me about the English boys."

Gideon felt as if he was taking his first breath. He knew Elsie wouldn't be able to tell her daed, but he had hoped she would tell her mamm. "I'm glad she did, and I told Solomon. I hope that was all right." Right or wrong, it was out, and the decisions were not his alone to make. He was too relieved to let the worries bother him. "You should have been told earlier."

Meredith shook her head. "It would just be more of us asking for them to stop and them probably ignoring us or it would entice them to do more."

Gideon grunted, knowing he'd missed the mark on the parallel. It was too obvious for him to live out what he'd been learning. Elsie had done better than him in applying what she internalized from the *Martyrs Mirror*.

When they reached the buggy, Solomon stepped out and took the bag Meredith held and walked to the back with Gideon.

"You have a very wise wife, Solomon. I think I've found one like her." He grinned, but Solomon was in no mood after hearing both good and bad news and obviously not knowing what to do with either.

"*Jah*, you already have," he mumbled and lumbered to the front of the buggy.

Chapter Nineteen

RACHEL SAT IN a rocking chair next to the couch stitching patches of pastel colors together. Rachel thought they had enough, but Elsie was sure they should have added at least one more color—the one Elsie always wanted to use. "We could add yellow."

"Just because it's your favorite color doesn't mean we have to use it on every quilt we make." Rachel stuck her finger with the needle. "Ow! That hurt." She held the tip of her finger with another one until the bleeding stopped.

"Are you okay?" Elsie asked, although it was a common occurrence when it came to Rachel sewing. Having all brothers gave her little time to do any more work than necessary. She could mend a sock in no time, but taking the time to sew a quilt was difficult. She was at a disadvantage with no sisters or mamm to help, but she was also stubborn about accepting assistance. She'd give, but she had a hard time receiving.

"If the thimble didn't get sweaty, I'd use it."

"I thought your brother was making you a wooden one with a soft tip inside at the top."

"*Jah*, me too. He's too busy with his girl. Every second he has is spent with her. He gets his chores done quickly and does them well so Daed can't complain. Although I do think Daed feels they are getting serious awful early." Rachel tested her fingertip and started in sewing. "Although courting will begin and weddings soon after in the fall."

While Rachel concentrated on not pricking her finger again, Elsie wondered if she and Gideon were spending too much time together. It seemed to be accepted due to the support Gideon usually gave to any needing comfort. But in Elsie's case he singled her out and spent time almost exclusively with her.

"*Ach!*" Rachel drew her eyebrows together in frustration and pain. "Can I borrow your silver thimble?"

Elsie could tell she was on her last nerve and didn't like giving into wearing the confining piece of metal over her finger. "Why don't you get us some water?" Elsie offered to give her a reprieve that she knew Rachel would appreciate.

Rachel jumped up and went into the kitchen. "Want me to make something? There's some peanut butter cookie dough in the cooler."

"*Jah,* with some milk." Peanuts was a crop they couldn't grow up north, and Elsie had acquired a taste for them, especially peanut butter.

As she sat sewing and smelling the aroma of cookies baking, the phone rang. Rachel's daed kept the phone in a side room that was about the size of a pantry so it wasn't a temptation for anyone to use unless absolutely necessary. Since the move from Virginia, they had become a little more relaxed about it.

"Are you going to get the phone, Rachel?" The unfamiliar sound of the ring drew Elsie's attention. She stood and studied the device she'd only used a few times in her life.

Rachel walked over to the black phone and picked up the receiver. She held it to her ear and quietly listened then watched Elsie. The whites of her eyes told Elsie it was something important—not the milk truck was having mechanical problems and would be late, or the weather was going to turn bad and to protect the crop. No, this was something unusual.

Rachel said a few words then turned to her. "Elsie, it's Katie." Her face was a light color of pink that spread down her neck. She stared then stepped away from Elsie to give her some privacy, but Elsie grabbed her arm to keep her close.

The phone shook in Elsie's hand, and her mouth went dry. She was ready when she made the call, but she wasn't prepared for Katie to call her. "Hello." Her voice was not her own; it was weak, just above a whisper. There was no response, so she tried to hear if the connection was still there.

"Elsie?" The sound of Katie's voice was so yearned for that Elsie had to take a deep breath to keep from letting go of her emotions.

"Katie, it's me." It seemed strange to be so proper. Their sisterhood needed no introduction in the past.

"How are you?" There was something different in her voice, maturity or a new seriousness that wasn't there before.

"I'm *gut*. And you?" During a short pause Elsie locked eyes with Rachel, who held the intensity. They were both so formal Elsie felt she was talking to a whole new person.

"Elsie, it's so good to hear your voice."

"*Jah*, I feel the same."

Katie laughed. "I haven't said an Amish word for so long it sounds funny to hear Pennsylvania Dutch again."

"Not even to…Jake?" Elsie realized too late how many different ways that could be interpreted. Jake wasn't what was important right now. And she didn't want to reveal any feelings she might have had. There was a long silence that made Elsie uncomfortable, but she didn't know how to back step after what she just said.

"I want to come home, Elsie." Katie's voice wavered slightly.

Elsie's heartbeat increased. "Then do. Everyone misses you." Although her daed loved his daughter, he may be the hardest on her if she did return home. It would be more out of hurt than anger, because her daed's feelings were easily bruised. And there would be the minister, deacons, and the bishop to deal with as they would expect her to be baptized. Jake had been, being a year older. Even if Katie wasn't shunned, being with someone who was would be difficult.

Elsie thought about Katie's baptism. She remembered Katie saying it was time due to her age, and she started the prep classes, but then she left instead. Thinking back, Elsie realized how much she saw signs of rebellion, questioning, and independence in

Katie that most didn't seem to have in the community. But she never thought it would lead to Katie leaving.

"Elsie?"

"Sorry, I was just thinking about what it would be like with you home again."

"Yes, that's what's kept me away. I know it would be hard for us to be accepted back into the community."

At the mention of Jake Elsie flinched. Her mixed feelings kept her from asking about him. She wrestled with the emotions that still rose in her whenever she thought of him. Elsie decided she wouldn't engage those feelings. Time with Gideon seemed to have curbed her desire for Jake, but obviously not as much as she thought.

"It will all work out. I'm glad you changed your mind, Katie. It will be so good to see you."

"I'm still not certain. But I don't really have a choice anymore."

"Is it getting hard out there?" Elsie didn't know if she should ask, but she was curious as to how Amish adapted when they left the community, especially since they lived in Virginia were it was more conservative and the congregation less in touch with the outside world.

Katie let out a long, hard sigh. "Elsie, you have no idea."

Katie was right; she didn't. Many that left the community came back with appreciation for the Amish life. She understood some people needed to satisfy their curiosity of what was out there, but from what she'd seen and heard, Elsie wanted no part of it. "Where are you now?"

"In a suburb of Dallas." She sounded weary now, as if she'd lost her stamina.

"Is that far from here?" Elsie felt naive and was sure Katie was more worldly now. She knew her home in Virginia and here in Texas. That was enough for her, and hearing Katie confirmed those sentiments.

"A few hours away. I'll be in touch."

"Can I call you?"

"No, it's better if I contact you."

"Talk to you soon then." Elsie had the sudden feeling she couldn't let go...that if she hung up, she wouldn't talk to her sister again. But that was out of her control.

Elsie gave the phone to Rachel, who had been by her side during the entire conversation. "Well?"

"They're coming home." Elsie sat down and clasped her thumbs together, trying not to twiddle. She stared at Rachel, trying to read her reaction.

Rachel crossed her arms over her chest. "Do you think she really will?"

"She said she is." Elsie looked into Rachel's questioning eyes. "You don't believe her?"

Rachel sighed. "*Nee*, I don't."

A rush of fear, anxiety, and wistful hope all hit her in the chest at once. It was more than just Katie. It was Jake coming back, the possibility of Gideon leaving, her daed's health, and the English boys all mixed together. The tangle of emotions fought with one another until she spouted something out. "You never did take to Katie. Do you want her to come back?"

"Part of me doesn't, if you want the truth." Rachel's gray eyes searched Elsie's. "I don't want to see you hurt or disappointed if she doesn't show up. You're so much happier than you were. You let go of the pain of losing her. I don't want you to go through losing her again." Rachel settled back in her chair. "And you're right. I never was fond of her. You and she are very different from one another."

"I'm sorry. I shouldn't have asked how you felt about her." Elsie had known what Rachel was thinking from the moment she heard Katie's voice. She just wanted to believe differently. "I can't help but hope she will return. She is my sister, after all." She'd had enough disappointment and didn't want Katie to let her, or the rest of her family, down. She couldn't ignore the question that kept nagging at her: Would Katie really come home?

Chapter Twenty

ELSIE GUIDED THE Holsteins out of the barn and into the west pasture once the milking was done. The sun peeking up over the horizon was bigger and brighter. Summer was right around the corner.

Aaron came running out of the house pulling up his suspenders. His hair was poking out like thistles, and his clothes looked like he slept in them. When he saw Elsie herding the cows away from the barn, he stopped and slapped his arms to his sides. "*Ach nein.*"

"I'm sorry, Aaron. Timothy and I finished loading the milk cans." She watched him drop his head to his chest and take slow steps to her.

"Can I?" He pointed to the long, skinny whip that she was using to guide the cattle. They rarely had to use it, but it kept the cows from straying.

"*Jah.*" She handed it to him and tussled his already messy hair. "Timothy asked about you." He always did, but if he ever forgot, she'd remind him so she could honestly tell the boys he had.

Aaron grinned. "He always does. I think he really likes us."

"Why do you like him so much?"

He shrugged. "He's a really nice English person."

"There's lots of nice English people."

"Some are not."

Elsie gazed down at him. "Why do you say that?"

"Like the boy at the market the day that Gideon talked to, was he nice?"

Elsie stopped walking and let the Holsteins find their own way. She only kept guiding them for Aaron's sake anyway. "How do you know this?"

"I heard you and Gideon talking about him."

"You shouldn't eavesdrop on people's conversations."

"*Nee*, but you shouldn't be mad at that boy."

"What do you mean?"

"He doesn't mean it."

She bent down, trying to understand what he meant to say. "Go on."

"Gideon helps people, so that's what he should do for him."

Elsie thought about the situation through her little brother's eyes and saw forgiveness. As much as she felt sorry for that boy, she still blamed him along with the others for causing the grief they had given her and the other farmers. Aaron's heart wasn't hardened like Elsie's, but she didn't realized it until now.

"Did it upset you to hear what Gideon said?"

"I didn't hear it all, only the part about the scared boy at the beginning. Then I left 'cuz I was eaves…dropping." He struggled with the last word, but she knew what he meant.

"Well, you're right that Gideon is going to do whatever he can to take care of it, and it's nothing for you to worry about." She smiled to unburden his little soul.

He stuck his hands in his pockets. "Oh, I'm not worried. God will provide."

Elsie smiled wide hearing the words her mother always said. "Let's get back to the house. I'm hungry, aren't you?" She stood and took his hand.

"Starving." He pulled away and ran ahead of her to the back door.

Adam walked in the kitchen holding his cheek. His face was pinched with pain. "My tooth."

Mamm bent down and made him open his mouth. "It's ready to come out."

"Do you want me to pull it?" Aaron offered as he wrinkled his nose at his brother.

Adam shook his head and started to cry, so Mamm set down on a chair and put him on her lap.

"Look at me."

He stared at her with big, puppy dog eyes as a tear rolled down his cheek.

"I'm going to use this napkin to get your tooth out." She put a hand under his chin and lifted until Adam agreed, then he opened his mouth. Mamm placed the paper napkin on his loose tooth and twisted very quickly.

Adam jumped. His eyes widened. Mamm opened the napkin to reveal a small white baby tooth. He smiled up at her and plucked the tooth from her hand. "That wasn't so bad."

"Mamm is the best at that," Daed announced with enthusiasm as he took a seat at the table.

With the excitement over, Elsie helped Mamm serve breakfast. But when she sat down, she lost her appetite. What Aaron heard wasn't bad. He had a good perspective of it, but she needed to start analyzing the circumstances. Since they told Omar and hadn't heard from him, she figured he felt there was nothing further to be done. And with the Amish, that was true; they wouldn't retaliate. But was there anything else they could do?

She was distracted throughout the meal. Her thoughts went from the scared boy to Katie and back again. Her mood was catching, and once the boys were gone, Mamm sat down at the table with her, leaving the dirty dishes on the counter.

"What's on your mind?" Mamm placed her hand on Elsie's cheek and waited. There was no option but to tell them both, but Elsie remembered what Rachel said and hesitated. What if Katie didn't come and she told her parents, only for them to be upset again? But she obviously couldn't keep what she knew to herself any longer. She felt she might burst into tears at any moment.

"The last couple of times I've been at Rachel's..."

Her daed's brows drew together, making her pause.

"When Daed was in the hospital..."

Her dead sat down next to her. His burly presence resonated next to her, causing her to stumble even more.

When she thought about everything, Elsie realized how much

she'd been keeping from them. Her mind went all the way back to the first incident with the English boys and everything up to the present. The spiral of events continued to compile into a bed of lies and secrets. When she stared at each of them, she wondered if they would ever be able to trust her again.

She turned to her daed and sucked in a breath. "I've talked to Katie." Elsie waited to let the shock sink in. She didn't intend to go round about it; just tell it straight out. But once she looked into her parents' faces, it wasn't that easy.

Her mamm's bottom lip dropped, but she remained speechless. Daed straightened and frowned. "Did you contact her, Elsie?"

Her mamm snapped out of her surprise. "You asked me if you should the day your daed was in the hospital." She turned to Daed. "It's my fault, Solomon. When Elsie asked, I was too worried about you to talk with her about it like I should have." Throughout the explanation Mamm fought away tears, tears that Elsie knew were from hearing her lost daughter's name and not from talking to Elsie that day.

"I cannot...will not talk about my eldest daughter." He stood and was about to turn away when Elsie grabbed his hand.

"She's coming home, Daed."

Her mamm and daed shared glances and then stared at her. Daed wiped his hand across his forehead. "I will deal with Katie if and when the situation arises. Not before then."

She wondered if he didn't want the risk of disappointment if Katie was back in their lives again like Elsie did. But this had been his reaction, when it came to Katie, from the day she left. His big heart burst when he found out.

When he started to walk away, Elsie spoke, "But Daed—"

He held up a hand and marched out of the kitchen, slapping his hand on the counter with a *whack*!

Mamm watched him leave and turned to Elsie. "You spoke to her on Rachel's phone that day...the day you asked if you could contact her?" She said it like a question, but she knew what Elsie had done.

"I never talked to her on the phone that day. But I thought she should know about Daed. Was I wrong?" Elsie felt the answer was yes to everything she was doing or had done. Were the things she'd seen and experienced so terrible, or was the guilt making her unsure?

Mamm smoothed a lock of Elsie's dark hair behind her ear. "You did what you thought was right. It's hard to know what to do when the unexpected happens."

Elsie didn't know if Mamm meant that for her or for herself. It had to be hard for her parents to follow the ways of their community when it was concerning their own child. But it wasn't for her to question.

"Mamm, there's been so much that has happened." Elsie felt like telling her mamm everything. Putting the burden on Omar wasn't fair.

Mamm smiled with tears in her eyes. "There is nothing you can do about your sister, and your daed will come around."

Elsie wanted to believe that her sister would come home and that Daed would forgive her and that Mamm's broken heart would mend. But she knew better than to expect everything to end up the way she wanted it to. It would only disappoint her. "I hope so."

Mamm patted her hand and stood. "Work is the best medicine. I'll clean up the kitchen if you get the boys going, and then we'll get the garden started."

Elsie's mood lifted at the thought. Neither of them had mentioned it with Katie gone. The three of them looked forward to gardening; it didn't seem like work to them when they did it together. "We're behind since we missed spring planting."

"We'll have to work all the harder then to catch up." Mamm smiled with satisfaction and turned to clean the dishes. "It's ironing day, so we'll need to make time for that as well." She took a brush and began to scrub a pan with vigor.

"I'll gather the clean clothes and sort the ones that need ironing and get the boys to gather the eggs." Elsie felt better all ready.

The boys were eager to get their chores done when Elsie told them about the garden, so she didn't have to prod them along. Elsie gathered the clothes and got them ready to iron. While Mamm finished up in the kitchen, Elsie took the boys to the back shed to gather flower bulbs, seeds, and tools they needed to clean up the garden. It had lain dormant over the winter. They learned from some of the owners of a nursery in town how to grow winter plants, something unheard of up north. Maybe next year would be better and they'd have some plants all year long.

They dug up the rotted vines and plants then tilled the garden with a handheld wheel with handles that loosened the dirt so they could make rows. The boys enjoyed that part the most, and by the time they were finished, there wasn't a spot that hadn't been turned over at least two or three times. The boys made it fun now that they were old enough to really help. But Elsie couldn't deny the void of Katie being gone. They worked through lunch until the boys started to lose their energy, so they stopped for a bite to eat.

Elsie pumped the well water to wash off her hands. She had dirt from head to toe as it seemed to go flying with the boys learning how the tilling worked. Try as she may, the dirt turned to mud, and she couldn't seem to get it all off.

"Looks like you need some help."

When Elsie looked up from the pump, Gideon was standing on the other side of the garden fence with his hands hanging over the top. He held a grin that made Elsie think he'd been there awhile. "Gideon, we're going to have some lunch. Are you hungry?"

"I can always eat." He gave her a once-over. "But it looks like you need some help cleaning up first."

Elsie glanced down at her bare arms and pulled down her sleeves. That covered some of the mud so he couldn't tease her that much. "It seems I keep making it worse."

He reached over and opened the wire fence door for her. He chuckled as she walked by. "It's worse than I thought." Then the boys came over without a lick of dirt on them. "How did you get so dirty?"

"We made the rows. We didn't dig in 'em like Elsie did," Aaron explained while Adam nodded.

"Afternoon, Gideon." Mamm went by and shooed the boys up to the house. "I hope you're staying to eat with us."

"I'd never say no to your cooking." Gideon gave her one of his smiles that brought out a dimple. He held the bucket of water while Elsie wiped off the dirt from her ankles and arms.

Gideon pointed to her cheek. "Missed a spot." He wiped it off with his calloused fingers and stared directly at her. "I was at Rachel's checking to see if her daed had gotten rid of that illness that's been keeping him down."

"Is he any better?"

"*Nee*, it's hanging on." He turned to her directly as he spoke. "She told me you talked with Katie."

"*Ach?*" She was enjoying the day and didn't want to put a damper on the high spirits everyone was in, but Gideon should know about Katie. "Did she tell you that Katie wants to come home?"

His brows lifted. "*Nee*. Do you think she will?"

Elsie felt a tinge of irritation at Gideon's question after hearing it too many times. "I don't know what to make of it, Gideon. But it's good news."

"I understand how you must be feeling." He looked down in thought. "If she does come back, you should have an open heart, without condition. I'm only telling you what you already know. It's just a reminder."

Elsie nodded. "I know. I need to be prepared."

He tilted his head. "*Jah*, you do."

She drew her eyebrows together. "I wonder why she decided to come back."

"She didn't tell you?"

"*Nee*, she said a lot of things had happened."

"A lot has gone on here with you as well. Did she ask you about that?"

Elsie hadn't thought about her not asking about the English boys or about her parents, or anything for that matter. "*Nee*, she didn't." There was a slight edge in her tone that she meant to keep inside of her, but she was with Gideon, so it slipped out.

Gideon was silent for a long while, and she knew he was analyzing everything she was saying. "I'm glad you're not letting her steal your joy." He scanned the garden that had Adam and Aaron footprints all over it. "This is what you love to do."

She slowly looked over the garden. Crates of flowers were scattered around the outside perimeter, ready to plant, and various vegetables as well. She was satisfied with the progress they'd made and realized she was smiling. "*Jah*, it is."

Adam opened the door and poked his head out. "Lunch is ready."

As they walked to the door, Gideon shook his head when he saw Adam's dirty feet. Then up to the smudge of dirt on Aaron's nose and chuckled. "And good luck getting anything done with those two around."

Chapter Twenty-One

THE MEN STARTED coming in with their flatbeds and work-horses as Gideon stood by his daed's field and kicked around some dirt. He leaned down to inspect the soil.

"What is it, son?" His daed bent toward where Gideon was intently staring.

"Wire worm." Gideon's gloomy edge gave his daed the motivation to squat down and study the brown dirt for himself.

"Looks like grubs too." He grabbed a handful of soil and squeezed. "Still haven't made peace with the earth down here in Texas."

"The organic matter is low. Once we get the balance right, we'll be ready to plant again." He didn't want to tell his daed he didn't know what was needed to correct the problem, but he'd find out today. He watched the swarm of men driving in and figured he'd have a harder time deciding whose advice to listen to more than finding the remedy.

The fields needed to be rotated, so no sooner was the spring planting done, then came cutting hay that had been planted in the winter. Now that the stalks were dry, they could bail them into rectangular chunks.

The men stacked the bales onto fifteen-foot flatbeds and trundled slowly along the side of the pasture. When they stopped for lunch, Gideon brought up the question about the soil. The men all stopped eating.

Davie relayed the latest information from the most well-renowned sources. "You need some essential mineral elements."

"Drip tape and some regular old fertilizer," Whitey Manuel

163

piped in as he pulled on his premature white beard that lent him his nickname.

When Elsie rode up with a basket full of food, Gideon stepped off the porch and waited for her. The conversation would continue without his presence, and his daed would make the final decision either way.

As she stepped down from the buggy, he thought there was a special glow about her. Maybe it was the way the sun was shining directly down on her or that the golden flecks in her brown eyes were especially bright. Or maybe it was simply that he'd become completely overwhelmed by her. He'd been her rescuer and confidant, but he wanted more, and at this very moment he decided that's the way it had to be.

"*Hallo* there," she chimed. Her mood seemed to be as bright as she looked. Elsie handed the basket to him and went to a spot on the grassy area tucked away from the large group but still visible.

"You're chipper today." The basket wasn't as full as usual, and his curiosity made him remove the cloth and peer inside.

She tapped his hand. "Just wait." She took the blanket that was tucked under her arm and spread it out for them to sit on.

Gideon set the food down and sat cross-legged in front of her. "What's this all about?"

She stopped taking food out of the basket, like she was plucking up the weeds in her garden, and smiled at him. "I made a lovely lunch and only want to share it with you. Very un-Amish of me."

He chuckled. "If there is such a thing." As Gideon watched her pull out the food, he was astonished to see that everything she made was his favorite. She handed him her mamm's cheese biscuits, mincemeat sandwiches, and for dessert her Aunt Fannie's chocolate cookies.

"How did you know what I liked?" He didn't try to hide his surprise. Only his mother and a couple of aunts knew what he preferred. He wasn't a picky enough eater for it to matter.

She handed him some sweet tea. "Because I know you, Gideon Lapp." Then she took a bite of her own food, sampling each one and making an "Mmm" noise when she chewed. "I did pretty well. Maybe not as well as your mamm, but she's had more time to practice."

His baffled state began to dissipate, and he enjoyed the meal, and even more so the company. "This was great, very *gut*."

"I'm glad you liked it. But you wouldn't tell me if you didn't." She smiled and leaned back to let the sun hit her face, closing her eyes. "You've been beside me through everything." She opened her eyes. "This was my way of saying *danke*."

Although Gideon appreciated her gesture, he wanted this to mean more, and he felt he needed to know where their relationship was going. "Elsie." His voice was louder and more serious than he meant for it to be.

She sat up with wide eyes.

"I've asked your daed for permission to court you." He felt a fire in his stomach that he pushed through. It wasn't usual for the young man to talk with the parents about courting, but because of their special situation, Gideon felt he could.

Elsie didn't show any sign of saying no; she just waited and stared. His usual ability to read her was lost at the moment.

"Elsie, would you consider letting me—" He lost his words. Never had he stumbled so badly. He didn't have a fear of speaking, and was actually quite comfortable with a healthy debate. But he couldn't find the last two words he needed to finish what he was asking. His mouth went shut and opened again, but there was not so much as a breath of air that escaped from his lips. What if she still wasn't ready? But what if he didn't ask her and someone else did?

He slowly regained his senses. He'd finally found the only girl he'd ever had true feelings for to allow him to court her, and he was at a loss of words.

She squeezed his hand. "Are you all right?"

"*Jah*, I have something important to ask you and..." He stopped short. By the look on her face he knew not to continue. It was as if he was causing her physical pain to finish what he set out do. Her forehead creased and she twiddled her thumbs, a sure sign she was worried. "It was hard for me to tell what you're thinking. I can with a lot of people. But not always with you."

"I can't live up to your standards." An awkward mood hung over them, with neither of them seeming to know what to do or say.

After a moment's time Gideon spoke his mind. "What standards have I put on you?"

"Not you, Gideon; the community, Omar, and the others would have certain expectations if we were formally together."

"God will put me where He needs me. Just as He will place you, and all who follow Him, on the path He has for us. *Jah*, I love the Word and studying, but that doesn't mean I'll preach or lead; it simply means I enjoy learning, and so do you."

"But is that what you want?"

"I want to serve others in whatever capacity God wants me to. And yes, if it means leading, then I will." He lifted a single eyebrow. "But if I don't know yet where I'll serve, how do you?"

"I don't, of course. But I have a pretty good idea, and if that happens, I don't know if I'm suited to be who you'd need me to be." She sighed and turned away then back to him.

He grinned. "You have big plans for me, more so than Omar or anyone else does, for that matter."

She stroked her cheek with her fingers. "God's plans. '*I know the plans I have made for you.*' His plans are the only ones you need to listen to, not to any of ours," she said in all seriousness.

Gideon held onto the verse and applied it not only to what he would be called to do but also to what commitment he might have with Elsie. He was disappointed, yes, but he forced himself to obediently wait for God's timing in courting Elsie. She clearly wasn't ready, and her understanding how important his calling was showed him even more that she was well suited for him. He prayed for patience.

As they were packing up, Chris walked by and stopped. "*Hallo.*" He waved as he greeted them.

166

"It's *gut* to see you." Gideon reached out to pump his hand. He clumsily clasped his and shook once, hard.

Then Chris reached over to shake with Elsie. As they twined their hands, Elsie put her other hand on top of his and looked him in the eyes. "Are you helping stack the hay?"

He shook his head. "Driving…" He stuttered then finished his sentence. "…the horses." His grin showed his appreciation for the task. April and May were the names of the two horses the Fishers were using. "Both girls."

Gideon took his time gathering the utensils and went around the corner of the haus to wash them off. Then he heard another male voice.

"Elsie, I've been looking for you."

"I didn't see you there," Elsie's voice sang out.

"Go find our wagon and tell Daed I'll be along, Chris."

Gideon popped his head around the corner of the clapboard haus to see Chris wave to Elsie.

Mose. It figured. He always seemed to be around Elsie. Gideon knew they shared the same plight with their siblings gone, but it still irked him the way Mose sought her out and the way their conversations went off the topic of Katie and Jake.

"Mose." He stood, pumped Mose's hand and moved away.

"Gideon," Mose answered in a flat tone and turned to Elsie. "Rachel said you talked with Katie."

Gideon wiped off the plates and listened to them talk.

"*Jah*, I asked Rachel to tell you. I didn't know how you'd feel about it. If your daed is like mine, I thought it best to wait and see what you wanted to know."

"Are they all right?"

Gideon didn't like the way Mose moved a step closer, almost touching Elsie. He wondered if she was comfortable with how near he was and was about ready to step in when he heard Elsie respond.

"Katie didn't say as much, but she didn't sound like herself. She wants to come home."

When Mose put a hand on Elsie's shoulder to comfort her, Gideon stood and turned around. He wiped the water from his hand on his pants and laid the plates and forks in the basket.

"Have you heard from Jake?" Elsie asked.

"*Nee*. It would be good to see him and find out how he is. Did she say when they would be coming?" Mose's eyes darted to Gideon's once quickly.

Gideon's gaze remained on Mose until he heard his daed calling for everyone to get back to work. "Mose, it sounds like we need to go." He turned to Elsie and grabbed the basket. "Let me help you take this to your buggy." He wasn't about to leave them alone together. Part of him wanted to tell Mose they were courting, but that was the sour part of him he didn't want to seep out and make him a liar.

"*Nee*, but I'll tell you if I hear anything more," she said as she folded the blanket and walked beside Gideon.

Mose went around on the other side of her. "I'll tell my daed and mamm so there are no surprises. It would be just like Jake to show up out of the clear blue sky."

When they both smiled at the scenario, Gideon felt left out of the conversation. He'd only seen a side of Jake that hurt Elsie; before that he was just one of the many Fisher boys, and not one he knew very well. He was missing out on something that the two of them understood about Jake and seemed to be amused. But Gideon felt sure he didn't want to find out what it was.

Chapter Twenty-Two

LSIE TOOK THE cover off the buggy. It was a nice day, and she wanted to enjoy it before the hot summer weather started. Angus was a large stud with one of the calmest dispositions in their herd. She preferred to use him when she wanted to take an easy ride and not trying to train a horse to pull the buggy.

She needed to go to the Byler's store to pick up a few items. Her farm was at the end of the community and the store was at the very front, just off the highway to Beeville. The neighbors were helping with a grocery shower for a widow who broke her leg in three places and was coming home from the hospital. There would be a supply of food waiting for her. Elsie also brought a baby blanket to sell that her mamm made.

Elsie passed by John and Annie's bed-and-breakfast that was next to the store. The two-story home, with five bedrooms, was larger than most. The three rooms they boarded were usually full this time of year. Elsie wondered if they would add on once they had more children. It brought them good and steady income to subsidize their farm. There were pots of fern, upside-down bunches of lavender, and herbs hanging from the trim above the railing. The couch and porch swing were empty, too early for the guests at this hour.

The door's hinges creaked, and the aromas of vanilla, dried herbs, and lavender vied for attention. As Elsie walked through the store, she decided what to buy for the widow Verna.

"Morning."

MaryAnn popped her head up from the box she was digging into.

"You're here bright and early. Gotta enjoy this weather before the heat starts up." She tucked a gray strand of hair behind her ear and rested her hands on her wide hips.

"*Jah*, for sure. I need to get some ingredients to make granola for Verna before she gets home."

"Ah, she does like her granola, especially Clara's recipe with coconut." She came out from behind the counter.

"And I have this for you to sell." Elsie laid the powder blue infant blanket on the counter for her to examine.

MaryAnn ran her hand over the soft flannel and fussed over it. "This is precious. And with the summer babies on their way, someone will be needing this—especially if a set of twins surprises some mamm."

She went over to an aisle with cooking and baking ingredients. They weren't commonly needed since they made a lot of their own but nice to have in a pinch. "Tell me what else you need."

"Oatmeal. The silverfish got into it, but I'll stop at Rachel's and borrow some from hers, so just the coconut."

She cringed. "That might be the one thing I don't have. I'll have to make sure to get some in town." She rifled through items on the shelves, shoving small bags and boxes around. "You have vanilla, maple flavoring, and vegetable oil?"

"And salt, of course. Don't need pecans." Elsie searched with her, hoping she wouldn't have to ask around for coconut too since she didn't frequently use it.

"Good crop this year for pecans." She continued to search for the coconut with success. "One small bag." She carried the plastic bag to the counter and added up the total.

The bell on the door jingled as Will walked in with Ruby close behind. "Little sister, I thought that was daed's buggy." He gave her a tight squeeze. Ruby's hug she barely felt.

"Ran out of oatmeal, of all things."

"And our place is too far to come over and get some from us?" Will smiled as though teasing, but she knew he meant what he said.

"But I bet you don't have coconut," Elsie countered. Bantering was the language Will related to. And Elsie didn't mind. She missed it, in fact.

Will turned toward Ruby. She shook her head. "*Nee*, I don't usually have it around." That opened the door for talk about cooking, so Elsie thought she'd take advantage of it.

"You can come over and help me make granola if you like." Elsie noticed the edges of her mouth turn up and considered that a yes.

Ruby shrugged at Will, who nodded to her. "All right." Her eyes shifted to the blanket on the counter. "Who made that?" Ruby reached over to it to feel the soft material beneath her hand.

"Mamm did. She usually makes bigger blankets, but I think she has grandbabies on her mind." Elsie smiled, but neither Will nor Ruby did. When Elsie looked at Will, he gave her a forced smile and put his hands on Ruby's shoulders.

"Come on, honey, you can ride home with Elsie, and I'll pick you up later." Will leaned down to kiss Ruby on the forehead and winked at Elsie then started to walk away.

"Where are you going?" Elsie inquired as she watched her tall, muscular brother saunter off.

"I'm not big on shopping. And I do have a farm to work." He grinned and was out the door whistling a tune.

Ruby and Elsie smiled at one another, and Elsie shook her head. "I don't know how you put up with him," she said in the most endearing way.

"He makes me laugh." Ruby's eyes softened when she spoke of Will. They seemed to be happy together, and Elsie hoped to have the same kind of relationship. Then she stopped, literally causing Ruby to run into her.

"Sorry!" Ruby moved past Elsie to see why she stopped.

It was if she'd forgotten she had the beginning of that bond with Gideon. They were, after all, almost promised to one another, or at least exclusively together. He had always been there, but moving their relationship to another level hadn't sunken in yet.

"Elsie?" Ruby's dark eyes were studying her face with intensity.

"I was just thinking." Elsie didn't know if she should tell Ruby about her and Gideon, being so close to moving their relationship forward. They might figure things out eventually, but it would be nice to share a confidence with Ruby. When she thought about telling Mamm and Daed, she smiled. Nothing would make them happier, except maybe Katie coming home. Her daed acted as if he didn't care, but she knew better. He was hurt and worried and didn't know how to express it. Mamm kept in good faith that Katie would return, and Elsie hoped she was right.

"About what?" Ruby's large dark eyes made Elsie decide she had to tell her. It might make her feel more a part of their family to be the first to know.

"I think Gideon wants to court me." She smiled wide.

Ruby's mouth lifted on one side. "What do you mean?"

"He wasn't himself, so I'm not sure of his intentions, but he was definitely trying to talk about us."

"So what's changed?"

Elsie paused. "I'm not sure." Ruby's blunt reply made Elsie realize she didn't have an answer. Whatever he tried to say was distorted by what his future held. That left her somewhere in limbo, but now, thinking back, she had put herself there.

Pop! Pop! Pop! Piercing bangs like the sound of a gun went off. Then the shrill whinny of a horse. Elsie ran out the door with Ruby right behind her. Angus was up on his hind legs, eyes white with fear. His nostrils flared as he went down on all fours. The buggy moved to the side and jackknifed.

Elsie went to him slowly with her hands out for him to catch her scent. Her wrist hit a hot spot on the axle. She cried out as her skin seared in pain. She looked down the road and saw a blue car driving slowly along the way. It sped up and took off, leaving a cloud of dust trailing behind. Angus let out short, hard breaths as she stroked his tense neck and chest. She climbed up into the back of the wagon and found what appeared to be shredded paper. When she picked up part of one, she realized by the smell of gun powder that it was fireworks.

"Is he all right?" Ruby walked behind her as she rubbed Angus's side.

Elsie jumped down off the wagon and brushed off her dress. "He's fine. He's heard plenty of gun shots, just not coming from the wagon attached behind him." They moved Angus forward to straighten out the buggy but weren't in any hurry to leave yet.

Ruby noticed the pink skin on her wrist. "Did you get hurt?"

"Something burned me." Elsie tried not to think about the dull pain and tended to Angus instead.

Ruby narrowed her eyes toward where the car parked. "Don't Englishers have work to do?"

"They must, but maybe not enough to keep them occupied." Elsie wrinkled her brow and looked down the road with her. "At least the younger ones don't."

MaryAnn burst out of the store, letting the door slap shut. She watched the car in the distance. "They're trouble. If those boys were mine, they wouldn't see the light of day if they pulled a stunt like that." She piped in with gusto. "I'm telling Omar about this. I know they won't do nothin', but I'm telling 'em all the same." MaryAnn turned and went back inside then brought out Elsie's coconut. "It's on the house."

Elsie took her time calming Angus. Although he adjusted quickly, she wanted to give him an extra few minutes before driving him home. His eyelids drooped as she and Ruby talked and stroked him. "Do you think MaryAnn will really tell them?"

"She's just blowing off steam." Elsie stepped up and sat down in the buggy. Ruby followed.

"Can't say as I blame her. I figured they'd tire of these stunts." She was only a bit shorter than Elsie but sat taller on the bench, her feet barely touching the footboard.

Elsie didn't want to talk about the English. She was tired of them in a way Ruby couldn't begin to understand. Angus slowed his trot, and his ears went forward. She clucked at Angus and

BETH SHRIVER

tapped his hide with the leather reins. Angus dealt with the situation better than they did, startled by a bunch of loud noise that didn't mean as much to him as it did to them. Another ridiculous prank done by wayward teenagers. How many more would there be before it all stopped?

Elsie's cheeks burned from turning them back and forth, taking one hit after another. Her mind changed with a new thought. Why was she the one on the path that day when it all started? Katie was there too, but once she left, they sought her out. She knew they were preying on her because she was young, defenseless, and was no threat to them, but why her? It was a selfish way of thinking. She wouldn't want anyone to go through this, but she wouldn't be human if she didn't wish it was someone else, like Katie.

Sometimes she worried that she wanted Katie back to share the burden and take the fall with her—and to have her walk from place to place and see how it felt to worry and wonder if they would show up.

"Elsie." Ruby's voice brought her back.

"Sorry, I was thinking about what you said. They have to get bored with it soon. I can't imagine that antagonizing people who don't respond can last too long."

"Why are you so preoccupied?" Ruby was either hurt or irritated; Elsie couldn't tell.

"Forgive me, Ruby." She glanced at her, thinking she owed her as much to know what was on her mind. "Those boys have been bothering me for months. Gideon has spoken with them, and Omar is eager to have a word with them. But there's nothing we can do but wait until they stop." Elsie sighed with relief. It felt good to tell someone else. There had to come a time when her burdens were lifted, for her parents' sake as well.

"Why do the weak try to prey on the strong?" Ruby looked up as if she'd find the answer in the skies.

Elsie needed to hear it in her head again to make sure she heard it right. "How do you mean?"

174

"It's much harder to resist retaliation than to abide by it."

Elsie was still digesting her words when she thought of the scared boy. He was battling between the two, the right way or the wrong. It was always a choice but not easy to do, and not at all in his situation.

"They know we could overtake them each and every time they come into our community, but we're strong enough not to. We don't have the need to oppress others, and they know that. That's the only reason they're brave enough to keep coming back." She wrung her hands as if to rid them of those unwelcome delinquents.

Elsie knew Gideon had a momentary impulse to fight back when he saw them with her that day for the first time. "We do have that instinct to fight. But by Christ's example we don't."

Ruby nodded. "This too will pass," she quoted the verse that was so appropriate for this situation.

Elsie smiled her appreciation and remembered their plans. So much had happened she'd almost forgotten. "We've got to get home and start baking granola."

"I've never made it with coconut; sounds good."

The rest of the ride was pleasant as they compared recipe ideas. Ruby did know about cooking; she just didn't have the practice she needed. Elsie didn't think she'd be teaching someone how to cook yet, but she liked that it gave them a way to get to know each other better.

As they drove down the lane to the barn, they noticed two buggies in front of the house tethered to the post. Elsie and Ruby took the harness off that attached to the buggy. Elsie thought Angus deserved a romp in the pasture, so she let him out and watched him run and stop short then throw his head playfully.

When they got to the house, they heard muffled voices. Daed's was the loudest, and he sounded angry. When she got closer, she could see Mamm through the window and two other people.

"Do you have company?" Ruby cocked her head to try and see who it was.

"*Jah*, but I don't know who." She studied the buggies and noticed one was Gideon's.

Ruby opened the door and stopped in the doorway. Elsie maneuvered around her and stopped in her tracks.

Katie sat on the couch and turned to see her. "Elsie."

"You're home." Elsie wanted to say more, but she was too shocked to think of what to say. "I thought you would call again before you came." Katie looked different. Her hair was shorter with streaks of brown mixed with her amber curls, and her face fuller, with rosy cheeks.

"I decided just to come." Katie stared at Elsie, in silence.

Elsie looked around the room then shifted one foot to the other. "Where's Jake?"

Gideon stepped forward from the other side of Ruby, and Elsie wondered if she should have asked.

"Jake's not here." Katie kept staring at her, waiting for her reaction. Elsie knew Gideon was too. But she felt nothing. A numbing sensation covered her mind and slid down over her heart.

"When you said it would be hard for *us*, I thought you meant you and Jake."

Katie stood, showing the bump in her stomach. "*Nee*, me and the baby."

Chapter Twenty-Three

THE ROOM STARTED to spin. Elsie made her way to the nearest place to sit, a footstool by the chair her mamm was sitting in. She looked over at Gideon, who had been staring at the floor. Her imagination went wild wondering what he might be thinking. Was he in as much shock as she was? Or was he upset she'd made mention of Jake? Her daed was pacing slowly between the kitchen and front room. He stopped and flexed his jaw. "Where is Jake?"

The same question filled Elsie's mind, and she shamed herself for it. The baby and her sister's health were more important, but she too needed to know the answer.

Katie stared at her daed. She seemed to have no remorse, but that was just who Katie was. She neither judged nor accepted judgment on her own behalf. But in this case it seemed only natural for her to show some sort of guilt. Then Elsie remembered her own long-suffering guilt, how it brought her to a place of withdrawal and depression when Katie left and the trouble with the Englishers began. Ultimately Elsie's guilt only made things worse. Katie's way of letting guilt slide off her like a discarded cloak was completely opposite. "He stayed in the city." Her gaze locked with Solomon's, and both fell silent.

The expression on Daed's face said he was close to bursting into a rage. He drew in a deep breath, seeming to give himself a moment to defuse. "Why isn't he here with you?"

Katie shrugged. "He didn't want the wrath of the community falling on us."

Daed took a giant step closer to her. "So he left you to bear it alone?" He glanced down to her stomach.

Katie wasn't afraid of their daed. She never had been. But she did respect him. She answered with a nod.

"You have nothing to say about his actions?"

"I am here and he is there. That's all there is to say."

Daed's breathing intensified as his eyes pierced into Katie's. "He is a dog to have left you this way." Although his anger was meant for Jake, he directed it at Katie.

"I left; he didn't."

When Daed's bottom lip began to tremble with rage, Mamm stepped closer. "This is Jake's responsibility too, not just yours."

"I know that." Katie's voice grew louder with each word.

"Don't raise your voice to your mamm." Daed walked away from them and stood in front of the window, looking out, his back to them. Elsie knew he was holding on, trying not to explode. For his daughter to be in this predicament, and to have an attitude, with no Jake, was more than he could take. It was as if all the underlying thoughts and behaviors she always had came out while she was gone.

Jake was as independent as Katie. Maybe he didn't want to leave the outside world, not even to accompany his wife home...but Elsie wondered how Jake could let Katie travel home alone in her condition. What made her return? Did she and Jake split up? Could it have been because of the baby?

For several minutes no one spoke. When Elsie couldn't stand it a moment longer, she broke the silence. "What are you going to do?"

All eyes were suddenly on her. Some because it snapped them back and others who were probably thinking her question but didn't want to ask.

"I'll fetch your bag, Katie." Gideon walked passed Elsie and to the door.

"I'll make something to eat." Mamm stood awkwardly and then gave Katie a forced smile. Ruby followed after her.

Daed was as still as a cornstalk as he watched Gideon out front. Elsie observed Katie as she put a hand on her stomach.

What must it be like to have a living being inside of you? And even though Katie wore English clothes, she was still Amish—or was she? Where would her place be here now? Then she thought of Jake, and her lips tightened together.

"How are you, Elsie?" Katie was staring at her with interest.

"I'm *gut*."

"Are you with Gideon?"

"*Jah*." Elsie didn't know why she said it. They weren't officially a "couple." But this whole situation with Katie made her want to be. Seeing what she and Jake were going through made Elsie lose all doubt concerning Gideon.

Daed turned slightly. "Praise God." He walked across the room.

Katie and Elsie watched him go, and Gideon came in. Daed embraced him. Gideon's arms were pinned to his sides and his eyes were wide as Daed tightened his bear hug. "God bless you, son." Daed released him and walked through the kitchen and out the back door.

Gideon stood unmoving, with a blank stare. "What was that about?"

"You and my sister together." Katie's eyes watered, but she sat up straight, took in a breath, and the tears disappeared.

Gideon sat on the footstool next to Elsie. "I didn't know myself, until now." Gideon looked at Elsie with question.

"It's not exactly official." Elsie caught his eyes and smiled, hoping he would too. It really wasn't fair of her to bring it about like this, but in this way, it truly came from the heart. She studied him, unable to imagine Gideon treating her like Jake was treating Katie. She hoped Jake would correct his mistakes and come to his senses. If not, what would she do?

"But now that your daed knows..." Gideon lifted his brows.

"Well, it's about time," Katie smiled. "You two belong together."

"I've always thought so," Gideon said but didn't look at Elsie.

They both knew she didn't return his feelings as quickly. It took many months of making himself helpful and noticeable before Elsie considered him. And then there was Jake.

"Do you think Jake will follow you here?"

Katie's smile faded. "I don't know. After I found out about the baby and wanted to come home, we got into an argument. He said we're now English and we'd have the baby just like the English do."

"Are you English?" Elsie's question slipped out. It was something she really wanted to know, and the bishop would ask along with the rest of her family.

"It's hard to fit in out there. But once I got used to it, I liked it." She shrugged. "So what does that make me?"

Neither Gideon nor Elsie answered. Elsie didn't even know for sure if she truly wanted them to answer. Besides, it was not her place to say.

Ruby walked in and folded her fingers together at her waist. "The food is ready."

Gideon jumped up, maybe to avoid the topic or simply because he was hungry, and took Elsie's hand to help her stand. Katie pushed against the back of the couch with one hand, the other hand on her stomach, and tried to catch her balance.

Gideon went to her, but Katie shook her head. "*Nee*, thanks though."

Ignoring her response, he reached out to steady her. Katie obviously appreciated Gideon's efforts and didn't want to bother him. The fact that he was doing what her husband should have been there doing wasn't lost to Elsie—and probably not to Katie either.

"I'm not usually so clumsy," Katie sighed. "Just tired, I guess."

Elsie wanted to know how far along she was. The last time she saw Katie it was winter, now summer was almost here. "When is your due date?"

Gideon stared at Elsie, possibly uncomfortable with her question.

"Second trimester, so maybe September."

Elsie waited for more information, but Katie didn't offer any. She was wondering if Katie knew the answers. She didn't seem happy, but was it from the humiliation of coming home, Jake, or something else?

Katie glanced at her. "I've only been to the doctor once to find out if I was pregnant. I was taken off guard and didn't know what to do or say. All I came away with was that we don't have insurance. I didn't know what else to do but come home."

"Alma the midwife is moving down this way, but in the meantime we're sharing a community doctor with the new Amish community."

"*Gut*, I feel better already."

Elsie smiled. "You said *gut*."

"I did, didn't I?" Her eyebrows drew together.

"You see, you're still Amish."

Katie shrugged. "Maybe home is where the heart is."

Elsie wondered what she meant specifically but didn't ask. Her opinion of Jake continued to decrease the more she found out about him. There was an exciting, impulsive side of him that Elsie found intriguing but knew better than to indulge in it. Katie was defensive and bitter, and Elsie was curious as to exactly why.

When they got to the table, Elsie wished it was only she and Katie. She had so many questions to ask. Everyone took a seat, but Daed's was empty. Mamm noticed when Elsie glanced at his chair.

"Gideon, you can sit in Solomon's place," Mamm offered.

Katie stared at her mamm. "He's not eating with us?"

"Not until he talks with Omar." Mamm began passing the food around.

Katie sat back in her chair. "In case I'm shunned?"

Mamm gave Katie a look that told everything, and Katie turned away. "Give your daed some room. He's beside himself with anguish."

"Meredith and I gathered up some luncheon meat and bread to

make sandwiches; help yourselves." Ruby set a plate on the table with cheese.

"Thanks for lunch." Katie ate more meat, bread, and canned peaches than anyone. "How's Will?" she asked Ruby.

"He's *gut*. He's missed you." Ruby moved awkwardly as if she wasn't sure what was appropriate to discuss. "Are you feeling all right, Katie?"

"*Jah*, only a little sick at first, but I'm fine now."

Mamm nodded. "*Gut*." She tried to eat, but she barely nibbled on some cheese. Mamm got up and left the table to start cleaning up in the kitchen. Elsie knew she was fighting with her emotions. There were rules to follow and traditions to respect. But what were they, and how did they apply to this situation?

Ruby got up and went to help, and Gideon left as soon as he finished eating. Once Elsie was alone with Katie, all the questions came forward. "Will you be comfortable in your old bed?"

"It'll be different to share with my sister again, but yea, I'll be fine." Katie continued to eat as if she hadn't for a week. She'd eaten almost a whole jar of peaches by herself.

"All of your clothes are in the closet or in the attic."

She looked down at her stomach. "I don't think they'll fit."

"We could let them out."

"I'll need to as I get bigger."

"Are you and Jake married?" Elsie watched Katie's eyes dart toward her.

"Yes." Katie looked back at her plate and took the last bite as if she'd just answered a question about the weather.

"So, you're Katie Fisher now." Hearing the names together threw her a little. She'd imagined her name with Jake's but never Katie's.

"We were before we found out about the baby." She leaned back and put both hands on her belly.

"I see." Elsie said softly as she absorbed what she'd just learned. It was good they were married first. Omar may go easier on her this way. But since she didn't know the dates exactly, Elsie hoped she was right.

Katie did a double take as if deciding something and then asked, "I know you and Jake were good friends. It must have been hard when we both left. But we couldn't see any other way to leave without trying to be talked out of it."

This was the first time Katie made any real reference to how Elsie felt about Jake, and now she knew why; she considered them just friends. Elsie never told anyone how she felt, but people probably knew by the way she acted when she was around him. Elsie wondered what Jake thought of their relationship. Had it been all in her mind?

"Gideon is a good man," Katie replied with meaning and a touch of sadness. "I'd like to lie down." Katie turned to stand.

"You're probably tired from the bus ride." Elsie instinctively went to help her.

"I can walk up the stairs, Elsie." Elsie was glad in a way. She needed some time to take this all in—and talk to Gideon about Katie, and even more, what was to come. "All right then. Get some rest." She watched Katie lumber up the stairs. From behind you wouldn't know she was with child. But she waddled as if it was difficult for her to get around.

She stopped and turned back. "Elsie, it's good to see you."

Elsie smiled, "You too." Her words were true, but the resentment of Katie leaving lingered. She hadn't even asked if the English men who harassed them were still a problem, among all the other events that had gone on. But then Katie had only known about the one incident, and she didn't want to upset Katie with yet another issue to deal with, but it was heavy on her mind. Elsie wished she could tell Katie what she really felt. But it was better this way. It kept her tongue as it should be, dull not sharp.

∼ Chapter Twenty-Four ∼

GIDEON PUT A hand-crafted playhouse in the wagon and strapped it down next to some lawn furniture customers had purchased at the bizarre. While he was in town, he also planned to check in with Minister Miller, who was at the new community that was growing on the other side of Beeville.

As he made his way to Yonnie's Gideon noticed the clouds rotating in the morning sky. The sun coming up was a dark, golden color covered with murky, twisted billows, like small tornadoes skittering across the sky. Betsy and Ross had extra pep in their stride, so Gideon let out some slack on the reins.

Yonnie and two of his brothers were walking along a skeleton frame of the dawdihaus they were building for his dawdi and mammi. They took turns balancing on a beam trying to knock the others off and be the last man standing. Gideon heard the whoops and hollers as one fell after another, with Yonnie's the loudest.

"Yonnie!"

Yonnie looked up, and his brother took the opportunity to knock him over. He got right back up and proceeded to push off two of his brothers. They landed on the ground, tucked and rolled, and then climbed back on.

"Yonnie, come on," Gideon called out, but he couldn't help but be entertained. He spent a lot of time doing the same stunts with his four brothers. But he wanted to get back so he could see Elsie.

"Hold your horses," Yonnie yelled back. He put his fists in front of him, against his chest, and stuck out his elbows to make his way through. He jumped out of the wooden frame then grabbed his shoes and socks. He hoisted himself up and sat down on the bench seat. Yonnie hiked a thumb over his shoulder. "You've got quite a load."

"*Jah*, we sold a lot at the last bizarre."

"The crowds are getting bigger this time of year with summer around the corner."

"Actually, today is the first day."

"By the calendar, not by our crop, if we're going to help the newcomers."

"We'll have a chance to find out. I'm going to stop by after we unload all of this furniture."

"*Gut*, I'd like to meet them."

"And see Minister Miller. He's been there for quite a while, so they must still not have chosen a minister."

"*Jah*, I wonder if he'll stay."

Gideon didn't want to consider that option. He was new to their own community and just learning his way with them. To start over with a new community so soon seemed to be a lot to handle. And then there was Zeke vying for the spot, which created mixed feelings. Gideon knew Jonathon Miller was the better choice, but he didn't miss Zeke leaving their community. "It's either him or Zeke."

Yonnie groaned. "*Jah*, that's what I'm worried about." He looked up at the sky as thunder rolled in the distance.

Gideon glanced up at the gray sky. "Heavy humidity today."

"So, do you want to talk about it?" Yonnie's face held no expression. His usual excitement and energy seemed to dissipate.

"You must mean Katie." Gideon tried to put his thoughts aside until he had more time to talk to Elsie. It would be so easy to judge or blame, but neither would result in anything good. But Katie's demeanor made it difficult for Gideon to unconditionally accept her decisions, choices that were now affecting her family. The painstaking months she was gone were difficult, yes, but living with the outcome of that choice was another thing all together.

"I hope it doesn't change your mind about courting Elsie."

Gideon turned to him. "How do you know I'm courting her?"

He grinned. "I didn't. I was just hoping." He slugged Gideon in the arm, which hurt almost as much as Solomon's back slaps. "I'm courting Beverly Zook." His grin grew as he tugged the blond hair from his eyes.

"Congratulations, my friend." Gideon felt great happiness for Yonnie, whom he thought might never find a bride. But this was just the beginning of a long and demanding process. There would be classes each week and commitments to the church to prepare for marriage. Gideon and Yonnie were baptized, but Elsie and Beverly weren't, so that would have to take place as well.

"What about Katie?"

"She came home."

"Well, that's *gut, jah*?"

"*Jah*, because she's in a family way."

Yonnie paused, but only for a second. "So, why don't you seem happy for them?"

"Jake didn't come with her."

Yonnie frowned. "What a rat!" He shook his head. "Katie will have a lot of help. It's *gut* she came back."

Gideon nodded but didn't want to discuss it any further, and Yonnie didn't seem to either.

It started to rain, and Gideon wished he'd attached a cover to the wagon. It didn't last long, but the sky continued to darken and the clouds overhead grew larger and spun faster.

When they got to town, they went straight to the drop-off point. The store owner came out to help them organize where to put it all and raved about the craftsmanship of their work. It made Gideon wonder what the English furniture looked like in comparison when hearing the compliments. After they finished, they kept going east through Beeville and to the new community. It wasn't hard to find when the signs started popping up—fresh country eggs, Guernsey milk, baked goods, and more goods for sale.

When they got closer to the area, Gideon stopped at the first white clapboard home, which was where Minister Miller was staying. They were greeted by an older man and his family. Gideon and Yonnie introduced themselves and stepped inside the immaculate home. The feminine touch of six daughters and their mamm showed in the decoration, furniture, and small details.

"You're just in time for lunch." Minister Miller came into the room and pumped Gideon's hand and then Yonnie's.

As they made their way to the large table, Gideon asked the minister how things were shaping up. "How many are in this community now?"

"There's about thirty-six, I believe." The minister rubbed his chin in thought.

"Thirty-seven with Janet's newborn." Ephraim, their host, pointed at Minister Miller with a chubby finger.

"We've kept the minister busy with the upcoming weddings and babies being born." The mamm tapped her daughter's hand to stop her staring at their visitors, and she started eating again.

"You've been missed. When will you be coming back?" Yonnie asked around a bite of potatoes.

Minister Miller looked up from his plate, and the instant Gideon saw his expression, he knew the answer.

"I won't be coming back."

"You're staying here, then?" Yonnie obviously needed the confirmation as much as Gideon did.

"I've enjoyed serving here, and they need a minister." Minister Miller's young face glowed with appreciation. "And there are many in your community who are capable to serve in my former position. I recently informed the deacon."

"God's speed to your work here." Gideon was glad for the minister but prayed for his own community, knowing Zeke would quickly replace him.

Gideon tried the shoofly pie even though whoopie pie was his favorite dessert. The flavors mixed together on his tongue and made his eyes water. He'd had this pie all his life, but it never tasted like this. "I was wondering if you'd had any problems with the locals in town."

"*Nee*, nothing more than the staring and the expected curiosities." His friendly demeanor didn't change. These behaviors were expected for the Amish living down south.

"We still get that and have been for over a year," Yonnie took a bite of the pie. Gideon watched Yonnie's eyes grow as he took another bite. They'd always had good cooking, but this was even better than they were used to.

The father dropped his fork on the plate. "I don't like some of the youths' comments to my girls, but they are good to ignore it."

That made Gideon pause and wonder exactly what was said to Elsie. Maybe he didn't want to know. The harassers made him want to do things he'd never thought of before. And when it came to Elsie, he had a harder time controlling those actions.

"This was an incredible meal," Yonnie said in a boisterous tone, making everyone smile slightly.

The girls brought a pitcher and poured more water and then served them seconds without asking. Their mamm kept a sharp eye on them, but when one young lady glanced at Gideon too many times, he decided it was time to leave. "We should go before this weather takes a turn for the worse. *Danke* for your hospitality."

Yonnie gave him a grave look and took once last glance at the girls then stood to go. "*Jah, danke* for the meal. One of the best I've had."

"We're opening a restaurant in town, *Essenhaus Style Inn*." The father grinned. "I already have a full staff."

Gideon smiled. "We'll try it out the next time we're out this way."

They waved as they walked to the wagon, inspecting the gathering dark clouds on the horizon. "Looks like it might hold." Gideon wanted to see Elsie even more so after the lunch they'd just had. Sharing a meal with six girls without her beside him made him a bit uncomfortable.

"Who can think about the weather after that meal." Yonnie's eyes widened. "And all of those young ladies."

"You're a committed man, my friend." Gideon reminded him.

Yonnie stared, still with shock on his face. "*Nee*, I'm just hoping for the sake of that daed there's a lot of young men in this little community."

Gideon chuckled, thinking that Yonnie was indeed faithful to his girl, Beverly. He wanted to continue his rounds to meet more families, but the sky was turning an ugly shade of black. He held tight onto the reins in case the horses spooked. Lightning hit the ground in the distance, and he waited. A clap of thunder made Ross lurch forward, but Betsy stayed a steady course with ears alert.

"Let's get home while we can." Yonnie leaned forward in the bench as if it would improve their momentum. "Glad that wagon's empty."

As they drove down Main Street, the car in front of them slowed down and stopped on the side of the street. People came out of stores to watch the ominous sky. Some stayed indoors, peering through windows in the local stores or restaurants.

"They act like they've never seen a storm before." It started to sprinkle, but Gideon worried about what looked to be a coming downpour. He wanted to try and make it home, but he didn't want to drag his friend through a storm for his sake.

"Stay ahead of it, and we'll be fine. I want to see Beverly as much as you do Elsie."

Once they left the town, they would have to spend almost two hours on the highway. A few farms dotted the landscape between town and home, but the distance between them was great. Gideon was glad to hear Yonnie agree. Extreme weather was part of living in tornado alley.

He kept the horses at an even trot. Ross wanted to forge ahead, but Gideon kept pulling him back. "Atta boy." Gideon tried to calm him, but he had to yell to be heard above the thunder.

"This is gonna be a long ride home." Yonnie wrapped his arms around his chest and blinked against the slapping rain. They didn't bring jackets, not used to the changing weather of this climate.

"Or a short one with the way these horses will run." After they'd gone a couple more miles, Gideon pulled over. "The wind is too strong." He climbed in the back of the wagon.

"What are you looking for?" Yonnie turned around to see what Gideon was doing.

"Is it this?" He held up an overhead cover that would help block the rain. "I don't know if it'll hold in this storm, but we can't keep getting pounded."

The two of them strapped it down and locked the cover into place. "Think it'll hold?" Yonnie examined the wind pushing against the back of the cover.

"Unsnap the back. We can make do with only the top and sides."

Yonnie complied. The sides stopped shaking, relieving the cover of the harsh wind that was blasting them in the face. The rain still kept them plenty wet, but some protection was better than none.

The weather seemed to get worse the closer they got to home. He watched Yonnie, who had his eyes closed and his head down against the gusts of wind. Gideon watched a windmill spin like it was going to take off into the sky.

"This is *narrisch*!" Gideon yelled over to him.

"There's a farmhouse up the way if you want to stop." Yonnie nodded forward to point out the house without removing his arms from around his chest.

As soon as he said it, a circular wall of clouds underneath the largest one created a funnel swirling and twisting faster and faster. Lighting scorched the ground as a dazzling rod of lightning hit the asphalt road behind them.

As they watched the light and sounds, a familiar car drove up behind them. Gideon couldn't miss the dark blue color and fat wheels. A pipe in the back made a loud purr as it drove up behind them. Gideon kept an even stride and did his best to ignore them, but he knew Yonnie couldn't.

"What is that car doing? They can go around." Yonnie was about to wave them on when Gideon put a hand on his arm.

"Don't. Those are the Englishers who have been giving Elsie a hard time. I don't want them to see me. It'll just make it worse."

"When did this happen?" Each time the car jumped forward Yonnie had to stop himself from turning around.

"A while ago. Just when I think it's over, they do something again." Gideon felt much more emotion than he was telling Yonnie. The one good thing was they were taunting him and not Elsie.

They revved the engine and tapped on the back of the wagon, giving the horses a slight jolt. "It's all we can do to ride against this weather, let alone be pushed around by some Englishers." They came up to the side of the wagon and moved closer until they were almost touching the side. Yonnie's angry voice pierced Gideon's ear. "They're gonna run us off the road."

"Hang on." Gideon whistled and then pulled taut on the reins. The horses stopped almost in sync. Gideon pulled on Ross's rein, and he moved back in line with Betsy.

The car moved ahead and stopped in front of them. Gideon held his ground, waiting impatiently for their next move. The car spun its wheels, fishtailed, and sped down the road with tires squealing.

Both horses took off full speed. Gideon tried to keep their strides in rhythm, but they were too frightened, which made for a bumpy ride. They blazed past the house and were in such a high speed the horses had them turning onto the road to home much quicker than they'd expected.

"Those two can fly." Yonnie watched both horses with astonishment.

"Ross, yes, but Betsy's been holding back on me."

Yonnie stared at the dark clouds covering the late afternoon sun. "Looks like it's simmering down."

"Do you want me to drop you off at Beverly's?"

"*Jah*, you'd think those Englishers would grow tired of being the only dog in the fight."

"They don't think the way we do. *Danke* for helping me with that load, and tell Beverly *hallo*." Gideon waved as he drove away without waiting for a reply. Yonnie waved as he ran up to her house, head down, tucked away against the wind.

Elsie's place was down at the end of the road and on the left. He was almost there but slowed as he passed by his family home. A few shingles were missing and a fence was down, but from what he could see, everything seemed to be in good shape.

As he turned down the lane, he looked out over John's cornfield to see the huge cloud gain velocity. It whipped through the ground like a top, chopping up the corn and sending the debris flying in every direction. Since they'd moved to tornado alley, this was the worst storm he'd seen, and he knew there would be more now that summer was here.

By the time he pulled into the Yoders', the Fishers' cornfield was ravaged by the fierce winds. Then the layers of clouds spread and the wind calmed. He watched them break apart into many small billows that continued to shrink until the sky was clear. What was so strong and powerful only a few minutes ago was now an innocent puff of air. Gideon felt God's authority in how He controlled the skies and was humbled. He would build Elsie's and his life together on the Rock, not on sand.

He examined the Yoders' house and grounds. There was minor damage but nothing too concerning, and he felt a sense of relief. Gideon slid down out of the wagon. His wet shirt was drying but still stuck to his skin. The cover of the wagon held out better than he thought it would. Maybe it was that good Amish craftsmanship the Englisher talked about.

As he walked to the house, he noticed the garden that only a short while ago was full of colorful flowers. The lines of vegetables had markers of wooden sticks with names of the plant at the end of each row in Adam's and Aaron's handwriting. The small gate into the garden had a broken hinge that hung to one side. The fence had surrounded the vegetation, and honeysuckle vines had been planted on the outside of the fence, but they were now scattered and torn. It was an amazing transformation from just a few days ago when he saw the beginning stages of cleanup after the winter. And now again it was in ruins and in need of repair.

The back door opened. Elsie came out and ran to Gideon. "I've been worried about you." She wrapped her arms around Gideon's neck, and when she did, the life storms, as well as the earthly one they'd just experienced, disappeared, and all was right for a few short moments.

Chapter Twenty-Five

I CAN'T STAY IN this house one more minute." Katie paced across Elsie's bedroom, stopped at the window, then turned and walked back again.

Elsie sat on the bed watching her fuming with frustration and anger. What Elsie felt was more hurt than anything. "Sit down and talk to him."

"Daed won't even look at me. How am I supposed to have a conversation with him?"

"Maybe when you go through baptism and the rest of what the bishop asks, he'll be better." Elsie knew how stubborn her daed was. His harsh behavior was caused by his broken heart, not that he loved his eldest child any less than when he first laid eyes on her.

Katie plopped down on the bed next to Elsie. "I talked to Will, and he said I was welcome any time." She lifted her upper lip.

Will had not taken the news lightly when Jake didn't return with Katie and knew how conservative their daed was, so he empathized with Katie. The idea took a minute to sink in, but then Elsie decided it could be helpful for Katie and Ruby to be together. "That might be a good idea."

"Really?" Katie studied her face.

"Ruby may appreciate the company. Will's had a hard time getting his crop started, and Ruby's family are all still in Virginia. I think she'd like the company."

"I'll pack my things." Katie was up and around before she finished the sentence. Then they went to tell Mamm.

"Do you two want to help me finish with the mincemeat

sandwiches?" When Mamm turned to see them, she stopped mixing and turned to Katie. "What is it?"

"I've decided to stay with Will." The way Katie said things hurt. She was always direct but even more so now.

Mamm wiped her hands on her apron and leaned against the counter. "Why?"

"It's too hard with Daed." As she spoke the words, Daed came in for the afternoon meal, keeping his eyes downcast, and sat at the table.

"Do you have something to say to me?" He didn't speak her name.

Katie rolled her eyes. But when Elsie looked closer, she saw the tears Katie was trying to push away. "*Now* you talk to me." She threw up her hands dramatically.

"You gonna go running off again?" He took his napkin and laid it across his lap.

"You don't want me here."

Daed stood abruptly and kicked his chair out from under him. "I've wanted you here for the last six months and thirteen days."

Katie stood at attention, her eyes wide with emotions. Their daed was a passionate man, but at this moment he was undone.

"If you leave again, don't come back." His large fists shook at his sides as he stomped out the door.

Katie fell into the chair he'd just abandoned and put her face in her hands. "I can do no right by him."

"You already have, by coming home," Mamm said to her. The boys came flying in, and she went back to preparing lunch. There was no need to upset them.

"Maybe my idea wasn't so good after all." Elsie felt responsible, but she would have explained her reasoning had she gotten the chance.

"This was your suggestion?" Mamm asked but didn't stop working long enough to look at her.

"*Jah*, I thought it would be good for Ruby." She didn't need to explain; her mamm knew of Ruby's struggles.

"Hmm, maybe so, at least until your daed and you can work this out." She placed a sandwich in front of Adam and looked over at Katie. "As long as you come over for a meal once a day."

"You mean to see Daed. Fine! It's better than living here." Katie mumbled the last of what she'd said, and Elsie was grateful. Although Mamm was patient, she would only take so much from Katie.

After they finished their meal, Katie said good-bye to the boys and Elsie got her bag. Will's place was at the other end of the community, so the ride took awhile. Only the sound of the steel wheels crunching on the gravel road was heard until Katie broke the uncomfortable silence.

"If he missed me so much, why does he ignore me?" She was quiet for a moment until Elsie didn't respond, then she started to complain again. "He always said he wished they could have had more children, but because I left, he doesn't recognize his grand-child?" Katie turned to her.

"You know Daed loves you and the baby you're carrying. He just doesn't know how to show it right now. Give him some more time." Elsie clucked at the horse.

"You sound like Mamm." Katie frowned, but Elsie considered that a compliment. Her mamm was a strong woman that Elsie hoped to grow into.

When they got to Will's farm, Ruby answered the door as if she was waiting for them. "*Hallo*, Elsie. Katie, you are radiant."

Katie smiled genuinely for the first time sense Elsie had seen her again. "I haven't heard anyone use that word."

"Ruby reads a lot. You should see the library she's started." When Elsie heard the back door open, she grew tense. If Will could accept this as doing something for his sister and forget that Jake wasn't here, maybe he'd handle this like he should.

Will walked through the kitchen and called out, "Who's here?"

Elsie was glad Will was there and not only Ruby. He was a much more progressive thinker when it came to the Amish ways. In this community he was able to live in a way that better suited him, so he would concentrate on Katie moving forward rather than focusing on decisions she made that the congregation didn't believe were appropriate.

He rounded the corner into the family room. He stopped and stuck his hands on his hips. "Well, if it isn't both of my sisters standing right here in my *haus*." He went to them and gave them both a tight squeeze then kissed them on top of their heads. "You staying for lunch and dinner?"

Ruby shifted her weight, so Elsie dropped the bag on the floor to distract from the talk of cooking.

"What's this?" Will stared at Katie. "You're not leaving again."

"I was hoping to stay with you." Katie's eyes darted between Ruby and Will.

Ruby stared at Will, her eyes pleading for attention before he agreed without her permission.

"Of course you can." Will glanced at Katie's stomach. "You'll have to tell us what you feel like eating. And you can have a room all to yourself down the hall."

Ruby turned pink and hadn't taken her eyes off him. "Will."

He let out a belly laugh. "Sorry, I'm talking too much. It's so nice to have family with us."

"*Jah*, I'd like to talk with you," Ruby told him as soon as he stopped blabbering.

Tension filled the room as silence fell. Katie turned to Will. "Daed and I aren't getting along, especially since Jake's not here."

"I don't blame Daed for that." He didn't seem to care about insulting her, just stared her down until she responded.

"He *is* my husband now, Will."

"You have enough to figure out without worrying about Jake."

Katie's face tightened from battling with Will's assumptions. "I'm not sure what's going to happen. All I know is I need a peaceful place to rest when this baby comes."

Will's eyebrows scrunched together. "You make it sound like it's coming right now."

"William," Ruby scolded, but that was just his way. He wasn't always proper like he should be.

"I'll get your bag after Ruby shows you to your room." He took Katie by the arm.

When Ruby walked by her, Elsie clasped her hand. "*Danke* for taking her in." It was strange to thank someone for doing what they did naturally, but Elsie felt she should to encourage her.

Ruby nodded and went to the stairway without saying a word. Elsie knew this was stressful for her and hoped she'd find some comfort once she got used to having guests. Their community was so large in Virginia that Elsie didn't know her until they moved down here, and even still it wasn't easy.

Elsie heaved a sigh as she left the house. It seemed right for them to be together. But Will's attitude would have to change about Jake, or he needed to keep his thoughts to himself, but that wasn't Will's way.

As she climbed into the buggy, Elsie knew she needed to talk to Gideon about the trouble at the store a few days ago. So much had gone on she hadn't had a chance to be alone with him long enough to tell him.

Riding up to Gideon's house, she admired the even lines of de-tassled corn with no tassels sticking out of the top. It was helpful to have five sons to work the farm, compared to only her daed and two five-and-a-half-year-olds. Will came over to lend a hand and Daed helped him, but mainly during planting and harvest.

Gideon was in the field with a pitchfork throwing hay on a flatbed. The summer sun was overhead beating down on the large field. Gideon's hat was off and his suspenders hung down, bouncing against his legs. His brothers were spread out throughout the field doing the same work.

Elsie stopped and waited. He finally saw her and yelled to his youngest brother to take over for him. As he approached, the straw hat went on, and he flipped his suspenders over his shoulders. "This is a nice surprise." He took out a handkerchief and wiped the sweat from his forehead and neck.

"I know you're busy, so I won't keep you."

"No worries. It's good for him to work by himself." Gideon gestured to his brother who looked like a younger version of him. "I'm glad you came. It breaks up my day."

"I've been meaning to tell you, the day I went to the store, Ruby and I had a run-in with the Englishers."

Gideon's eyebrow lowered as he listened.

"We heard some loud popping noises. Sounded like gunshots. Once I got Angus settled, I saw a bundle of fireworks in the back of the buggy." Gideon's face twisted into what she thought would be anger, but he just shook his head.

"MaryAnn told Omar about the Englishers causing trouble at her place, but he didn't tell me that you were involved."

"I suppose he thought I'd tell you." The run-ins with the English boys were becoming part of their lives to the point it wasn't so much of a surprise anymore. What would it take to make it end? Maybe it wouldn't, and it was their plight.

"They caused us trouble on the way home from town the other day. Tried to run us off the road during that storm, so it turned out to be quite a challenge to get 'em off our tail. Then we got busy doing repairs so I didn't tell you either."

"We should tell Omar, Gideon."

"*Jah*, I'll give him the details you told me. He keeps a record of it all in case something turns around on us."

"He writes it all down?"

"*Nee*, keeps it in his head."

Gideon reached for Elsie's hand and met her eyes. "My favorite story from *Martyrs Mirror* is about the martyr Dirk Williams. He was imprisoned and put in a castle, but he escaped by tying cloth together and shimmying down the side. When a guard saw him, Dirk ran across a frozen lake, making it safely to the other side. The guard pursued him, broke through the ice, then yelled for help. Dirk Williams went back and saved his captor." He smiled faintly. "This will pass."

"Those martyrs sure gave us a lot to live up to." Elsie grinned and gave him a quick kiss on the cheek. He responded by squeezing her hand.

"How is everything at home?" His reluctance was obvious by the way he asked. He glanced over at his brother.

She wanted to tell him what was on her mind, about her daed and Katie. She also wanted to hear his opinion about Katie staying at Will's. But then she decided to enjoy this moment they had together, knowing it wouldn't last long.

⌒ Chapter Twenty-Six ⌒

TIMOTHY'S SILVER TRUCK came roaring down the lane, stopped for a moment, then drove on, leaving a cloud of dust behind. Elsie could see his friendly smile and blond hair as he got closer.

She told the boys to keep an eye on the milking and waited for him. "I'm surprised to see you out in this *narrisch* weather."

He lifted an eyebrow in question.

She saw him almost every day and sometimes forgot he didn't understand most of their Pennsylvania Dutch words. "It's crazy, unpredictable."

"Is everything all right here?" He took a glance around the place. "Looks like the weather vane has gone missing, and the garden needs some CPR."

She furrowed her brows, knowing how he felt only a moment ago not understanding her words.

"It needs help," Timothy explained, and then turned back toward the dirt lane leading to their home. "There's a guy under a tree out front. I've never seen him before, not that I know everyone in the area yet, but pretty darn close."

Elsie glanced at the large maple. Long thick branches covered with healthy, red leaves created a circle of shade around the tall tree. Elsie's curiosity piqued, but with the Englishers persistent intimidation, she didn't want to approach this person alone.

"I'll go with you," Timothy offered, as if reading her mind. "I've heard about some teenage boys bothering the Amish. Has anything happened here?"

Elsie thought about how much had happened over the last year—from moving to these Englishers and to friendships, one of which was with this man she'd come to know and consider a friend. "*Jah*, they like to pick on me. But they may have also done some vandalism in the community too."

Timothy slowed his walk. "What did they say to you?"

"Told us to leave and…said some other things that I don't want to repeat."

Timothy clenched his jaw. His face held the same stone expression Gideon's did when he found out about them. "If this guy is one of them, I'll take care of him for you."

"*Nee*, we don't believe in violence."

"Yeah, but I do." Timothy met her eyes and sighed. "All right, but I'll be sure and get the word out in town. I haven't been paying much attention, but I will now."

"*Danke*. Did you talk to him?"

"Yeah, he said you knew him, so I figured it was all right for him to be here, even though I thought it was strange that he'd plant himself there instead of coming up to the house."

Elsie stopped, realizing who it was. "You don't need to walk me any farther. I'll catch up with you at the barn."

He stood still but kept his eyes on her. "How do you know this guy isn't one of them?"

"*Nee*, this one I know." She started walking again, trying to get a better look at him before he turned around. When Elsie saw his profile, there was no question. His blond hair was cut short, not the Amish way that covered the earlobes. Instead of a bowl trim, his hair was in layers and came up high on the back of his neck. He was wearing denim pants and a T-shirt, nothing like the clothes he wore for the first twenty-two years of his life.

Timothy stayed put as Elsie got closer to the tree but kept a sharp eye on her. She was glad he did, but not for Jake's sake.

"Jake Fisher, what are you doing lying under my maple tree?" She crossed her arms over her chest and stared down at him, wearing a frown. When he opened his eyes, she prepared herself. The sharp blue color melted into hers, bringing back familiar feelings. But they soon passed, replaced with thoughts of Gideon.

"Elsie." He grinned, revealing the dimple in his left cheek. "I've been waiting for you." Jake sat up and put his arms on his knees.

"You could have come up to the door." Anger had built up over the months he was gone, and she had no intention of hiding it. But he didn't seem to know or care.

"And get a berating from your daed? No thanks." He stood then brushed off his pants and ran his fingers through his hair.

"Well, you deserve it."

"Oh, you too, huh?" He seemed amused, not having seen her this upset before.

Elsie turned away. She held her arms tighter in front of her chest and tightened her lips together in frustration. Then she felt him touch her shoulder.

"I owe you an apology. I just don't know how to say it." Then he fell silent. She didn't respond, waiting for more, until he squeezed her arm.

She shrugged his hand away and looked him in the eyes. "That's not good enough."

"I didn't mean to let you think there was more between us then there was. I take the blame for that." He put his hand on his chest as if confessing something of great importance. But she still wasn't satisfied.

"Well, you did."

"I'm sorry." He held out his hands then dropped them to his sides.

"Did you ever tell Katie how you felt?" Then she stopped her thoughts. If he didn't think there was anything between them, why would he?

He shook his head. "I didn't want to upset her or you."

Elsie scoffed. She'd played the fool. Any attention he'd given her was frivolous. The ache in her heart was slowly mending as she spent time with Gideon, and at that moment her feelings for Gideon grew even more.

Jake stared over her shoulder, his eyes squinting. The sun shone down on his face and made his eyes twinkle. "Who's that?"

Elsie almost forgot Timothy was there, but when she looked at him, she didn't seem to be the one he was angry with. "His name is Timothy." She gestured to him.

"I deliver the milk in to town." Timothy came over but didn't offer his usual smile.

Jake offered his hand, and when they shook, Jake's grin grew. "Haven't shaken a hand like that for a long while."

"I don't usually either, but it's become habit since doing the milk runs here."

Elsie liked how Timothy was learning the Amish customs from being around them. He wasn't one that did his job and left; he grew in learning their ways.

"I've been gone for a few months."

"Did you just get here?" Elsie wasn't surprised about Jake's sudden arrival, but others may need more warning than she did. The decisions may be harder with her group from Virginia than the less conservative one that was already here.

"About an hour ago. It took you long enough to come see me down here." He pointed up at the thick trunk.

She let her arms drop down to her sides and squeezed her hands into fists. If Timothy wasn't here, she'd like to tell Jake how mad she was at him—and hurt. "It's not every day I expect someone to be under my tree."

"Better get to those cows." Timothy had been quietly observing, unlike his usual talkative self. He was close enough to catch some of their conversation. Elsie could see it in his eyes; he didn't like Jake.

"I don't miss that. Especially in the summer, hot like it is today. The flies buzzing and the cow's tails slapping around with manure on them. And I always got the kickers. I put a boot on 'em most every time."

"Maybe it's the one milking and not the cow that needs the boot." Timothy walked ahead to hurry them along.

"The Holsteins don't like you to be late when they're gorged with milk," she added to buffer Timothy's comment. "What kind of work do you do in the city?"

"It's only a short-term position."

She stood there waiting for more information.

"I work in a factory, on the line, assembling parts." His wistfulness was gone for a moment but returned when he glanced at her. "It's temporary until I can find something better."

"Why don't you use the carpentry skills your daed taught you?"

He chuckled. "Just as expected, you always try to make everything right." Jake grinned, and that dimpled cheek appeared again.

Elsie felt her forehead tighten. Jake's intuition about her was painfully correct, and she didn't want to hear it. She analyzed everything, to the point of frustration at times. "Does Katie know you're here?"

"No, I've been trying to build up my nerve to go knock on the door." He turned back at the maple tree. "That's why that nice big tree with some green grass under it was so inviting."

It didn't take long for Elsie to realize, but she didn't miss his nonchalant talk or behavior. He'd always been carefree but not to this extent. "Are you planning to stay here all day?"

He shrugged. "If need be. I don't want the door shut in my face."

Timothy turned to leave, and Elsie would much rather help him milk than try to get Jake to muster up his courage to see Katie. But there was her sister to think about. She was so bitter when she first came home, maybe she'd soften with Jake here.

She marched up to the house with Jake at her heels. When they were next to the door, she threw her hands on her hips. "Why are you here, Jake?"

He scoffed. "It's where I should be, right? With Katie and the baby?"

"Why didn't you come with Katie from the start?"

He shifted his glance from the farmhouse to the fields and back to her. "I never felt like I belonged here; still don't," he grunted.

"You were different is all. That's not wrong, but there are rules to follow for the sake of everyone, not just you."

"Here it comes." The bitterness permeated his every word. She didn't know he felt this way. He used to ignore the talk and reprimands when he'd do something that was considered disobedient.

"Once your group came down here, it only got worse, everyone going back and forth on what we could or couldn't do. I guess you use the phone here now. That's why Katie's coming back wasn't a surprise." He turned away. "But I'm sure the baby was." He didn't turn back for a long while.

"Did it scare you?" As strong as Jake was, bringing a new life into the world had to have weakened him.

He nodded and rubbed his nose. "They were only away a few days, and I thought I was gonna go out of my head being away from them."

She smiled at his acknowledgment that there were two separate people in his life now that he was beholding to. "You did the right thing."

He grinned. "Something about this baby makes me think I will." He tightened a fist. "I should have come with them." He shook his head with passion. "But I couldn't stomach the thought of all the rigmarole that they're going to put us through."

"But now you're doing it together." That much she could give him credit for. It couldn't have been easy for him to come back here. She could see him leading an English life, and Katie. But they didn't have the means to have the baby and came back to their family. That's what Amish do, support one another.

"Yeah, and it scares the heck out of me." He stared over to the barn. "Are the boys in there helping you?"

Elsie nodded, wishing she was in there with them. Her anger toward him was mixed with so many things that were slowly dissolving it away. There was a baby on the way. No matter what the circumstances, a new life brought great joy.

Jake followed Elsie into the kitchen and watched her mamm's jaw drop. Katie walked in and yelped, as if she'd stubbed her toe.

208

That brought Daed in to eat his morning meal, but when he saw Jake in his kitchen, his face turned a shade of red Elsie had never seen before.

"I'm going out the finish the milking." Elsie squeezed Jake's shoulder. "Godsend to you." Elsie turned and went back outside. She took in the fresh air and quiet. Timothy was finishing up when she entered the barn. "Almost done. Is everything all right?"

"*Nee*, but hopefully it will be. *Danke* for helping the boys." Aaron and Adam picked up the newspapers used to clean the teats and threw them away. Timothy finished filling the tanks, and Elsie put their bottled milk in the cooler.

"Everything will work out for you and your family, Elsie." With that he nodded and walked to his truck.

Elsie took the boys to the haus. They were full of questions that Elsie didn't want to answer. Once inside they walked quietly until they got into the kitchen. Mamm was hustling to get breakfast on the table so the boys could eat and get ready for church. Daed left as they were coming in, obviously upset, and Katie looked like she was going to cry or yell, one of the two. Jake was nowhere to be seen.

Oh, how she wished she could be taken away from all of this. And then she decided she could be. None of this was hers to deal with at the moment. She went up to her room and got ready for church, needing time to be closer to God without all of the distractions.

When she went downstairs, she sat on the porch and waited. Soon Adam came out and sat down with her, and then Aaron. She was beginning to think no one else was going to join them, which would be unthinkable. But under these circumstances anything was possible.

"Look!" Adam yelled and pointed at a buggy coming down the lane.

"It's Gideon." Aaron ran off the porch, with Adam soon after him. She followed, thanking God with every step she took.

Chapter Twenty-Seven

GIDEON WATCHED THE rows of cotton fields blowing in the wind as they made their way to the Fishers' house. They were going to help the family with the field that was destroyed by the storm. Gideon heard the bishop was coming over to talk with Jake and Katie as well.

"Why does it take something like this to make you appreciate the people in your life?" Elsie glanced over to the field he was admiring.

"Only time with the Lord could help you discover that revelation after everything that's gone on." Gideon appreciated her positive attitude, one that most people in her place wouldn't have.

"The other day I was mad as blazes at Jake, and Katie too. But now I'm glad to have them home again."

"You do have a forgiving heart, Elsie. I only wish you'd do for yourself what you do for others." He watched her and knew she was thinking.

"You mean forgive myself?"

He nodded. "*Jah.*"

"I didn't realize I..."

"If someone measured every thought and deed they did, would you encourage or discourage them to continue?" It was to the point Gideon didn't need to hear her question herself; he could read it on her face when she doubted a decision she'd made or something she'd said to someone, and the list was much larger than that. He was sure once she stopped being so hard on herself, she wouldn't think he was more than just the man that he was.

She tilted her head. "It's been difficult to discern what rules to follow since joining this community. But I suppose I've always been that way to a certain extent."

He smiled, enjoying the morning sunlight catching the lighter colors in her hair. "The English say you're your own worst critic." He tapped her on the nose. "That's you." He let her consider his observation while he tethered the horses.

"Morning." Mose gave the horse a pat on his side. "Omar asked for you."

"*Danke*." Gideon responded flatly then helped Elsie with the food she'd brought. She joined the women who were sizing up the goods.

When Gideon walked into the Fisher home, he remembered how similar this house was to his. The male-dominated room was quite the opposite of the family with six girls. The garden grew a few flowers and many vegetables, unlike Elsie's, which was the reverse. One wall was adorned with a calendar with pictures of landscapes. His own mamm didn't even have that much to look at.

"Omar." They pumped hands. "Unfortunately there was another incident with the English. I thought you'd want to know."

Omar lowered his head and looked down at the wooden floor. "Hmm, our prayers continue, thus keeping us close to the Lord."

His gentle ways kept Gideon where he should be, long-suffering, resembling Omar's example.

Omar put a chubby hand on his shoulder. "Gideon, I would like you to be the scribe while we meet."

Gideon nodded. Documenting wasn't usually done, but due to the two different groups meeting for the first time formally about something of this nature, maybe they felt it necessary.

"Morning, Gideon." Jake's voice was so similar to Mose's it made Gideon pause.

Gideon turned to face him. Katie was by his side, her cheeks rosy, and she had that glow that women have when they're with child. How could that be bad? But the actions they did against the church he understood. Bishop Raber from Virginia may feel differently. He let a lot of rules go, but using a phone or playing Eck ball was much different than what Jake had done.

"Jake, Katie." Gideon felt the need to keep the meeting formal. If the bishop asked him to be a part of this, he needed to be respectful and observant. When he sat down with the others, it felt right, as if the Lord was telling him this was his place.

The elders came in with Minister Zeke. Once everyone was greeted, they all sat down facing Katie and Jake. Gideon sat beside the bishop with pen and paper.

As they went through the process of gathering information, Gideon took down the accounts of Jake and then Katie. The elders and deacon were silent as the bishop asked questions, but not many. Jake convicted himself for what he had done simply by explaining that he'd left without a blessing, married outside their community, and broke his vows. Katie's hands shook when she tried to recall the timing of everything that had happened. Jake was less remorseful but gave a full confession of going against the church.

The bishop was silent for a long while, digesting everything he'd heard. "Jake, do you wish to be a part of this congregation?"

Jake turned to Katie then back to the bishop. "*Jah*, I do."

Zeke stepped in before the bishop could continue. "Discipline is given with great reluctance and only when there is no other way—"

Omar raised a hand to quiet him. The blotchy color of Zeke's face darkened with either frustration or embarrassment that the bishop stopped him. Omar looked to Gideon and made a line in the air to scratch the last comments.

"If you want to be a member of the body, you need to rededicate yourself to Christ, the church, and to the rules of this community. Upon repentance the relationship will be restored and what is in the past stays there." He studied Jake with pensive eyes.

"I suggest you and Katie be married and baptized in the church to be recognized by the community as a wed couple. The congregation takes baptism commitment seriously. The statement is meant to be lifelong. Breaking it means breaching your commitment to the Lord Jesus and the body of believers you will make your vow with. Note that I said *with*, not *to*.

He turned to the elders and Zeke. They conversed with one another, and Omar shook his head, which Gideon assumed meant they had nothing to add.

"We will meet again on the last day of the sixth week from today." The bishop concluded.

Katie nodded her understanding. Jake offered his hand, and the bishop accepted. They had a silent prayer then stood to leave.

Gideon caught Omar's arm. "That went well, but did everyone really agree?"

"We all met before and knew most of what went on. The minister and I made the final decisions after listening to everyone. You know we can't have communion unless the matters are agreed upon. We still have a long way to go to get these two groups to be as one. Thank you, gentlemen." The bishop grinned with satisfaction walked out into the sunshiny day, followed by the others. "Looks like we have some work to do."

Gideon waited for Katie and Jake to come out, and when they did, he clasped a hand on Jake's shoulder. "Are you all right?" he asked Katie, now that Jake would be socially shunned.

"I'm not sure about where I want to be, here or out there, but I can't imagine not being with our families once the baby comes." Katie waited for Jake to meet her eyes, and when he did, tears filled them.

"It sounds like you have some choices to make. I'll pray for discernment." Although their ways were demanding, the expression of repentance was powerful when you were corrected by those who want you to live a spiritually prosperous life.

Gideon looked for Elsie sitting among the women, and as he watched her, he felt blessed. When she caught him staring at her, she raised her brows. He smiled so she'd know all was well and walked out to the field. Nothing unexpected happened; everyone would know the consequences. Now it was up to Katie and Jake as to what they wanted.

Gideon took in the fresh air. Working the earth was considered communing with God and living a sacred lifestyle. The community integrated almost daily to help one another with their farms. Gideon prayed he would always be able to live off the land.

When he went to find his horse, he saw him hitched up to Mose's tiller. When Mose saw him, he stopped at the end of a row. Gideon asked him, "You forget your horse this morning?"

Mose nodded. "Something like that. He came up lame, and Elsie said it would be all right to use Ross."

Gideon was speechless. He glanced over his shoulder to see Elsie staring back at him. Was this a coincidence, or was she trying to get them to play nice? "Sure, mind if I lead?" Gideon was already walking to the driver's side, but Mose waited until he was right next to the wagon to move over. Gideon had never been angry with Elsie, but this might be the first.

The bench seat wasn't long, so their sides touched as they went along. A bump would knock them together, and each time Gideon thought of another unkind word to say to his lovely bride-to-be. He tried to stop the thoughts but couldn't, and somehow he knew how Elsie must feel constantly telling her conscience to turn around and shape up. And it was exhausting.

"Elsie didn't tell me you were coming back out." Mose decided to share after a good twenty minutes of silence.

"Oh?" Gideon didn't want him to have any satisfaction that he might be upset with her, but he wondered how obvious it already was.

At the end of another row Gideon noticed the women bringing out the food. "Praise God for small favors," he mumbled.

"Did Elsie set us up?" Mose was staring at her too.

"I believe she did."

"I suppose we're supposed to tell her everything between us is good."

"It would be if you'd stop giving her so much attention." As soon as it flew out, Gideon wanted to grab it and shove it back in, and instead of feeling better, he felt worse.

"We're never gonna get off this thing if you go in that direction." Mose said it politely, considering it was him.

"What do we need to do to satisfy her?"

"Get along I suppose."

It was silent again except for the steel wheels crushing fragments of corn stalks. "We're courting now."

"I figured." Mose turned his head and stared at Gideon. "Congratulations."

"Do you mean that?"

"I think so." Mose grinned and then started laughing. It was catching; Gideon started in too.

"Well then, *danke*." Gideon wasn't totally comfortable telling Mose, but he was one person Gideon really wanted to know they were a couple, and he hadn't laughed like that for a while. "What about you?"

Mose grinned. "I'm not in a hurry." He pointed to the row so Gideon would know they were not on line. "You're off."

Gideon held onto his temper, or pride, whichever it was. "This isn't gonna work with the two of us, and it's my horse."

"It's my tiller," Mose shot back.

Gideon shook his head and let out the breath he was using to hold his temper in. This was going to be a long day.

Chapter Twenty-Eight

BEADS OF SWEAT covered Elsie's face as she jolted up from her sleep. She flopped back down in her bed and squeezed her eyelids together trying to remember what she'd dreamed. She knew she wouldn't be able to go back to sleep, so she got up and knelt by her bed to say her morning prayer. The dream seemed further away now, so she got ready for the day. She remembered tonight was youth singing. That took her mind off of her heavy heart. Now with Jake and Katie settled in, her mind refocused on the Englishers.

The flash of a picture in *Martyrs Mirror* came to her. She'd looked up Dirk Williams, the man who saved his pursuer. There was a reason Gideon introduced her to *Martyrs Mirror*. He didn't know it at the time, but the timing was all God's. How many occasions had she referred to the book since the recent trials in her life started? More than she could count. She learned from Gideon's example to look at the past to better see the future.

"You're up early." Daed stood in the open doorway as Elsie pinned her kapp. He was always the first one up to feed the livestock and get the milking started if he got to it before Elsie did.

"Bad dream."

"Sorry, honey. What was it about?" When he tapped her on the nose, she thought about how differently it felt when Gideon did the same thing. Elsie didn't know she could admire a man as much as she did Gideon. Growing into the woman she wanted to be was even more important because of him. Although the trials had been difficult, Elsie decided they wouldn't defeat her. Yet following through would still be a challenge.

She sat on her bed and Daed came closer. "I can't remember, only that it was unpleasant?"

"Have those Englishers stopped their mischievousness?" He frowned. "They've still not hurt you? Not even a hair on your head."

"*Nee*, they've become more of a pest than anything." That is, if they didn't start the fire, but she didn't want to mention that.

"They have to tire of us sooner or later." His chubby cheeks filled with a smile. "It will pass."

She tilted her head. "That's what Gideon says."

"Then it must be true." As Daed walked out, he hummed and went downstairs. His mood was so different than when Katie was there, as if he built a wall against her to shut out the hurt and the pain. That only made things worse between them, but both were too stubborn to drop their guard.

Elsie met her mamm in the kitchen. After the morning meal Mamm held out a box of preserves, pickled vegetables, and some stewed tomatoes. "Would you take these to Ruby's for me?"

Elsie grinned. "I'm sure Katie is eating well at Ruby's."

Mamm quickly glanced at her. "Well, of course she is. With our family shrinking by the day, I don't want this food to go to waste."

"I don't mind the ride over. I'd like to see how they're getting along." Elsie was almost out the door when her mamm spoke.

"Ask your brother if they need anything, will you?"

"*Jah.*" That was Mamm's way of saying see what he missed eating and she'd make it for them.

When she got to Will's, she watched him working in the field. His thick brown hair glowed in the sunshine and his muscles bulged from the strenuous activity. He was tall like her daed. He seemed lonely, all by himself—so different than when they were growing up when he and Daed worked together.

Elsie rapped on the front door and stepped inside. "Ruby." She heard someone bustling around in the kitchen and headed that direction. She placed the basket of food on the counter and turned to her sister-in-law.

Ruby's face went flush when she saw her. "Oh, Elsie, I'm so glad to see you." She dropped the potato in her hands and wiped them on a towel.

"Is something wrong?" Elsie thought of all the things that could be upsetting her. Was Katie being her difficult self? Or did Jake come by and say something without thinking, which was so common for him to do. Or was it Will?

"Katie seems upset, but I don't know why." She glanced over Elsie's shoulder and continued. "I've tried to talk with her, but she says she's fine." Katie came in, and they both turned to her.

Katie's face turned almost the same crimson color Ruby's did when Elsie first walked in. "What brings you here, sister?"

Her tone warned Elsie to be cautious, but she wouldn't play into her antics either. "Is everything working out here for everyone?" Elsie looked at Ruby first and then to Katie.

"Sure," Katie rummaged through the basket, deterring the conversation. "Thank goodness, homemade jams."

Elsie looked to Ruby for her answer. "I'm not sure."

"What do you mean?" Elsie asked Ruby but was looking at Katie.

Katie huffed out a breath. "It's hard to be here is all."

"Where, at our home?" Ruby's eyes misted. Elsie put a hand on her shoulder.

"I'm sure it has nothing to do with you, Ruby." Elsie stared into Katie's eyes.

"*Nee*, it's..." She exhaled. "Are you going to singing tonight?"

Then it all fell into place. "*Jah*, oh, I see." Elsie's eyes softened, and she went to her sister. She was hard to love at times, but deep down she had a soft spot, and Elsie was grateful to see that side of Katie again.

"I used to have so much fun at those." She loosened her arms from around Elsie's waist. "It's times like these that I don't feel ready to have a baby." She put a hand on her belly that Elsie noticed had definitely grown since she moved in with Will only a few weeks ago. "But then I feel this little one move or kick, and I fall in love with her all over again."

"Her?" Elsie smiled.

"Just a guess." Katie grinned back. "It's hard for Jake to be at his parent's house and me here. But I know it's temporary."

Ruby stared at the two of them, bewildered. "So, it's not my cooking?"

A bubble of laughter trickled out, and then Katie joined in. Ruby smiled her relief.

"You've gotten better, Ruby." Katie's encouragement was exactly what Ruby needed, and Elsie gave a little prayer of thanks. She bid them good-bye so she could get her work done in time for singing.

As Elsie made her way back to the buggy, she heard the pounding of a hammer behind the house. She curiously walked back to see a skeleton structure of a small building, a shed or maybe a chicken coop. Jake gingerly stepped across the wooden beams as he made his way over to her. "What brings you here?" He jumped down and landed on both feet, bending at the knees.

"That was quite a jump." Elsie looked up at the distance he'd cleared and shook her head. He was never cautious when it came to the barn raisings or building dawdihaus's for the grandparents in the community. He always took on the wildest horse in the herd to break and was the first to take a dare. This was one of those times she appreciated Gideon even more. "How are things here with Will and Ruby?"

"*Gut*, but it's strange not sharing a room with my wife."

"*Jah*, I can see that, but you will be soon enough."

"Living here makes me want our own place." He stuck a thick blade of grass in his mouth and chewed. "Think we might stay."

She was relieved for the two of them and their little one on the way. She wanted to be a part of this child's life, and not from many miles away. "I'm glad to hear that. Have you told anyone?"

"*Nee*, but I plan to at the baptism."

"And Katie agrees?"

"She's why I'm doing all this." He spit the wad of grass out of his mouth.

Elsie paused. "The commitment you're making isn't for Katie; it's between you and God."

"I know all that. It's about doing the right thing." He said it so proudly, like he was doing a favor for someone.

Elsie wasn't sure how to approach this. Jake knew what the commitment meant and what his part in that was. He met with the leadership council before church each week to be reinstated. They had gone over all of this with him. But was he doing this for the right reasons? "Have you talked to the deacon or bishop about your motivations in joining the church?"

"Ah, Elsie. You are always so good to follow the rules." He cocked his head to the side and grinned.

"If that were true, I wouldn't be talking to you." The first weeks had passed by quickly, but it had still not been the full six weeks since Jake was shunned. Yet Elsie was too concerned about her sister's welfare because she couldn't talk to him.

He grunted, amused by her response. "But still, how can I compare to your ideals?"

She pulled back as if a gust of wind hit her. "This has nothing to do with me. It's about you and why you're going through ceremony and why you should live here or not." He had done it again—pulled her in and shocked her back out again. But this time she wouldn't let him persuade her to fix this. Gideon was one being considered for the ministry and would be observing the ceremonies; whose better hands to leave Jake's fate to?

"I'll be praying God's direction for you, Jake. And patience for me." With that she turned away, knowing the conversation wouldn't go where she wanted it to. Then she realized she'd given too much favor to Gideon. It was in God's hands.

Elsie took quick steps away from Jake when she heard him chuckle at her last words. She got into her buggy and went straight home. Then Elsie got ready for singing and waited for Gideon on the porch swing. Solomon came out when Gideon pulled in. He walked over to Gideon as he rubbed the back of his neck.

"I'd like you to keep the top off when you go to singing." The more conservative groups rarely put the top on, especially when there wasn't a chaperone. Gideon's group was not concerned, but Elsie knew he would respect her father's request.

"I have no problem with that, Solomon, unless it rains," Gideon grinned.

"Don't even say it." Solomon wagged a finger at him. "Have fun you two." Solomon shook Gideon's hand instead of giving him the usual slap on the back, tipping Elsie off that he must be feeling sentimental.

As soon as he turned the horse around, Elsie was filling Gideon in on her day. "Why are you so quiet? Am I talking too much?"

"*Nee*, this is different for me to go to singing with you instead of with Yonnie."

She laughed. "Did you hear they picked out names? The Virginians are the Purple Martins and your group is the Meadow Larks, along with the new community."

"They are a 'higher' group like we are, so it makes sense."

"I've never liked being called the 'low' group."

"You conservative Virginians." He grinned and shook his head in jest.

"We're not near as conventional as we used to be."

"Are you comfortable with the changes?" His eyebrows drew together as he waited for her answer. These were decisions they would have to seriously think about when they were announced as a couple.

"In some ways, yes. But it's become more confusing, and that's caused problems that we didn't have before. Everyone used to know what the customs were and the consequences if you didn't follow them. Here everything is questioned between the two group's councils, and when they don't agree, there's friction."

"True, but overall our two groups have done well together compared to some others who couldn't get along. Some even went so far as to pack up and go back up north." Gideon steered Betsy up the lane and parked beside the many decorated carriages.

Some were dropped off, but others from the Purple Martin parents who had younger teenagers stayed to supervise, as well as the parents who were from the new community. The ages ranged from sixteen to well into their twenties. This time together wasn't so much testing their limits as it was a time to socialize and find a life partner.

Volleyball nets were set up in a row on a grassy area in Omar's yard. The teams were varied as far as age and gender. They played with vigor, diving and flying up to spike the ball. This went on for hours until it was time for supper.

Gideon found Elsie in the crowd and wiped the sweat from his brow. "Great group of newcomers."

"*Jah*, that's *gut*." It was nice to finally meet the new Amish. She also wished Katie was part of this. But she was married and with child, living a completely different life than before she left.

They filed into Omar's home, which was set up the same as when they had church. The men went into the kitchen, and the women sat opposite of them in the other room. The first song was chosen, and one member stood up and led. The chorus was always loud, but with the added group their voices were even louder. Gideon grinned at her, obviously feeling the strength from the added voices.

The temperature in the room increased due to so many people together and the gas lamps. In the second hour they sang faster tunes, all in German. Elsie watched Gideon sing with the boys, belting out notes from deep inside of him. Then she sang with the girls during another part of the song. Cups of water were passed around to cool down parched throats.

The parents sang along with them and then left to prepare the snacks. Plates of cookies, small whoopie pies, popcorn, and chips were passed around, as well as drinks. The low mumble of voices filled the room and warmed the bishop's home.

They slowly wandered out, leaving in their buggies. Some of

the guys asked a girl if she needed a ride home, which was their way of showing interest in courting. Others went to the barn where they sat and talked a while longer.

"This was our first singing," Gideon mentioned as Elsie walked with him to his buggy.

"We've been dozens of times; do you mean with the new group?" Then she realized what he was saying. She beamed at him and stopped. "*Jah*, it was."

He took a step forward and reached for her hand. "But you've never let me hold your hand at singing before."

She scanned the area to see if anyone was looking, pushed up on her tiptoes, and gave him a playful kiss on the cheek. "And you've never kissed me at a singing before."

"I'd like to, but I'm trying to be a gentleman." Although Gideon was a couple years older than Elsie, he still knew to be discreet. But he wouldn't be treated like a youthful teenage boy either.

She watched him look around and meet eyes with Omar, who smiled and gave him a nod.

"But I think I just got permission."

Chapter Twenty-Nine

ELSIE TUGGED AT the weeds creeping into her garden. The chili peppers were starting to come in. She was partial to the spicy vegetable, which they didn't have in Virginia. The sweet potatoes and tomatoes were growing strong, but the squash wasn't doing so well.

The end of the summer was full of work for the upcoming autumn events. Those being baptized or married would need to complete their preparations, attending meetings with the church leadership until the ceremonies. And there would be the announcements of those courting. Then fall harvest would consume their time until the winter months.

"You're working hard." Jake's voice used to waken her spirit, but now she anticipated something was wrong each time she saw him.

"I shouldn't talk to you, Jake." It was well after the noon meal with plenty of chores to be done.

"Came to see Solomon." He stuck his hands in his pockets, something most Amish didn't have, and watched her analyze him.

"He's in the back of the barn." She wanted to ask him what he was up to but didn't want to give him the pleasure. Daed hadn't given him a second of his time since he'd returned and most likely wouldn't until Jake made himself right with not only the ceremonies but also with the family.

"Is he doing some woodwork?"

She nodded. He didn't move, as if reluctant to talk with Solomon. She gestured to the weeds she'd let get the best of her vegetable garden.

Jake didn't respond. Time in the city seemed to change his

desire to work the land. Maybe working on an assembly line was more satisfying for him.

"I'll see you on my way out." He started toward the barn and looked back a couple of times. Her curiosity grew when she saw him stand by the barn door for too long, second-guessing himself.

The next thing Elsie heard was her daed yelling. She jumped up and ran to the barn. When she got there, Daed had his back to the door and Jake.

"Solomon, I'm not leaving until you hear what I have to say." Jake waited for a moment. When Solomon didn't respond, he started in again. "I'm sorry about the way things happened. Katie knew you'd be upset about her leaving, so we left without telling you."

Daed turned on his heel to face him. "You dare to blame my daughter?"

"*Nee*, it was both of our decision. I should have left without her, but she wanted to go with me."

Solomon leaned forward, his neck stretched like a chicken. "Your role as a man is to protect your wife, not take her to outsiders who don't know or care about you or her."

"I take full responsibility, Solomon, and you can stay angry with me, but for Katie's sake, talk to her."

"I don't know you or her until you have made your vows under God." His voice softened slightly, but the rage was still in his eyes. Elsie didn't know if he'd even seen her standing there, but he was so upset it didn't matter.

"I'm doing this for Katie. I can't stand to see her so upset because you won't acknowledge her. Ignore me if you will, but don't keep pushing Katie away."

Elsie was stunned by Jake's words. He was as confident as ever, yet respectful, and spoke with emotion. As hard as Daed was on the outside, he was soft as jelly when it came to matters of the heart.

Daed turned back to the thick wood table where his latest project set. Jake's jaw twitched, and he ran his fingers through his hair. "It's one thing to ostracize Katie, but there's the baby to think of."

At that moment Solomon moved away from the project he was so protective of. Elsie's breath caught when she saw a beautifully hand-crafted cradle. The birchwood with a deep brown stain brought out the etching of clouds in the headboard, one with an angel floating on top.

Elsie turned to Jake. His mouth opened, and his eyes darted from Solomon and back to the cradle. He wiped his nose and nodded to Solomon. "*Danke.*" Then turned and walked past Elsie and out the door.

The next day Elsie watched Gideon pull up in front of her house with the trailer. The service was being held at their home today. She was glad. It would be good for Jake. He was overwhelmed and uncertain about all that was expected of him. He and Katie went to the marriage classes with Elsie and Gideon. Katie and Elsie were going to be baptized today as well. Most importantly, Jake needed to make a confession to be reinstated into the church.

"Morning, sunshine." Gideon was carrying one of the new benches that were made to replace the chairs. "This is an important day."

She smiled as he walked into the house. Elsie felt a certain contentment hearing Gideon's enthusiasm for the step she was about to take. She had no doubt in her mind about what this meant to her and the community. Without a formal commitment the church would become meaningless and weak.

When Jake's family drove up in their buggy, they gathered benches to take into the house. Jake rode with Katie and Ruby in Will's buggy, but he went over to help his family. Although there was no talking, his actions spoke volumes. His mamm's eyes misted, and his daed gave Jake a skeptical nod. His brothers' responses ranged from a glance to completely ignoring him.

Elsie's mamm and daed never doubted she would be baptized and dedicate herself to the church and that she and Gideon would marry. She was the daughter that "didn't give them any surprises," as her daed said. Elsie wondered what made Katie rebel against what he felt was sacred.

As she watched Jake take a seat in front of her, she remembered back to the previous Sunday when they were at their last session. Jake had gone to the session this time and went over the process. Candidates had a final chance to change their minds. When they reminded the male candidates they were also committing to the possibility of serving the church ministry, Jake looked at Katie and then to Elsie.

When the two sermons were over and songs from the Ausbund were sung, the deacon and Bishop Omar stood before the congregation and asked the candidates to stand. One at a time they knelt and were asked questions. Then Zeke poured water through the bishop's hands and over the individual's head. The bishop gave a holy kiss to the males, and Omar's wife gave one to the females. They then stood and joined the congregation. They went through the process one by one until the very last candidate, who was Jake.

"Have you read and understand the *Dordrecht Confession* and what that founding document represents?" The bishop's face was stern with no inflection as he waited on Jake's response.

"*Jah*, I have," Jake said without hesitation.

"Do you renounce the devil and the world to commit to Christ?"

"I do."

"Will you, Jake, honor Christian values and follow the guidelines of the Ordnung?"

Jake stood stone still with no response. The congregation was silent. The women stopped fanning themselves even though the heat was suffocating in the house full of people.

"Jake, will you abide by the rules of this church district?"

Jake turned to the side and caught Katie's eye. Her pale cheeks flushed, slowly moving down her neck. Elsie saw Katie look down.

Elsie shut her eyes, and as she did, she prayed, hard. She heard the bishop ask one more time.

Zeke stood and lifted his finger in the air and opened his mouth to speak, but Omar turned his hands down for him to sit. He turned back to Jake.

"Do you confess your sins against God and the body of this church, Jake?"

Elsie didn't ask for him to say yes, or no, but for God's divine plan, whatever that was for Jake, Katie, and their unborn child. When she opened her eyes, Jake was walking out the door.

"*Nee*," she whispered. "This can't happen." She struggled to follow through with her offer for God to decide. She scanned the room to see faces filled with astonishment and heard the soft buzz of conversation. Elsie went after him. She hadn't gone too far before she saw him walking down the main road. "Jake, where are you going?"

When she got closer, he stopped abruptly. "Why should I be shunned for what I did?"

Elsie searched for patience. Why was he so incredibly selfish? "You were married in a courthouse, not under God. Many couples go to premarital counseling, like you did when you came back here. 'To do the right thing,' remember? And you left the body of the church with no discussion or permission. Besides all that, didn't you ever think about how worried we all were?"

"There's so much to get back in with this place again." He scanned the snakelike creek that flowed behind the haus. "This is why I didn't come back right away. I can't do this."

She heard steps behind her crunching on the gravel road. Others were waiting and wondering. "The bishop was very good to reinstate you, and this is what you do with that gift?" She was as mad as he was and wasn't scared to let it show. Whatever he did, Elsie feared Katie might follow, and she didn't want to lose her sister again.

"How is that a gift?" His brows puckered.

"For someone who cares enough to help you get back on the right path is the greatest gift one can give or receive."

"To the Amish I may have broken the rules." He put his hands on his hips and looked to the sky. "But I didn't feel I was on the wrong path." He turned to Elsie.

"None of us do, Jake. That's why we go through baptism so the body of the church can help us along the way." Elsie knew he understood all of the teachings, but somewhere during his time away he changed his view of them and what they stood for.

"I thought about what you said the other day, about who I'm doing this for. I'll take my chances on my own."

"You're leaving?"

"Katie and the baby will be better off without me." He looked over Elsie's shoulder, took a deep breath, and then jogged down the lane.

Elsie didn't know what to say, so she let him go without a word. As hard as this was, maybe it was for the best. But getting Katie to see that wouldn't be so easy.

"Where is he going?" Katie came up behind Elsie, laboring from the short walk. She held her stomach and watched Jake walking away. "Why didn't he finish the ceremony?"

Elsie didn't have the answers, and what little she did understand, Katie didn't want to hear. She was hurt and confused for Katie, not knowing what to do or say. "I don't think he feels comfortable here."

"That makes three of us." Elsie heard Katie's breathing increase. "If he leaves now, I don't ever want to see him again." Katie turned and marched back into the church where people stood waiting. She needed to. Someone had to face reality.

Chapter Thirty

GOING OUT FOR a meal was rare, but Gideon thought it would be a nice gesture to support the Amish family who opened up their own restaurant. And after all that happened with Jake, he thought it would be a good diversion for everyone. The two people hurt by Jake's actions the most were too stubborn to talk about it. So Solomon and Katie kept the fire smoldering inside just big enough that made them impossible to live with.

He wanted to have time alone with Elsie, but when he drove up in his buggy, Katie was the first one out the door. "You're moving pretty quickly, considering." He smiled and she tried to reciprocate, but the corners of her lips refused to lift.

"Does your daed know I'm here?" Although Gideon knew that Solomon trusted him, he followed along with protocol.

"*Jah*, of course."

He went up the stairs and followed her to the two blue rockers on the porch. "How are you feeling?"

"You mean about the baby?" She waved a hand at him and nodded. "I was ready to do this alone when I first came back, but then when Jake came here, I started to think we could really be a family." Her shoulders sank. "He didn't even ask me to go with him."

Besides Gideon's surprise that she would come to someone for advice, he hadn't seen Katie vulnerable. Even her actions were not her usual calm but sharp demeanor, but then this was important. He had to tread lightly to earn her trust.

"I think he did what he thought needed to be done." Gideon

didn't expect to make her feel better. He would be lying to tell her anything different than what he thought was true.

Katie's forehead wrinkled in confusion. "Leaving us? How can that be right?"

"He felt he couldn't fulfill his responsibilities."

"Why do you think that?" She paused and started again with a boisterous voice. "I know he wasn't ready. The pregnancy wasn't planned, but then most aren't here, so I thought it would be the same with ours." She stopped and rubbed her belly. "If we wouldn't have left the city, I think we might have stayed together."

Gideon moved closer to her so he could speak softly and hopefully persuade her to do so as well. Her anger was understandable, but he wanted to have a calm conversation. "Then why did you leave?"

"I was scared. And when you're scared you go home, right?"

Gideon appreciated her admitting she was frightened and felt more empathy for her. "I wouldn't know. I've never left my community. But if you do decide to stay here, it would do you well to surrender your bitterness."

She stared at him as if he'd asked her the impossible, and right at this moment it probably felt that way. "But I can't let this go."

"Not offering forgiveness is a heavy load to bear. To forgive is to trust."

She grunted. "I can't trust Jake."

"I suppose I'd feel the same. But it's not about Jake; it's trusting in God."

"How can I do that? I'm so mad at Jake I can't imagine letting him get away with doing this to me and our baby." Her face contorted, fighting off a sob.

Gideon remained silent until she composed herself. This was a lot to ask of her, so out of her nature, it would take obedience and encouragement to get her to where she needed to be to find peace.

She met his eyes with hers full of tears. "How can you forgive someone who has so completely wronged you?"

"Grace, God's redemption. I don't know God's answer for you, but I do know that He'll show you the way." He knew of Katie's independent ways, so he didn't want her to think there was any other way then His way.

She shook her head. "I can't do what you're asking."

"Follow your *glaawe*, faith. I'm not saying it's easy. But if we offer up our anger to God, evil loses power." The silence that came was comforting. Katie sat back in the chair and rocked slowly.

"Jake said to me once that leaving the community for him was like looking down into the unknown but knowing you have to jump."

When Gideon heard that he became concerned. It would be difficult to forgive someone with such reckless abandonment. But no, he wanted to believe in her.

"I don't feel so good. I think I'm going to lie down." Her face went pale, and she took deep breaths.

"I'll go in with you and get some water."

"*Danke.*" She got up with difficulty and made her way into the house. Dinner out could wait for another time when everyone could go. When he got a whiff of the food from the kitchen, there was no doubt they'd be eating an early supper at the Yoders.

"And your daed may need help." He was installing crown molding, corner blocks, and long pieces of layered wood strips along the ceiling edges.

"Nice work." Gideon placed his hands on his hips and watched Solomon standing on the top of a ladder.

"I've been wanting to do this since I took up carpentry." He climbed down and admired his work with Gideon. They discussed how to proceed together on the project as the women quilted. Gideon couldn't help but hear them talk, although he found it distracting him from his work at times.

"Ouch!" Rachel jumped.

Elsie grinned as Rachel stuck a finger in her mouth.

"It's not funny, Elsie." Meredith frowned at her. "Are you all right, Rachel?"

"*Jah*, I do that all the time." She turned to Elsie. "But you don't have to be so amused by it," she teased.

Ruby scanned the intricate piece of work. "This is going to be a beautiful quilt. Are you going to sell it at the bizarre?" Gideon sensed that Ruby felt comfortable quilting with everyone. The tension had lessened even more when Jake left.

"*Nee.*" Rachel looked over at Elsie.

"We're going to give it to Katie." Elsie glanced at Katie, who was lying on the couch.

Katie sat up and stared at the quilt, then at Rachel and Elsie. "Really?"

Gideon and Solomon stopped working for a moment. Everyone did, including Katie, who sat up trying to get comfortable.

Elsie smiled. "We thought you would appreciate it."

"It's a comfort quilt after all," Rachel justified.

"You mean you think I need it."

Gideon cringed. It was hard to know how Katie meant what she said. Gideon saw Elsie put a hand on Rachel's shoulder to let it pass. If Katie only knew how long it took Elsie to talk Rachel into giving the quilt to her, she would be eating crow, maybe.

"Well, I will need it. It's no easy thing to have Jake leave," Katie said, but she didn't meet Rachel's eyes.

They had done well to stay in the same room together for as long as they did. Watching the dynamics of a group of women was interesting but painful at times.

"*Danke*; it is a beautiful pattern." Katie stroked the quilt. It was earth tones to settle the soul.

"I have something for you too." Ruby handed Katie a blue baby blanket. "Your mamm made it."

Gideon watched Elsie's eyes dart over to Meredith, unsure of what to think of the gesture. They knew Ruby wasn't a great cook; maybe she couldn't sew either.

"I wanted to keep it in the family. It's so beautifully made."

Ruby admired the blanket Katie held up. It was one of Meredith's vintage blankets that all the women raved about.

"Maybe it's time for a break." Elsie smiled at Ruby as she stuck the needle in a pin cushion. "I've made some comfort food." That got a good laugh, and everyone made themselves useful in the kitchen. Elsie opened the lid to the pot of chicken and dumplings she'd made that morning.

Gideon couldn't help but give Ruby a glance. By her facial expression he saw her discomfort. Ruby had made great strides, and he hoped she continued to. It wasn't always a given that everyone in a family, especially a large one, would all get along.

"And there's vanilla pudding for dessert for Katie," Meredith announced.

"I wouldn't have gotten through this pregnancy without vanilla pudding." Katie waddled over to the table and sat next to Rachel before she had a chance to maneuver to a different seat. Gideon shook his head. They were permanently in the third grade when they were together.

Gideon looked around at the bustle of people in the room and scooped another spoonful of dumplings. He went out onto the porch where Elsie was sitting in a chair with her plate on a small spindled table. He sat beside her, and she put her cheek in her palm, watching him.

"Thanks for helping Katie."

"I don't know that I did, but you're welcome." He took another bite in thought. "She's going to need a lot of courage to start a life over without Jake."

"Katie's brave."

"This is different, not leaving your home and moving into the city. This is walking away from someone you care about to live a fruitful life."

"I see." She poked her fork around in her potatoes then dropped it onto the plate.

"I hate to see her go through this. I hope she'll find meaning in the suffering."

"I guess it's as they say, it will be a new normal for Katie."

Elsie's face became hard. "All because some don't believe the rules apply to them."

"You mean Jake. *Nee*, he didn't believe in what the Ordnung stands for. But it's good he admitted that before he took a vow he didn't accept as truth."

They finished eating and moved to the porch swing. Will came to pick up Ruby and stayed for a short time, then everyone left. Silence slowly covered the house as darkness filled the sky. The click of Meredith's shoes traveled to each room as she closed up the house.

When all the lights were off but the porch lamp, Gideon moved forward. "I guess I should go."

Elsie pushed him back into the swing and took his hand in hers. "The sun hasn't set yet."

He chuckled. "All but a sliver."

"Daed said we could be alone out front as long as the sun was up."

"I think the rules will change once the minister announces our marriage, at least a little."

"That sounds nice, *our* marriage." She stared up at him with her milk-chocolate brown eyes that held such a look of contentment he couldn't help but stare. He had been long in waiting for her to finally come to him, and even now he had to remind himself that she felt the same way he did.

He kissed her palm then held her close. It was at that moment he questioned if she ever truly would, really could, care for him the way he loved her. For the Amish love was not always the main reason a couple would wed. Theirs was more of a practical union. You were fortunate if you also had a great affection for your mate and them for you.

When the last streak of sunlight fell behind the horizon he stood, taking her hand as she reluctantly followed one step behind him.

"Good night, Elsie Lapp." He grinned and started down the stairs one slow step after another.

She giggled. "I'm not a Lapp yet."

"Just wanted to see what it sounded like." And as it rang again in his ears, he liked what he heard.

Chapter Thirty-One

As they trotted down the road into town, Gideon kept an eye out for the young men who nearly drove him off the road the day of the storm. It was one thing for him to take the chance of meeting up with them, but he didn't want Elsie in harm's way. He noticed she hadn't been in town for a while, but he wanted her to see the new arrival of buggies with him.

As they pulled into town, Gideon noticed Elsie scanning the area. It had been long enough since she'd seen the English boys he hoped she wouldn't worry.

"It's early to eat lunch. Do you want to look around?"

"*Jah*, one place in particular." His grin gave him away. She stared at him with suspicion.

"And where might that be?"

Gideon tethered the horses to a coin meter. "We're standing in front of it." He took Elsie's hand and guided her into the shop. They went outside to the side of the building where the buggies were lined up to show. Multiple colors of white, yellow, black, and gray were only a few that were displayed; tops were optional.

"Look, Gideon, sliding doors." Which was unlike the side curtains they both had on their family buggies.

"Turn signals. I wonder how these are powered."

"Car battery." Jonas walked up and pumped Gideon's hand. He was short with a thin frame and lived in their community.

"I was hoping you'd be here."

"You should have told me. I don't usually work Saturdays. Elsie, how's your family?"

"Very well, *danke*." Elsie smiled then listened to them banter.

Gideon was enthralled with all of the options. There were

Plexiglas windshields with wipers, hydraulic brakes, rubber wheels, and many other decisions to make. When he'd narrowed it down, he turned to Elsie. "So, which one do you like?" He watched her eyes widen.

"It's not for me to decide." Her eyebrows drew together in question, so he explained.

"The buggy is for us." He smiled.

She put a hand on her chest. "But Gideon, that's a lot of money."

He nodded. "I've been planning for this for quite a while." He and his daed had saved for a long time, even before Elsie ever came into the picture. Money wasn't an option, but he knew her well enough to know that she'd be frugal.

She took her time studying the various buggies lined in a row. "I don't know if I'm bold enough to get a bright color, maybe gray instead of black."

He chuckled to himself. "That's probably wise. We wouldn't want to upset the bishop."

"Some Amish are getting the colored models." Jonas pointed to a yellow one next to them. "But they're from the new community east of here."

"If things keep changing, maybe we'll end up with a bright blue one someday," Gideon teased, and Elsie gasped.

Jonas and Gideon went over the paperwork as Elsie looked out the large picture window. She looked up and down the street at the tourists and families who walked down the sidewalks shopping or buying produce, mainly Amish made. Some of the shop owners were disgruntled with the Amish moving in on their sales, but most appreciated them bringing in the business.

As Gideon waited for Jonas to get their affairs taken care of, he watched Elsie look up into the hot summer sky and then in front of her. An English boy walked her way. He noticed her put a hand to her chest and draw in a breath as he approached. He slowed his gait when he noticed her staring at him, but he didn't stop walking. Gideon tried to discern if it was one of *the* English boys as he passed her, but before he could get a good look, the young man was gone. Elsie seemed to be doing the same. She took a deep breath and found a place in the shade, waiting for Gideon.

When he finished with Jonas, he joined her outside. "Are you all right?"

"I keep thinking I'll see one of them."

"Fear is guiding you, and there is nothing *gut* that will come of that."

She seemed to shake it off. "*Jah*, it does no *gut*, only brings more worry."

Gideon beamed as he moved closer to her. "We are now proud owners of our own gray buggy."

She clapped her hands. "When can we take it home with us?"

"Today! That's why I brought two horses. Jonas will have it ready for us when we've finished eating."

"I know you're not supposed to be proud, but I appreciate your diligence in saving for this."

"I am a little proud, but don't tell anyone." Gideon grinned then clasped her hand and led her to the Essenhaus Style Inn. The front windows were adorned with flower boxes filled with multicolored tulips. The house was a light shade of yellow with white trim.

Elsie read the sign. "The eating house?"

"Most of the customers will never know what that sign says, but by the looks of it, they like the food." Patrons came in and out one right after the other. People stood waiting for tables with fussy children in hand.

When they entered, Gideon was greeted by one of the daed's fair-haired girls. "Gideon, I'm glad you came." Her blue eyes twinkled then set on Elsie. "*Hallo*."

Elsie nodded. "Were you expecting us?"

"We were hoping Gideon and Yonnie would come visit our restaurant. Come this way." She led them to a booth and got them both water.

She handed them a menu. "Hasenpfeffer is the special. Take your time, and I'll be right back."

"I haven't eaten rabbit in some time."

Elsie scanned the selections with interest. "I think I'll stick with pot roast."

She read the menu and read the descriptions. "They are very authentic."

"The tourists probably like it. I hope they know what they're getting." The waitress came over, and they told her what they wanted, adding a side of corn fritters.

"Save room for some Schnitz pie." She wrote down their order and rushed off. They were busy, but as their daed said, they had a lot of waitresses.

They watched the commotion as they ate. The tourists were interesting to observe as far as what they wore and their behavior; some were peculiar, while others seemed like regular folks.

A young man ambled in and studied the room. When his eyes met Gideon's, they locked for a split second.

"Who was that?" Elsie watched the boy walk away. "Was that one of them?"

"*Jah*, the boy I talked to at the bazaar. He looked right at me. I'm sure he doesn't want anything to do with us."

"Well, that's what we've hoped for." As soon as she said it, Elsie seemed to know it wasn't what he wanted for this one. There was something that young man had that the others didn't, a sense of regret. He was being bullied yet knew right from wrong.

"You tried to talk to him, Gideon." Elsie put a hand on his as he glanced back to where the boy had been.

"Let's go get that buggy." He smiled and stood to go, taking glances at the door. The boy obviously came in to eat but left because he and Elsie were there. If the boy came back, he wanted to be prepared with what to say to him.

The owner came by as they were leaving. "Gideon, I wanted to catch you before you left." He turned to Elsie. "And you might be?"

242

"This is Elsie." Gideon watched his eyebrows lift.

"Your sister?"

"*Nee*, we're courting."

The daed's mouth shut, and he stood straight. "Oh, I see. Congratulations."

Maybe Yonnie was right about finding suitors for his daughters. "The food was *gut*."

Elsie looked at the daed. "You have quite a business going."

"I hope it lasts." He smiled.

When they went outside, people were hovering on the sidewalk gawking farther down the street.

Elsie stood behind Gideon. "What is it?"

Gideon watched a trail of black smoke lifting to the sky. He followed it to where it started down the block. His mind snapped into gear and he ran, realizing it was coming from the buggy store. He prayed he was jumping to conclusions. But when he got closer, he didn't think he was.

He stopped and looked behind him for Elsie. He didn't see her but heard Jonas yelp. Gideon kicked at the gate of the six-foot fence that enclosed the outdoor show area. He felt the heat blast him with each kick. Smoke filled his nostrils. The heat hit him in the face as the gate fell with a *slap*! Flames flew out on every side as it burned.

"Jonas!" Gideon yelled at the top of his lungs.

"Here!" His gravelly voice could barely be heard with the growing flames and crackle of burning lumber.

Gideon followed the sound. "Jonas!" No answer. He followed where he'd heard his voice and called again.

"Over here." Jonas held a hose, blasting a buggy with water.

Gideon stopped quickly and reached for the hose. "We have to get out of here."

"I got this." Jonas choked but wouldn't stop dousing the buggies with water.

"If you don't go, I won't either."

"There's nothing for you to do." He barked out a cough but

continued to spray the area as he walked down the row of buggies lined up by the side of the building.

Jonas was being a stubborn fool, so Gideon decided he had to take drastic measures. Gideon went over to him, picked him up, and draped him over his shoulder.

He heard loud male voices coming by the entrance, so he headed that way. Jonas was a small man, but he felt like a load, slung over Gideon's shoulder.

When they got to where the gate had been, Gideon used all of his power to get through that threshold and to the street. He reached out to move the gate that was still fuming so he could fit through with Jonas on his back. He yelped with pain as the heat seared his fingers; then he dropped his hand. "Stupid!"

Gideon pulled his shirt over his head and used it to push the burned gate to the side. Once outside of the buggy area he was engulfed by smoke that flew downwind of him. The smolder tasted like burnt rubber that made him gag. He held the shirt up to his nose.

Just when he thought he didn't have another ounce of strength to hold onto Jonas, he pushed him up and drug himself forward.

"Put me down," Jonas begged. Gideon looked outside the show area where a group of people stopped to observe. Gideon decided Jonas had probably had enough and tried to set him down easy, but he was too weak and Jonas landed on his behind. "Promise you won't go back in there?"

Jonas nodded and gasped.

Gideon led the way from the heat as chunks of canvas material burned off the buggy and fell to the ground. Fires poked up and spread throughout the rest of the buggy's frame.

"*Danke*, friend." Jonas' voice was a whisper, but Gideon watched his lips.

"*Wilkom*." Gideon moved closer and squeezed Jonas's hand.

The heat scorched his skin as the wind shifted their way. Gideon had just taken a breath to calm down when one of the glass windshields blew. They all ducked, even though they were yards away, as shards of glass flew behind them. Close behind explosions popped off throughout the area by the buggy that was on fire.

An English doctor came over and offered his help. Jonas was placed on a cot and examined as Gideon sat and watched.

"He'll be fine," the doctor informed them. "Just keep an eye on him."

Someone gave Jonas and Gideon some water. It burned as it went down but took away some of the pain. He spit brown saliva onto the ground as beads of sweat dripped on the cement.

Then he felt a soft touch on his shoulder. "Elsie." His scratchy voice failed him. He turned to her and held her in his arms. Emotion built up and spilled over into tears of relief. Elsie tried to pull away, but he held on tight.

"Gideon, thank God you're all right." Her hands rubbed his bare back, soothing and comforting him.

"Jonas is a stubborn mule," he huffed out the words.

"*Jah*, he is. It was good of you to help him."

"He would have done the same for me." Gideon's throat stung with each word.

Gideon looked over at Elsie. "Will you sit with Jonas while I talk to the doctor?"

"*Jah*, sure." She kissed Gideon on the cheek and followed Jonas.

When Elsie slipped away, a coldness gripped him and he went numb. He lifted his head and wiped his mouth. The sirens quieted as the firefighters parked by the shop, the smoke smoldering in surrender.

Gideon didn't have the strength to move forward, but he forced himself, pushing ahead. People were starting to leave. Some were still inspecting the buggy area. He looked over to where his horses were along with another tethered to a post across the street.

One buggy had burned, one single buggy out of all of them. Then it hit him. He bent over and spit, but this time it wasn't from the smoke or fire. This time it was because his money and his brand-new buggy had all gone up in smoke.

Chapter Thirty-Two

T WO BROWN HORSES pulling black buggies clopped down Main Street. As they entered the town, Elsie read the green sign with gold letters announcing the Beeville name and the population of 12,529. A few cars lined the curbs shaded by potted trees. When they passed the white columns of the courthouse, she noticed the stone steps were worn and smooth by years of weather and footsteps. She wondered if this event would take them here one day.

It seemed like a dream, or rather a nightmare. Elsie couldn't believe it happened to them. *Jah*, they'd been pursued by these young men for months, but for them to take it this far was unnerving. She could tell by the taut line of Gideon's jaw that his patience was gone, tolerance nonexistent. Elsie didn't know how he would find the forgiveness necessary to let go of this.

"Elsie." Gideon's warm hand covered hers. "You look angry."

She pushed the air from her lungs. "I'm concerned." She turned to him. "And angry, but not as much as you are."

His jaw twitched. Normally he'd offer a Bible verse or calming words, but this drove him to a place she hadn't seen before. For a man to treat another in this manner with no provoking or reason had finally made him bitter. This was a side of him she didn't know and was unsure how to approach. They'd spent most of the day in Beeville yesterday, and well into the evening, talking with the authorities and going over the sequence of events again and again.

Omar, Minister Miller, and Zeke stepped down from their buggy and walked over to Jonas, Ephraim, and Officer Mayer, who were having a conversation.

The policeman kept his voice low. "We've found enough evidence to press charges, but we'd like to keep investigating."

"Sure, you do what you need to and we'll do the same." Jonas responded with an edge to his voice.

"We'd rather not have you or anyone else on the crime scene except the officers, Jonas." The young man in blue was polite but insistent.

Jonas obviously didn't want him in his store. His business would suffer the longer this went on. "I need to have access to the inside of the shop. As far as I'm concerned, what's done is done."

Officer Mayer tipped his head up a notch. "And what does that mean?"

"I won't be pressing charges."

"No?" The officer's brows lifted.

Jonas smiled. "Can't make me, can ya?"

The cop shook his head. "Yeah, I know your vow of no resistance and all, but don't you people get tired of getting pushed around?"

"Of course, no one likes to be mistreated. Yet I wouldn't feel any better filing a complaint."

"I guess that doesn't surprise me after working with enough of you Amish. We have a good idea of who the culprits are from the description of witnesses. The judge will want to punish these hooligans. They've done a lot more than this."

"We'll work something out," the bishop confirmed.

"What will happen to them if they are found guilty?" Gideon stood behind the group listening with Elsie. His dark eyes were filled with a coldness she'd never seen.

"I don't rightly know." The officer shrugged. "Get 'em off the street and scare 'em straight, that kind of thing I suppose."

Gideon looked to the ground and bit the side of his cheek. Elsie watched as he slowly lifted his head and glanced back at the buggies. His shoulders stiffened.

They walked away from her to the area again and went over every detail. How could she get Gideon out of the state he was in when they had to relive it again, and it wouldn't end even after today? Mamm was home with the boys and Daed was helping Will harvest corn. She would rather be either place than here, and she wanted Gideon out of here even more.

She searched for Gideon and followed him to the area where his buggy was. As she came closer, she looked at what he was staring at. Nothing had been tampered with. The first three buggies were in show condition, the one next to Gideon's had minor damage, but his was almost unrecognizable.

When she stood next to him, he put his hands on his hips and flexed his jaw muscles. "I'm sorry, Gideon." She moved closer and put a hand on his chest. He flinched and took a step back.

"I'm going to go talk to the Officer Mayer alone for a minute." He didn't look at her and took long strides without turning back. She expected him to turn around and apologize for his strange behavior, or even better, say he was ready to leave. "Elsie." Timothy's voice was welcome. As she turned to him, she fought away the emotions churning inside her. "I heard about the buggy catching on fire." He glanced over her head. "Were you involved?"

"The buggy was Gideon's." Her eyes watered when she said the words. She felt so badly for Gideon. It wasn't fair, but then the Amish knew that about life; Gideon had forgotten that temporarily.

"Tough break." He glanced back to the burned gate and through to the buggies. "Was his the only one burned?"

"*Jah.* They think it's those boys who have been bothering us."

"Is that still going on?"

"It comes and goes, but nothing for a while."

He rubbed the stubbles of his blond beard. "I see them around sometimes while I'm driving my route. It appears they're looking for trouble. But this seems like a big jump from their usual mischief."

He might be right. If they kept escalating their harassment, they might mess up their lives so badly they may not be able to pull out of it. "There is one boy who Gideon talked to that seemed to want out of the group."

"Might be Nick Hansen. I've seen him with them a few times. Surprised me at first. He's a good kid, but got a terrible family life I've heard."

"I'm sorry to hear that." So Gideon did pick out the one who was there for all the wrong reasons. Not that they all weren't, but he seemed to be the one that didn't fit.

"You'll be even sorrier when you hear the word that's going around. The talk is he's the one who lit the fire."

Elsie shook her head as her heart filled with disappointment and concern about how Gideon would feel hearing that. "The officers won't say, so I only have your information to go on."

"It's only hearsay, but word gets around in this town." He put an innocent hand on her shoulder and looked into her eyes. "This too will pass, right?" Englishers were more apt to touching than the Amish, but everyone in the community knew Timothy.

She smiled back and nodded.

"Timothy." Gideon stood next to her and greeted him in a cold manner. His voice was sharp and his eyes piercing. "You two seem to be having a serious talk."

Elsie gave him a stern look, her forehead drawn trying to make out what was wrong. "Everyone is serious today, Gideon. Are you about ready to go?"

"*Jah*, now I am." He nodded once to Timothy and didn't offer his hand as he usually would. It was all Elsie could do not to say a word to Gideon, but it would have to wait. She had no place to chastise him in front of someone, but his behavior wasn't acceptable, and it wasn't like Gideon.

They walked in silence, Gideon stuffing his hands in his pockets as if keeping down a tempest about ready to blow. Elsie marched ahead of him more than ready to go home. She'd never wanted to be away from him, but at this moment she did, and it saddened her.

They drove silently as all of the procedures and questions

twirled around in her head. Why did the English spend so much time on such matters? What's gone is gone, and as Jonas said, what's done is done. Dwelling on such things were dangerous to the mind, heart, and soul; Gideon was proof of that. But something more was bothering him. His behavior had changed too drastically. But given his frame of mind, she wouldn't get anything out of him now.

When they were almost home, Elsie thought she'd try. "Gideon."

He didn't answer but finally looked her way.

"What's wrong? I mean *really* wrong?"

He kept his eyes on the road, and by his lack of response and eye contact it seemed as if he didn't hear her at all. He only shook his head as if maybe *he* didn't even know.

"Is this about the buggy?"

His eyes narrowed, and his response was a one-shoulder shrug. It seemed painful for him to so much as even think about it.

"I know it's a disappointment." She stared at him for the longest time. He was so disconnected she gave up. He was beyond reach.

He stopped, and she quickly got out of the buggy and began to walk up to her house. Tears pricked at her eyes, and she willed them away.

"Elsie." His eyes were downcast as he picked at the leather reins in his hand. "It's not about things, but I did want the best for you. This is about something else." He lifted his eyes up to the sky and then closed them.

They were both silent. A row of black crows left their perch on the wire fence, squawked, and took to the air.

"I need to figure some things out."

She waited to hear more, for him to explain what he needed to think about. Elsie hoped he'd admit to overreacting and to have placed too much value on a material thing. Instead he sat there feeling sorry for himself, and for the first time since they started courting, she doubted his virtue. She had her reservations about him from the time they'd moved here, but that was more to do with her and her worthiness. This was different. Elsie gave him her heart, and he was putting a materialistic object between them? Again, she told herself there was something more. But she was in no mood to try and pry it out of him. Everyone had had a long night and day.

She made it as far as the front door and then shed a tear. On the way to her room she was grateful no one saw her, wanting to be alone. She shut the door behind her and knelt to pray. "God, You helped us through the trials of moving here, to cope with storms that destroyed crops and to withstand harassment, but this is tearing us apart. Please help us now."

When she was finished complaining, she sat down on the bed and searched inward. She didn't like what she found. She saw a selfish soul who felt she rose above another's grief. She knew what it felt like to lose something you cherished, her sister. Those months without her, and even still having her here but so different from the girl she grew up with. The hole was smaller, but the loss was still there. For Gideon this incident triggered something. His plans had been altered; maybe that was enough for a man with big expectations. She didn't know.

Elsie waited for Gideon to come visit the next day, but he didn't. He didn't come the following day either. Elsie decided if she didn't see him by the end of the next day, she would go call on him.

So she put herself to work like always, but to extreme. She went out early the following morning and hung laundry in the hot, summer sun. She didn't stop until every last piece of clothing was hanging on the line. The hard work made her feel better, but her body ached from pushing so hard.

She came inside, out of the heat of the day, and filled a wash-basin, then splashed water on her face. When she looked in the mirror, she knew to keep searching inward to keep herself humble. And by doing so maybe she'd figure out what was really on Gideon's heart.

Chapter Thirty-Three

KATIE'S HAVING THE baby!" Aaron yelled as he came running to the garden where Elsie was gathering vegetables. She lifted her dress rimmed with mud and stared at Aaron in shock. Had it been nine months already? Elsie felt unprepared for this, so Katie must feel so even more.

Aaron stomped his foot. "Now!"

Elsie jumped up and started running to the back door, then followed Aaron up the stairs. When they went into Katie's room, Mamm was sitting beside Katie and Daed was pacing while rubbing the back of his neck. Katie was most definitely in labor. Elsie sat next to her and watched as she tightened every muscle and then released. "Oh, my, we need a doctor."

"The doc is in the other community past Beeville. What if he can't get here in time?" Daed started to pace a little faster, and Elsie wished Gideon was there, resenting the time he was spending away. Three days felt like a year.

"Well then, what about the midwife?" Mamm was the calmest of any of them. Maybe because she'd given birth to four children she was more comfortable with the process. "Daed can; he's done it before?" Elsie mentioned in a panic.

Daed threw his hands up in the air and started to sweat. "I've helped more than one farm animal give birth, but that doesn't mean—"

"Daed, do something." Katie's plea stopped everyone. "But don't deliver the baby."

They'd hardly spoken to one another since her first day back. No matter how stubborn her daed was, he couldn't possibly disagree with anything she wanted right now. Elsie held her breath waiting for Daed to answer.

"I'll go get Alma," Daed informed whoever was listening.

Mamm stared at Daed with disgust. "*We* can deliver the baby."

"*Nee*, we need help," Daed answered with irritation. He was obviously flustered over the many implications that went with this situation. Besides being upset with Katie, being witness to your daughter delivering a child had to be awkward for him. Not that it was unheard of, but it was not ideal.

"I'll go." Elsie knew her mamm and daed would be more help than she was, and she could ride a horse faster than either of them.

"*Nee*, I will." Gideon stood in the doorway.

Elsie was so relieved to hear his voice she sighed and turned to see his strong, handsome face.

Daed seemed to relax a little. "Gideon, good man; always here when we need an extra hand."

"I'll go to Rachel's and use the phone to see if we can get the doc or find Alma." He let out a breath in obvious appreciation he'd found something useful to do besides play doctor as he did with Isaac. "Although I'm familiar with Solomon's touch. I've seen it before when I helped him birth a foal last spring," he said tongue in cheek as he turned to leave.

Elsie followed after him. "Gideon, *danke*."

When he stopped and turned to her, she felt everything would be all right. He'd always made her feel that way, and he seemed more like himself again.

"Well, I didn't want to be Solomon's assistant this time." He grinned.

"*Nee, danke* for being here." The timing told her he was already on his way here without hearing about Katie's labor. That gave her hope he was ready to talk.

He gave her a nod and hurried down the stairs.

Elsie and Mamm took over taking care of Katie. Daed went downstairs to keep the boys occupied, but Elsie could hear his boots wearing a hole in the floor. Soon her grandparents came, and other folks brought everything from food to baby blankets and knitted booties. By the time Gideon showed up again, the haus was a revolving door of people, food, and gifts. The most welcomed guest was Alma when she tapped on the bedroom door.

"Today is a day the Lord has made; rejoice and be glad in it!" Her five-foot-nothing stature didn't fit her loud personality. She was in charge, and a person knew it after her first sentence. She preferred to work alone unless the helper was trained under her supervision.

"Thank God you are here." Elsie stood so Alma could have the room.

"If you don't mind, I'll stay, Alma." Mamm wrung her hands with worry.

"*Jah*, I'll let you know if I need you." She was quickly at work opening her satchel, pulling out towels and making Katie comfortable. She was so unusually quiet Elsie would be concerned, but she knew how Alma's ways brought comfort to even the most distraught mother-to-be.

Elsie descended the stairs slowly and worked in the kitchen even slower as she prepared food for guests who were coming and going. She was more tired emotionally than physically. She loved her sister but couldn't tolerate her snappy words. It would be different with Alma there.

Elsie made her way through the house and out the back door. She took in the warm evening air, glad to be alone. The sound of the footsteps of one of her brothers approaching made her weary, expecting them to need her help.

"Want some water?" Adam held out a cup and sat with her on the stump of an old tree.

"*Danke*." Elsie didn't realize how tired she really was until she sat down. The anticipation for Katie's baby and spending the morning with her in labor had taken it out of her. She took a long drink even though he'd only filled it halfway.

"Where's Gideon?" Adam's eyebrows puckered with worry.

"He's been busy taking care of some things that happened in town a couple of days ago." That was true as far as she knew. He was working with the authorities on the vandalized buggy, but it didn't take up this much time. He was avoiding her.

"About his buggy that got burned?" Adam kicked his boots against the stump but didn't make eye contact; he rarely did.

"*Jah*, he is very sad about it."

"Why? He still has Betsy and Ross."

"But he needs a buggy for the horses to have a job to do." She tilted her head toward him.

He cocked his head too. "I miss him."

Elsie sighed and took another drink of the now lukewarm water. "Me too." And when she said it, she realized how much she meant it. She'd become accustomed to his daily visits. Then Elsie worried *she* was the problem he was sorting through.

"What are you two up to?" Gideon stood a rock's throw away, standing with one foot propped on a small hill.

Adam was up and off the stump in a flash. He ran to Gideon and hugged his leg. Gideon lifted him up and walked up next to Elsie. She couldn't hide her pleasure that he was there, although she was upset with him for taking so long.

Adam wiggled away from Gideon. "Gotta go."

"To the bathroom?" Elsie asked.

"*Nee*, Mamm said if Gideon comes to hightail it to the house." Which he did, lickety-split.

Gideon almost smiled watching Adam run off. But when his face tightened, she knew this was a serious visit, not the reunion she'd hoped for. "So, you're about to be an aunt?"

"*Jah*, and Katie is going to be a single mother." Hearing it out loud made it seem like a reality. No matter how much Katie thought she liked the worldly life, she would get a good start here. And Elsie was glad she could spend time with her nephew or niece.

"There's enough love to go around for this little one." His facial expression didn't match his hopeful words. There was too much of something else on his mind.

"Where have you been?" She stared at him, wanting to take in all he was feeling and thinking. He took so long to respond she eventually turned away.

"I never knew something like this could affect me this way. I've been wrestling with a lot of hatred." He looked straight at her, searching for something. An answer, a rebuke, what, she wasn't sure. One thing she did know was that Gideon was familiar with hate, but not so much with self-hate.

"How does the hate feel?"

"It's eating me up inside." He rubbed his hands together as if to rub the sin away. "I need to ask God to take it away so I can forgive."

She took his hand. "You will. It's only metal and rubber, things that turn to dust."

His eyebrows drew together. "You don't understand. It's not so much losing the buggy as having to testify that boy was the one who did the damage." He forced his lips together in frustration. "It's more important that I help that boy, not put him in juvenile hall."

Elsie took the information in slowly. What she thought was all selfishness on his part was quite the contrary. She shamed herself for thinking he was more worried about his own loss than anything else, including her. "Gideon, I had it all wrong..."

"*Nee*, I was angry about losing the buggy too."

It was if he didn't hear her and continued with his confession.

"I should have told you what was eating at me. This was something I hadn't dealt with before. The English think our ways are so harsh and demanding with so many rules to follow. But it seems the opposite to me. They don't forgive when a person breaks their laws. If this boy is who I think he is, being put in one of those places could change the direction of his life in a way he'll never recover from."

When she finally had a second to cut in, she asked what she

thought was most important. Her own confession could wait. "Have you talked with the boy?"

"*Jah*, his name is Nick, and he claims he's the scapegoat. I'm not so naive as to think he could be lying, but I don't believe he is."

After seeing Nick at the bazaar that day, Elsie tended to believe him as well. He'd confessed too much and given in too easily, unlike the other boys when Gideon tried to talk with them. "We believe in a God of second chances. Maybe you can share that with him."

"And the judge, if he'll listen."

"Because you feel so strongly about this, you should be there. To tell them what you told me."

He looked into the orange sun slowly going down. "I am going to court tomorrow. I have to see how this all works."

Elsie paused, unsure of how she felt about him dealing with the English ways. "What does the bishop say?"

"I'm not going to defend myself; I'm asking for a reasonable punishment for Nick."

"That's *gut*." She couldn't read him well enough to know what else he had on his mind. She hoped it had nothing to do with her.

"It might help if you're there, in case you saw or remember something I didn't."

She paused and shook her head without thought. She had no intention of going, even if he would have given a better reason. If he would have asked for her moral support or just to be with him, she might have felt obligated, but his only concern seemed to be this boy. Before she could answer, Mamm walked in. "Elsie, your nephew is here." Mamm stood at the back door waving them in.

They looked at one another. "You have a nephew?" Gideon asked sheepishly.

"*Jah*, Uncle Gideon." She thought surely that would break him from this trance he was in concerning a stranger rather than the family he was promised to. She waited one extra beat, waiting for a response, a smile, or anything that showed he cared. When he finally stood, but quietly, she picked up her dress and took quick steps up to the house leaving Gideon behind her.

Aaron met them at the door. "I'm an uncle!" He took Gideon's hand and dragged him through the kitchen. Elsie did her best to keep up with Gideon but finally let him slip away. She watched them climb the stairs together, and Gideon glanced her way. But instead of the usual feeling of warmth, the disconnection between them lingered.

Chapter Thirty-Four

THE HOUSE WAS unusually quiet as Gideon stood at the front door peering in through the screen. He knocked again, then heard footsteps coming from the kitchen.

Elsie walked through the entry room and opened the door. She kept her distance and hesitantly went through the kitchen. He could read the signs through her actions, guarded and careful around him. He would make it up to her, but this wasn't a good time. "Sorry, I was helping Mamm with breakfast before we left."

"Are Katie and the baby awake?"

"*Jah*, little Solomon sleeps a lot, but Katie doesn't." Elsie tapped on the door that was open and stuck her head in.

He stepped into the room behind Elsie. The sweet smell of lavender filled the air from the piles of pale colored blankets and the white diapers stacked on a small oak table. Then a cradle caught Gideon's eye. The workmanship was unmistakably Solomon's. So the stubborn man was letting go of his pride long before he let on. Love for his unborn grandchild poured out in every detail, especially through the cherub on the top.

"Morning, Gideon." Katie's eyes were soft, and her relaxed composure was comforting to see. She held little Sol swaddled in a blue blanket, tiny tuffs of reddish hair sprung up on top of his head.

"How is little Sol?"

As he stroked the baby's pink cheek with his finger, he heard heavy boots behind him. Solomon slapped Gideon's back, but much gentler than usual. "He has a good name."

"*Jah*, he does. I can't imagine how he'll live up to it."

Katie smiled at her daed. Gideon watched the eye contact

between daed and daughter. It took new life to bring them together again. Gideon hoped it stayed that way.

"So you're going into town today." Katie looked up from the baby and turned to Elsie. "I didn't realize how hard it was with the Englishers after I left." Katie twisted at the waist to comfort him. "I didn't think they'd continue to bother you."

"That's what I thought as well, but hopefully it'll be over now."

Katie seemed sincere and gave Elsie a long look. "*Jah*, me too."

As they left the house, Elsie's face tightened. He knew he had a lot to say to her, but he wanted to get through this day, just one more day, and he'd smooth things over with her.

"Are you ready for this?" He reached over to clasp her hand, but she moved away.

"As best as I'll ever be." Elsie was making it clear she didn't want to go, and he didn't blame her.

Gideon didn't want to speak in the courtroom; it was not the Amish way. He wanted Nick to have consequences that would make him a better person, not punishments that would leave him embittered by the English system. He found himself wondering why *this* boy instead of another. The blond-haired leader of the group seemed more deserving of punishment. Gideon stopped the thoughts and wondered why he felt so protective of Nick. Their conversations were brief, but maybe that was enough. He felt God's tug and pull to take action on behalf of Nick, and he would obediently follow.

He helped Elsie into the buggy and saw her clench her hands together, knuckles white in her lap. The concern he had for himself overshadowed Elsie's obvious dread of facing the English boys again. He put a hand on hers before she could stop him. "If you are uncomfortable with this, you don't have to go into the courtroom." He stared at her. "I mean that."

"I'll be seeing them again one way or another since we come into town to do business." She looked out at the ripe corn ready for harvest. "Best it's in a controlled environment like today."

"All right then, *danke* for supporting me. This might do us all some good." He knew he had a lot of forgiving to do, and so did Elsie. This would test their faith in ways that were new to them. It was one thing to pardon an Amish brother or sister in the Amish way. Gideon knew how to approach one of his brethren, but would the Englishers accept their offer to move on and live in peace?

As they got closer to town, Gideon could see Elsie tense, and she didn't say a word once they passed the Beeville sign. She scanned the area, alert to everyone they passed by. Elsie usually enjoyed going into town, shopping and selling her handmade goods. Now it was as if a forbidden boundary wedged between them, and once crossed she was in *their* domain.

"Elsie." She jumped when he touched her arm. "Why don't you go to Ephraim's restaurant? I'll come and get you when it's over."

She took a deep breath. "*Nee,* I'm going in with you."

He offered his arm, and she grasped onto him, staring at the scar on her wrist. She'd been burned by a hot axle trying to calm the horse when the fireworks were thrown in the buggy and around the horse. He swallowed hard. His motive for bringing her to Beeville to rise above her fears may backfire on him. But he felt she had to try, or those visions would continue to haunt her. He stopped at the doors to the courthouse and met her eyes. "Refuse to listen to the voice of fear; listen instead to the whisper of courage."

She looked away as tears filled her eyes. "I should be the one encouraging you."

He patted her hand then laced his fingers with hers. "You are by being with me."

Gideon ushered Elsie into a windowless room covered by dark paneling and filled with rows of wood benches. His skin tingled with a chill of foreboding that matched the coldness of the courtroom. Jonas slid down and made room for them.

Many young people, too many in his opinion, were seated with their parents. Across the room Nick slouched on the bench next to a stout man. What little was left of the man's hair was white.

Deep lines creased his face, and the years had bowed his back. A folded walker rattled in front of him when a younger man in a dark blue suit settled in on the other side of Nick. Gideon guessed the man was Nick's lawyer.

Waiting through the proceedings was daunting, but finally Gideon heard them call Nick's name. The elderly man patted the boy's shoulder, and Gideon could see the concern that clouded the man's watery blue eyes. Nick took the stand but wouldn't take his eyes off the floor.

The judge grew tired of his one-word answers and not looking up when he spoke. "You didn't do this alone. Now tell us who helped you."

"No one."

"I've heard of this Amo-bashing; it isn't done by one individual." The judge leaned toward the boy, his voice firm. "Others were involved. What are their names?"

Nick clenched his jaw in determination. "It was only me."

Gideon shook his head, remembering what Nick said about belonging to the group. Nick was choosing to take the blame alone rather than have the other boys out to get him.

"I'll be right back." Gideon moved away from Elsie and maneuvered up to the bench behind the defense attorney.

The judge glanced at Gideon and narrowed his gray brows. Gideon sat back and waited for a chance to talk with the lawyer, which came when the judge went over a file from the police department.

"Did someone press charges?"

The lawyer evaluated him from top to bottom, taking in the straw hat he held, suspenders, and boots. "You must be the Amish man involved."

"*Jah*, Gideon Lapp." He held out his hand and gave the lawyer a surprise pump of his hand. "Who pressed charges?"

"The owner of the store in front of where your buggy was parked. Burning debris caused damage to his property too."

That shop was owned by an Englisher Gideon had done

business with. Now that he mentioned it, Gideon remembered there was some damage in other areas. "What will happen to Nick if this goes through?"

"Juvenile Hall in San Antonio." The lawyer glanced around the room. "There are a few people in town who want an example to be set for the vandals around here. This boy is taking the brunt of it."

Gideon's throat became dry, and he knew his emotions were showing. His nostrils flared and he felt his face grow hotter. "Are you going to let that happen?"

"Order." The judge looked directly at them, but Gideon couldn't let this go. There had to be a way to fix this.

The lawyer sat down, assuming there was no recourse by Gideon's silence. "Let me think of something," Gideon whispered to the lawyer.

He didn't turn around but answered, "This kid is the only minor; that's probably why the gang gave him up."

"Nick didn't want to be in the gang."

"How do you know this? Do you know the boy?"

"*Jah*, he told me he had to do whatever they asked him to do to stay in or get out."

The lawyer turned to face him. "What's the recourse?"

"Order, counselor." The judge seemed as curious as irritated with them.

"What if he works for me, on the farm?"

The lawyer rubbed his cheek and watched the judge give him an ugly frown. "Do you really want that responsibility, Mr. Lapp?"

"Would you gentlemen like to share something with me?" The judge looked down at them over his bifocals.

Gideon turned to glance at Elsie. She stared back and lifted a shoulder, not understanding what was happening. "*Jah*, I do."

The lawyer stood. "Your Honor, may I approach the bench?"

"You may, but this better be important."

"It is, and can Mr. Groder, owner of Groder's Hardware, approach the bench as well?"

The judge nodded.

Nick finally lifted his head and noticed Gideon. His forehead wrinkled then softened as if absorbing what was happening. Gideon didn't take his eyes off of him, praying he was doing the right thing and that he would give good guidance to him. By the time he finished his prayer, the lawyer was back in his chair, and so was Mr. Groder.

Gideon held his breath. The district attorney and the judge left the room. Minutes passed, and hushed conversation filled the silence. A door clicked open. Everyone stood while the two men returned to the courtroom. After the judge settled in, he bent over the police report in silence. Gideon's heart pounded in his chest. The judge shuffled papers then reached for the gavel. *Bang!*

"Counsel has suggested I sentence Nick Hansen to one hundred hours of community service, to be completed on weekends. During this time he will be working for Gideon Lapp or Harold Groder, making restitution for their losses. The court accepts Counsel's recommendation." The judge pounded the gavel and sat back in his swivel chair. The bailiff called the next name.

Nick's face was ashen and his eyes wide with surprise and confusion. He looked over at the judge as if he needed to be told again that it was over. He watched as the elderly man huddled in conversation with the lawyer who had helped decide his fate. Nick slid from the chair and walked to Gideon first. "What just happened?"

Gideon enjoyed seeing the bewilderment in his eyes with only a slight amount of the bitterness he'd seen before. "I hope you have some muscle on you. You'll be learning how to work a farm."

"Yeah, not burn it!" Mr. Groder walked by. "Some of those hours will be at my store cleaning the mess you made."

Nick kept the sour look on his face, but he nodded compliantly.

The lawyer shook Gideon's hand again as Nick made his way up to the judge. "I hope this goes as well outside of the courtroom as it has here today."

"*Jah*, me too." Gideon knew he was in for a challenge. But to think of the other option the boy was given, he felt he had no choice.

They all turned to the rattle of wheels. "That's my grandpa." Nick pointed to him.

The old man clutched the handles on his walker. "Good thing you did for the boy. After his folks died, he's been hard to manage." His eyes narrowed as he stared at Nick. "You do what these men say."

Nick hesitated for a moment then nodded.

Gideon noticed his resistance but was determined to win him over. "I'll pick you up bright and early tomorrow morning. Be ready."

The boy's shoulder's rounded. "I will."

Nick's grandpa cleared his throat. "I told your lawyer who those boys were. Even if there's no proof against them, the police should be talking to them."

Nick rolled his eyes. "That's just great," he mumbled sarcastically.

Gideon hoped that would be enough. God had blessed him so far, he would trust Him with anything that may happen later. Then he heard the rustle of skirts and saw Elsie approaching. Her bright smile of approval lifted all the dark clouds that had been hanging over him. With the love in her eyes, she brought him a rainbow.

Chapter Thirty-Five

M ORNING." ELSIE STEPPED lively down the stairs of her house and to Gideon. "It's nice to have Nick stay more than one night now that he's out of school."

"We have gone to Beeville a lot lately for supplies with the houses that need to be built anyway." He gave her a sideways glance with half a smile.

Gideon hadn't talked much about if they would be living with her family for a while or building a place of their own once they were married. Now that fall was almost here, the weather would be pleasant to build a home. Then she had an idea on how to possibly get a hint of what he was thinking. "What supplies do you need today?"

"The regular restock items, and we need a lot of seed to get the wheat planted. We have about eight weeks before the weather changes."

Since he didn't have the wagon, it was obvious he wasn't getting lumber or anything he'd need to start construction on a home. He did have two horses, but that was due to the weight of the seed.

On their way through the community they passed by Gideon's family farm. Nick was in the field with Gideon's brothers hefting hay bales onto the wagon. He stopped to wipe the sweat off his brow. The noon sun was blazing down on them. One of Gideon's brothers tossed him a straw hat. Nick caught it and put it on. Another brother patted Nick's back. Elsie smiled, knowing Nick would be just fine.

After they got the supplies, they went to the buggy shop. Elsie felt Gideon's arm wrap her waist as he guided her to Jonas's. A black buggy that looked almost new was in front with no horse hitched to it. Elsie was hopeful Jonas had made a sale.

She looked at Gideon. "I'm still grateful for your gesture in buying the buggy. We'll have one soon enough." As much as she meant the words, they both knew it would take years to save the money again.

He gave her a forced smile. "*Jah*, or we could just ride Betsy and Ross into town and church on Sundays."

She softly laughed as they met Jonas at the door.

Jonas held out his hand. "God be with you, Gideon."

"If you're referring to Nick, it was a challenge at first, but he's coming around."

Jonas scratched his beard. "*Jah*, it was good you helped that boy. If ya need a hand with the youngster, let me know. And since we're doing good deeds, I think you're due."

"I'd like to see how the repair is coming along." Gideon looked around to where the fire had been. Elsie knew Gideon felt bad for Jonas. That shop was his livelihood, but the damage could have been a lot worse if more than one buggy caught fire. That was one of many things she was curious about, if they purposely targeted Gideon's buggy.

"You don't need to see any more of the fire damage. Besides, you had a long ride here and another going back ahead of ya."

Jonas pulled at Ross and harnessed him to the buggy they'd walked by. "Betsy is still hitched up where you parked her," Jonas informed them.

Elsie turned at Gideon with surprise then to Jonas. "What are you doing, Jonas?"

"That buggy is yours."

"*Nee*, Jonas—" Gideon started to protest.

Jonas stood his ground. "Now don't ruin this for me. You did for the boy. I'm giving to you." He smiled. "It's the Amish way, *jah*?"

Elsie gave him a gentle hug and watched Gideon as it all soaked in. He seemed reluctant, but she could see how elated he was by the way he was looking at that buggy. It didn't have all the accessories and showed some wear, but it was his, and she thanked God for their friend helping Gideon with his need. Jonas and Gideon shook and shared mutual satisfaction for doing a kind deed. "I don't know what to say; *danke*."

Jonas nodded. "Now get in your buggy and follow Elsie home."

Gideon stroked the smooth leather seat with longing in his eyes. Exposure to the sun made a crack on the bench covering, otherwise it was beautiful.

Elsie insisted that she go behind so she could admire Gideon in his buggy. She watched the dust kick up on the road from Gideon's new-old buggy as he went down the lane to his home. He unharnessed Betsy and parked his daed's buggy then climbed into his buggy.

Gideon grinned. "What a day." He patted a spot next to him on the buggy seat.

"That was a kind thing Jonas did for you."

"For *us;* that buggy is ours." He went down a path behind the Fishers' farm that was only tumbleweeds and dry ground.

Elsie sat back and stared at Gideon. "Where are we going?"

"It's a surprise." He narrowed his eyes.

She smiled. "What are you up to?"

"If I tell you, it won't be a surprise." His grin made her more curious.

He stopped at the top of a hill that stood out over the Rio Grande River in the distance, the spring of life for their crop, their ability to exist there.

"This is a nice view." Large oak trees in full bloom lined the river, and overgrown bushes with colorful leaves hedged the waters edge.

He pulled her close, and she laid her head on his shoulder, resting after a long day. "I'm glad you like it. We'll be spending a lot of time here."

"What do you mean?" She turned to look him in the eyes.

Could she dare to think he was saying what she'd been waiting for?

"This land is ours with a little help from your daed and mine." He smiled, watching her reaction.

"I'd hoped for a home, but this is more than I could have ever imagined." She whispered, hardly able to believe it. "And a buggy too."

He boldly moved forward and kissed her. "Will you marry me, Elsie Yoder?"

Although it was assumed, Elsie loved hearing the words. Her lips slowly rounded into a full smile. "*Jah*, I will, Gideon Lapp."

They stayed there watching the sun easing down and the water sparkling across the river. He kissed her again, and she snuggled into his chest, knowing they needed to leave but not wanting to ever let him go.

Glossary

ach — oh

Ausbund — hymnal

bruder — brother

daed — father

danke — thank you

dawdi — grandfather

Dietsch — Pennsylvania Dutch

Englisher — non-Amish person

glaawe — faith

Gott — God

gut — good

hallo — hello

haus — house

jah — yes

kapp — prayer covering

mamm — mother

mammi — grandmother

narrisch — crazy

nee — no

Ordnung — order of Amish ways

rumspringa — teenagers running around

shunned — disregarded

Um zu essen — come and eat

wilkom — you're welcome

wunderbaar — wonderful

COMING FROM BETH SHRIVER IN FALL 2013

Healing Grace

BOOK 3 IN THE TOUCH OF GRACE SERIES

Chapter One

MOSE FISHER WATCHED Joe Lapp walk out of the office. If he got a job at the shop, it would be awkward. Ever since Elsie Yoder had chosen Joe's brother, Gideon, over Mose, he hadn't found anyone to take her place. Their community hadn't grown much since their move to Texas, and the new community on the other side of town was still unfamiliar to him. Mose wasn't one to go looking for a wife, but being twenty-two years of age, he should be. He shook his head, pushing away thoughts of her.

He'd finished his work early, so he figured he'd leave and avoid Joe. He walked through the shop and to the curing and painting area next door. He'd almost made it when he heard Joe call out, "Mose, wait up."

Mose turned and watched him walk over. He looked a lot like Gideon, with dark hair and brown eyes, but he was shorter and skinnier. "Joe."

Joe offered his hand. Mose lifted his, which was a greater gesture than Joe could realize.

"The boss man just hired me." He was smiling from ear to ear. It wasn't always easy for daeds to let their sons leave the farm and take work in town, but it had become a necessity to make ends meet, at least for a short time, now and then.

"Congratulations." Mose couldn't think of much to say, so he turned to leave again.

"*Danke.* This is sorta like barn raisings and setting up Sunday church together."

He was making his point well, so Mose conceded. "*Jah*, just

277

like it." He couldn't keep the sarcasm from his words. He started to turn again, but Joe continued.

"I'm not my brother, Mose." Joe gave him an even gaze, and Mose felt a sliver of respect for him zip up his spine.

"*Nee*, I guess you're not," he mumbled, and walked away. He and Joe had always gotten along, were tight friends since moving from Virginia. It was time to let go of the grudge of which Joe should not bear the brunt.

The sun was hot as blazes. Sweat drenched Mose's shirt as he drove down the asphalt highway in his buggy with no top. His brother had taken a group to singing, and their daed always wanted the top off, but Calvin never put it back on, and Mose hadn't had time to deal with it earlier.

He'd finished his business in town early. He was always done before the English woodworkers and felt somewhat guilty taking off before the rest, but the owner didn't go by a clock. He'd learned to judge by the quality of a man's work. Mose missed working the land, but this was a season to grow, not to harvest or plant, and he liked the extra income.

He blinked as he looked down the road. A few yards ahead of him a car zoomed by a truck pulling a horse trailer. The driver swerved drastically, causing the trailer to fishtail and dip into the shoulder and off the road. The tires screeched as the driver yanked the truck to the left, but the weight of the trailer pulled it into the ditch.

It happened so fast, Mose felt like he was moving through sludge as he jumped out of the buggy. The smell of burnt rubber wafted to his nostrils as cars whizzed by, creating a gust of wind that blew off his hat. He ran toward the trailer that lilted to the side as the horses squealed and kicked, trying to get out.

An older man and young woman crawled out of the truck and came his way. Mose got to the rear gate first and grabbed the handle. Finding it jammed, he put all his weight into it.

"Let me try." The young woman didn't look at him, just moved his hands and wiggled the lever until it clicked. Mose strained to

pull the metal gate open. The angle of the trailer made it difficult, so she grabbed on and pulled with him. The squeak of the
hinge as the door opened caused the horses to thrash around in
the large trailer.

When one of the horses started to calm down, Mose took the
opportunity to move forward. He felt a hand grip his forearm.

"I've got this." She spoke in a calm tone to the two equines
as she made her way to the front of the trailer. They pranced
around nervously as she moved forward, landing a kick to her leg
and nearly a blow to her back, but she moved quickly and didn't
stop until she untied them.

Mose held out his hand. "Give me a lead." She took two seconds before giving him the rope and grasping the other one, then
started to urge the bay filly out of the trailer. Mose gave them
room and then clucked to the black gelding. As Mose made his
way to him, he took in the missing tufts of hair, swayback, and
worn hooves. When he kicked, he had little range of motion, but
it wasn't because he was hurt. He was old as the hills.

Mose spoke sweet nothings to him to let the old horse know
where he was, due to the cataracts in his eyes. Old Blackie moved,
slow but sure, and made his way out without much trouble at all.
Mose checked for injuries and found him to be in good shape.

"Let me see if I can get this rig out of here." The older man
walked to the truck and started it up. Mose barely had time to
shut the trailer door and step out of the way.

When the old man hit the gas, the tires sped until they caught
the asphalt, causing the filly to spook. She tried to run, but one
of her legs couldn't take the weight.

"She's hurt," he informed the young woman while holding on
to Blackie.

"I know. I hope it's not too bad." She met his gaze before
holding out her hand to shake his. "Thank you for taking care
of Wart." Her bright-blue eyes and frowning, yet beautiful, face
was frozen with worry. Maybe it was from the shock of the event,
or maybe it was that her daed didn't seem to have any manners.

"Wart?" Mose preferred his name for the old black horse. The English didn't seem to think of good horse names.

When he clasped her hand, he felt a connection and looked at her to see if she noticed it as well. Her eyes were focused down at their hands. She quickly tried to pull away, but Mose held on a second longer. "I can help you load them back in, if you like."

She glanced at the truck and then back to him. "I can manage."

Mose put his hands in his pockets, not ready to leave just yet. "You gave me Wart because you didn't think I could handle the filly?"

"I just bought her. Spent a lot of money too." She looked down at the horse's damaged leg.

Mose had a passion for horses and hated to see one in pain that he couldn't get his hands on to doctor. "Do you want me to take a look at it?" he offered, but by the way she kept looking over her shoulder, he already knew the answer.

"No, I better not." She looked at him straight-on but still hadn't changed her expression.

He could have continued the debate but wanted to ease her discomfort, and the only way to seem to do that was to leave. "What's your name?"

She hesitated, taken off-guard that he changed the conversation. "Abigail."

"That's a mouthful." He grinned, but she didn't. "Pretty, though." The Amish used nicknames, made it friendlier. He wanted to know if she went by one, then wondered why he cared. "Mose Fisher."

"Thanks, Mose." She turned away. The expression on her pretty face remained frozen during their entire conversation. Mose wondered what she'd look like if she smiled, but didn't figure he'd find out.

"Abby!" The older man came around the trailer.

Her expression thawed into anxiety as her hair fell over her face, covering her pinched forehead. She immediately moved away from Mose and began to coax the filly into the trailer. It took everything he had not to help her with the horse, but he knew his services were no longer wanted.

"Get those horses loaded." Her daed nodded to Mose and walked off.

Mose tethered Wart and turned to leave. He looked back once, to see her look away.

Abby.

He'd remember the name.

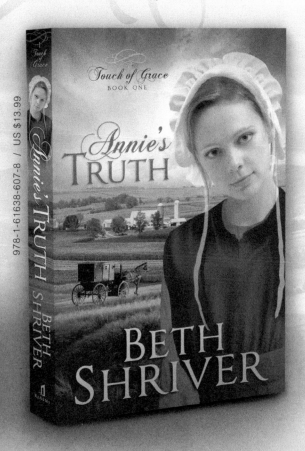

AN OUTSIDER

TORN BETWEEN TWO WORLDS

After learning the truth about who she really is,

can this prodigal daughter be accepted back into the safety

and security of home?